Zhang Boduan

Awakening to the Real

Zhang Boduan

Awakening to the Real

ISBN/EAN: 9783742823656

Manufactured in Europe, USA, Canada, Australia, Japa

Cover: Foto ©Andreas Hilbeck / pixelio.de

Manufactured and distributed by brebook publishing software
(www.brebook.com)

Zhang Boduan

Awakening to the Real

AN ANNOTATED TRANSLATION AND STUDY

OF

CHAPTERS ON AWAKENING TO THE REAL (ca. 1061)

ATTRIBUTED TO ZHANG BODUAN (ca. 983-1081)

by

PAUL B.M. CROWE

B.A., The University of Calgary, 1988
M.A., The University of Calgary, 1993

A THESIS SUBMITTED IN PARTIAL FULFILMENT OF
THE REQUIREMENTS FOR THE DEGREE OF

MASTER OF ARTS

in

THE FACULTY OF GRADUATE STUDIES

(Department of Asian Studies)

We accept this thesis as conforming to
the required standard

THE UNIVERSITY OF BRITISH COLUMBIA

December 1997

© Paul B.M. Crowe, 1997

Department of _Asian Studies_

The University of British Columbia
Vancouver, Canada

Date _December 22, 1997_

DE-6 (2/88)

Abstract

The *Wuzhen pian* (Chapters on Awakening to the Real), composed by Zhang Boduan during the Northern Song dynasty (960-1127), is one of the most important texts describing the Taoist method of cultivation known as *neidan* (inner alchemy). *Neidan* texts, including the *Wuzhen pian*, contain a complex array of symbols which draws on sources such as *waidan* (outer alchemy), the *Yijing* (Book of Changes), and the *wuxing* (five phases) in addition to earlier Taoist texts. One of the most influential representations of *neidan* literature is found in volume five of Joseph Needham's monumental reference work, *Science and Civilisation in China*. It is held here that this representation, while rich in detail, is flawed in its portrayal of the *neidan* process of cultivation. Needham and his colleagues present *neidan* as a form of proto-science which is concerned almost exclusively with physiological processes.

An argument is made for understanding the *Wuzhen pian*, which is taken as representative of *neidan* literature in general, as primarily a spiritual document detailing a process which leads to an experience of enlightenment and transcendence rather than as a chapter of early proto-chemistry in the story of the evolution of modern science. This argument is based on the author's annotated translation of the edition of the *Wuzhen pian* found in the *Xiuzhen shishu* (Ten Compilations on the Cultivation of Perfection). The annotation pays close attention to the various commentaries included in this edition of the text as well as the other editions found in the *Daozang* (Taoist Canon).

The main argument and the translation are preceded by a discussion of Zhang Boduan's (ca. 983-1081) life which is based on the hagiographic materials found in the *Daozang* and several gazetteers. A summary of the various major influences on the text and an overview its structure has also been included.

Table of Contents

List of Tables

Introduction

The *Wuzhen pian* was composed during the Northern Song dynasty (960-1127) which places

its author in the midst of a civilization undergoing great changes and enduring considerable and

unremitting pressures at its northern and western borders from the Jürchen and the Tanguts. The

results of these pressures were felt in the heavy economic burden incurred through having to

maintain a large army. Despite the difficulties associated with appeasing and fending off the Jürchen

and Tangut peoples the Song had a very well organized civil service which held considerable power

due to the freedom it was granted to manage the affairs of the kingdom. According to the *Zhejiang*

tongzhi[1] Zhang Boduan occupied a position in the civil service as a Magistrate (*fuli* 府使) in his

home district of Lin Hai. Also, after having been banished, he is said to have assumed the position

of Military Commissioner (*jiedu zhizhi shi* 節度制直使)[2] near the western frontier at Chengdu.

As an official Zhang would have been a member of the educated elite given to the enjoyment

of the arts such as poetry, music and calligraphy rather than the harsher, more brutish pastimes of

the Tang aristocracy whose prestige was still bound up with their military prowess and exploits. The

Song dynasty, which has been characterized as a renaissance in opposition to the medieval Tang, is

supposed to have been a time during which those who served the state had the resources and

therefore the leisure to think. Gernet describes this moment in history as one of an emergence out

from under the domination of Buddhism with its fantastical "phantasmagoria" of demons, animals,

---

[1]   *Zhejiang tongzhi, juan* 200, *xianshi* 3.

[2]   Hucker, *Official Titles*, 156 / 949. Within this title, *jiedu* (節度) is a prefix attached to many important titles but especially to that of Military Commissioner (*jiedu shi* 節度使). Ibid., 144 / 772.

and infernal beings.[3] Concerning Buddhism and Taoism during the Song, Hucker states that "Neither doctrine independently produced a major new thinker or work."[4] A new age of rationality and empiricism was at hand and much of the new thinking drew upon the ancient texts which involved a resurrection and reinterpretation of the *Mengzi, Lunyu, Daxue* and *Zhongyong*. All this culminated in the development of Neo-Confucianism. According to Hucker, it was only insofar as Taoism or Buddhism contributed to Neo-Confucianism that they could be said to have had any importance.[5] Isabelle Robinet sees the situation somewhat differently, describing Taoist inner alchemy as an important innovation.[6]

If this representation is accepted then Zhang was a remarkable individual as he seems not to have followed the Confucian revival which many of his peers favored. And indeed, rather than rejecting Buddhism, he embraced it as a helpful mode of thought for those who followed the great way of inner alchemy. The *Wuzhen pian* is usually described as a work which brings together the three teachings of Buddhism, Taoism and Confucianism, however, the presence of Confucian ideas is muted at best. Zhang's focus was squarely upon a Taoist means of cultivation which drew also upon Buddhist insights.

---

[3] Jacquest Gernet, *A History of Chinese Civilization* (1972, reprint; New York: Cambridge University Press, 1989), 330.

[4] Charles O. Hucker, *China's Imperial Past: An Introduction to Chinese History and Culture* (Stanford: Stanford University Press, 1975), 358.

[5] Ibid.

[6] Isabelle Robinet, *Taosim Growth of a Religion*, trans. Phyllis Brooks (Stanford: Stanford University Press, 1997), 215.

Other than what might be inferred from the claim that Zhang acted as an official, it is very difficult to state the circumstances in which he studied, wrote, and preached. Information about Zhang's life is provided in four hagiographies in the *Daozang* (see pages 6-13 below) and in a handful of gazetteers from regions in which he traveled. The *Zhejiang tongzhi* (compiled 1723-1736),[7] *Shanxi tongzhi* (compiled 1893), *Taizhou fuzhi* (compiled 1723-1736) and the *Sichuan tongzhi* (compiled 1796-1821)[8] all state that he received the teachings of the inner elixir from Liu Haichan who came to be recognized as the first of the five patriarchs of the Southern School. There are no works by Liu Haichan in the *Daozang* and virtually no hagiographic data on his life. A work entitled the *Jinlian zhengzong ji* (TY172, DZ75-76) compiled in 1241 mentions that he was a native of Yan shan (燕山) in Hebei and that he received his teaching from *Zhongli quan*.[9]

The teachings of inner alchemy were passed on from master to disciple by means of direct oral transmission though the written text appears also to have played a subsidiary but important role. Although the *Wuzhen pian* appears to relegate the written text to a secondary status it should be noted that some of the gazetteers and hagiographies state that Zhang passed his book on to an associate telling him that it contained his whole life's work and that he should make sure that it gets

---

[7] For the sake of brevity, references to primary and secondary works in Chinese will be given only in *Hanyu Pinyin* romanization. The Chinese title and an English translation are included in the bibliography.

[8] *Zhejiang tongzhi, juan* 200, *xianshi* section; *Shanxi tongzhi, juan* 252, shenxian section; *Taizhou fuzhi, juan* 239, *fangwai* section; *Sichuan tongzhi, juan* 167, *renwu / xianshi* section.

[9] *Jinlian zhengzong ji*, 1.9a-11b. This reference is given in Judith Boltz, *A Survey of Taoist Literature: Tenth to Seventeenth Centuries* (Berkeley: Institute for East Asian Studies University of California Berkeley, 1987), 173. Texts from the *Daozang* will be cited using the system found in the *Daozang tiyao* (TY) and will include the fascicle number of the 1976 Shanghai reprint of the *Zhengtong Daozang* (DZ). These numbers will be provided only in the first reference to each work but are also included in the bibliography.

disseminated.[10] Furthermore, the afterword to the *Xiuzhen shishu* edition explains that those who are predestined (have the bones of an immortal in a past life) will be able to understand its true meaning. The *Siku quanshu zongmu tiyao*[11] mentions that once people began to be aware of Zhang's book the Taoists transmitted it from hand to hand. It is also mentioned that the Confucian scholars rarely taught it.

It is possible that the text may have been chanted or sung as sections of the text were composed according to the *zi* tune known as the moon over the west river (*xi jiang yue* 西江月). This is a sophisticated poetic form which attests to Zhang's standing as a scholar. Also the afterword cautions the reader not to consider the verses of the *Wuzhen pian* as mere songs. The titles of many Taoist texts include the character *zhou* (咒) meaning to intone or chant and the chanting of texts remains to this day an important component of Taoist liturgy. No mention is made in the *Wuzhen pian*, or in any of the sources cited above, of the employment of the *Wuzhen pian* in a ritual or liturgical context. It appears to have served more as a kind of procedure manual for adepts.

Concerning the existence of a sect associated with Zhang and his book the main body of the text is silent. The afterword does mention that after receiving the teaching of the Golden Elixir, Zhang actively sought out disciples though it seems none of them had the requisite abilities to comprehend his teachings. It is also said that Zhang tried to pass on his understanding of inner alchemy despite the shortcomings of his disciples and met with punishments from heaven. Both the *Zhejiang tongzhi* and the *Taizhou fuzhi* state that a temple was built in Zhang's honour on a

---

[10] See for example the accounts in the *Taizhou fuzhi*, *juan* 239, *fangwai* section and the Xiaoyao *xujing* (TY1452, DZ1081), 2.33a.

[11] *Siku quanshu zongmu tiyao*, *zi* section, *Daojia* subsection.

mountain named Baibu ling (百步嶺) and the *Taizhou fuzhi* adds that a school of immortals who followed his teaching flourished there. Both Isabelle Robinet and Judith Boltz are of the opinion that nothing approaching a formal sect can be attributed to Zhang Boduan. Boltz refers to the Southern Sect (Nanzong 南宗), as a term "which came into use" rather than as a bona fide sect.[12]

The chapters below are organized as follows: Chapter One will examine the details concerning Zhang Boduan's life such as they are, based on the hagiographical information which is available in the *Daozang*. A section of this chapter will also be devoted to describing some of the important influences which helped to shape the ideas expressed by Zhang in the *Wuzhen pian*. The chapter will conclude with an overview of the structure of the text. Chapter Two consists entirely of an annotated translation of the edition of the *Wuzhen pian* which is found in the *Xiuzhen shishu*, a repository of inner alchemical works. The focus of Chapter Three is an analysis of the text's contents which provides a response to the excellent and detailed work of Joseph Needham and his associates represented most famously in *Science and Civilisation in China*. The response questions the accuracy and the usefulness of approaching Taoist inner alchemical texts primarily as documents of proto-science and, even more specifically, of proto-biochemistry. An argument, based on the contents of the *Wuzhen pian*, will be made for viewing this centrally important representative of inner alchemical literature, as a religious or spiritual text which describes a means for achieving transcendence.

---

[12]   Boltz, *Taoist Literature*, 173.

In the midst of black there is white which is the mother of the elixir;
within the male is contained the female and this is the sacred foetus.
Supreme unity resides in the stove; [you] ought to guard it carefully;
the three [elixir] fields gather what is precious and correspond to Three Terraces.

Chapter One
An Introduction to the Text and its Author

This chapter is intended to provide a general overview of Zhang Boduan's (張伯端) life and

his place within Taoism. Also included is a brief outline of the *Wuzhen pian* (Chapters on

Awakening to the Real) (TY262, DZ127-128), one of three inner alchemical texts ascribed to him.

For the purposes of this chapter, discussion of the text will be confined to its structure and a broad

description of its content. A more detailed analysis of the text's contents will be reserved for Chapter

Three.

I. Zhang Boduan

Very little information is available concerning the details of Zhang Boduan's life. Most of

the information provided here is taken from four hagiographic biographies found in the Taoist

Canon. The first, very brief, biography is included in the *Sandong qunxian lu*[13] TY1236, DZ992-995

(see *ce* 992, 2.9b-10a) which was compiled and edited by Chen Baoguang (陳葆光) in 1154. Chen

was a *Zhengyi* (正一) Taoist Master at Jiangyin in present day Jiangsu. This collection of

biographies was assembled by Chen in order to support his belief that with careful study and effort

the achievement of transcendence could be attained by anyone and was not entirely predetermined

---

[13] Hereafter *Junxian lu*.

by one's innate and naturally endowed aptitudes.[14] Chen's biography provides no detail concerning

the life of Zhang Boduan. Instead, very cursory comments are made concerning the content of the

Wuzhen pian. The second, and longest of the biographies, is found in the *Lishi zhenxian tidao*

tongjian[15] TY295, DZ139-148 (see *ce* 148, 49.7b-11a). This collection of biographies, the largest

in the Canon, was compiled and edited during the Yuan Dynasty (1260-1338) by the Taoist master

Zhao Daoyi (趙道一) (fl. 1294-1307) who resided at Fouyun Shan (浮雲山) in present day

Zhejiang.[16] The third biography is included in Weng Baoguang's (fl. 1173) synopsis of the *Wuzhen*

pian, entitled *Ziyang zhenren wuzhen pian zhizhi xiangshuo sansheng biyao*[17] TY143, DZ64 (see

15a-16b). The biography of Zhang Boduan is included in a section of the above text which was

added in 1337 as a supplement by the editor of the text, Dai Qizong (戴起宗) (fl. 1335-1337).[18] The

Xiaoyao xüjing[19] TY1452, DZ1081 contains the fourth biography (see 2.33a-34a). This very short

work is comprised of only two chapters (*juan* 卷) and was edited by Hong Zicheng (洪自成),[20] a

Ming dynasty (1368-1644) Taoist master who was a native of Xindu (新都), now known as the city

of Chengdu in the province of Sichuan.[21] This work contains the biographies of sixty three Taoist

---

[14]   Ibid., 59.

[15]   Hereafter *Tongjian*.

[16]   Boltz, *Taoist Literature*, 56-59.

[17]   Hereafter *Sansheng biyao*.

[18]   Boltz, *Taoist Literature*, 317, n. 447.

[19]   Hereafter *Xujing*.

[20]   *Daozang tiyao* (Beijing: Zhongguo Shehui Kexue Chubanshe, 1991), 1158.

[21]   *Daojiao da cidian* (Beijing: Huaxia Chubanshe Chuban Faxing, 1995), 749, s.v. 洪自成.

Immortals beginning with Laozi and ending with Chang Sanfeng, the Taoist sage often claimed as the discoverer of *Taiji quan.*

The dates for Zhang Boduan's life are not clear and none of the four biographies provide a year of birth. Concerning the year of his death the *Tongjian* states:

> On the fifteenth day of the third month of the *yuanfeng* (元 豐) reign (1082) [he] sat down cross-legged and transforming, [he] quit the world. At the age of ninety-nine years [he was] delivered from the corpse.[22]

The *Xujing* provides an almost identically phrased passage which gives the same date for Zhang's death. If one assumes that the ninety nine year lifespan given in these texts is accurate it would mean that Zhang was born in 983. Livia Kohn[23] appears to have taken this approach while Isabelle Robinet[24] and Judith Boltz[25] have taken the safer course of offering only a date for his death. Among contemporary Chinese sources the *Daozang tiyao*[26] gives Zhang's dates as 984-1082 as does the *Daojiao da cidian.*[27] The scholar and modern practitioner of Taoist inner alchemy (*neidan* 內丹), Wang Mu (王沭), claims Zhang's dates to be 983-1082.[28]

---

[22]   *Tongjian*, 49.10a. The phrase "delivered from the corpse" is a translation of *shijie* (尸解) a term referring to the transformation which takes place at death. The translation is taken from Isabelle Robinet, "Metamorphosis and Deliverance from the Corpse in Taoism," *History of Religions* 19 (1979): 57-66.

[23]   Livia Kohn, *The Taoist Experience: An Anthology* (New York: State University of New York Press, 1993), 313.

[24]   Robinet, *Taoism*, 221.

[25]   Boltz, *Taoist Literature*, 173.

[26]   *Daozang tiyao*, 1223.

[27]   *Daojiao da cidian*, s.v. 張伯端, 582.

[28]   Wang Mu, *Wuzhen Pian Qianjie* [hereafter *Qianjie*](Beijing: Zhonghua Shuju Chuban, 1990), 1.

All of the biographical accounts are agreed that Zhang Boduan was a native of Tiantai which is located approximately fifty kilometres inland from China's coastline in Zhejiang province. The *Tongjian*[29] and the *Xujing*[30] briefly allude to Zhang's youth, stating that he was an avid scholar though they furnish no further details concerning the nature of his studies. The *Daozang tiyao* mentions that in his youth Zhang was a student of Confucian teachings and also made a cursory study of texts associated with all of the "three teachings" (*sanjiao* 三教) of Buddhism, Taoism and Confucianism. In addition he studied astrology, healing-divination, astronomy, and geography.[31] This list is supplemented in the *Daojiao da cidian* with the addition of law, mathematics, medicine, and military strategy.[32] Contrary to the above information, the *Sansheng biyao* appears to state that, prior to establishing his name, Zhang did not study and instead wandered freely about. It is possible that Dai Qizong incorrectly copied the phrase in question from whatever source document he was working with. The wording is very close to that found in the biography included in the earlier *Tongjian*. The two lines of text read as follows:

少無所不學浪跡雲水

[In his] youth there was nothing [he] did not study; [he] wandered freely [amid] clouds and rivers.[33] (*Tongjian*, 49.7b)

---

[29] *Tongjian*, 49.7b.

[30] *Xujing*, 2.33a.

[31] *Daozang tiyao*, 1223.

[32] *Daojiao da cidian*, s.v. 張伯端, 582. Wang Mu includes a comparable list in *Qianjie*, 2.

[33] "Clouds and rivers" (*yunshui* 雲水) is a term which, by the Tang dyansty, was used to refer to a wandering monk or travelling Taoist master. *Ciyuan* (Beijing: Shangwuyin Shuguan, 1987), 1811, s.v. 雲水.

少無名不學 浪跡雲水

[In his] youth [when he was still] without a name (reputation) [he] did not study [but] wandered freely [amid] clouds and rivers. (*Sansheng biyao*, 15a)

Certainly the writer of the *Wuzhen pian* demonstrates a high level of literacy and a sound understanding of the *Yijing* as well as some knowledge of the constellations. Also, many direct quotations from and allusions to the *Daode jing* and the *Zhuangzi* are scattered throughout the alchemical portions of the text. A large section of the text also employs a wide range of Buddhist terminology and shows that the author had gained considerable insight into Chan Buddhist doctrine. Finally, references to various points and regions located on and inside the body demonstrate some familiarity with various anatomical and medical theories which were established long before and were current during the Song dynasty. It must therefore be concluded that the writer of this text was well educated and well read though it is possible also that Zhang waited until later in life to concentrate on matters of education as it is evident that he composed the *Wuzhen pian* in his later years (see below).

During his later life Zhang travelled extensively throughout various regions of China. The biographies provide no information on Zhang's early life, but focus instead on the period leading up to his meeting with an enlightened master and his subsequent composition of the *Wuzhen pian*. During the Zhiping (治平) reign of emperor Ying Zong (英宗) (1064-1067) Zhang served under a military official named Lu (陸)[34] who was stationed at Guilin.[35] Subsequently their garrison (*zhen*

---

[34] Lu's name is given variously as Lu Longtu gong (陸龍圖公), Longtu Lu gong (龍圖陸公), Lu gong Longtu (陸公龍圖).

[35] *Tongjian*, 49.10a.

鎮)[36] was moved and Zhang followed Lu to Chengdu in Sichuan. The *Sansheng biyao*[37] mentions that Zhang was given the title of Military Commissioner (*jiedu zhizhi shi* 節度制直使)[38] and acted as a Consultant (*canyi* 參議)[39] to the Military Commission (*anfu si* 安撫司).[40] According to the *Tongjian* and the *Xiaoyao xujing*, it was at this time that Zhang is said to have met a master, Liu Haichan (劉海蟾), and received Liu's teachings concerning inner alchemy.[41] The *Sansheng biyao* does not mention the name of Zhang's teacher. It says only that in 1069 (*jiyou sui* 己酉歲) Zhang met an extaordinary person (*yiren* 異人) who transmitted to him the secrets of the fire phase (*huohou zhi bi* 火候之秘).[42] It is unlikely that Zhang actually met Liu Haichan, who has frequently been the object of mythical lore in a similar manner to the Taoist immortals Lü Dongbin (呂洞賓) and Zhongli Quan (鐘離權). Judith Boltz notes that during the early fourteenth century, approximately the time during which the *Tongjian* and the *Xiaoyao xujing* were being written,

> . . . a number of texts came to assert that it was Liu [Haichan] who conveyed the teachings of the venerable Chung-li Ch'uan and Lü Yen to Wang Che in the North

---

36   Charles O. Hucker, *A Dictionary of Official Titles in Imperial China* (Stanford: Stanford University Press, 1985), 121 / 371. In references to Hucker, the page number is given first and the individual reference number second.

37   *Sansheng biyao*, 15a.

38   Hucker, *Official Titles*, 156 / 949. Within this title, *jiedu* (節度) is a prefix attached to many important titles but especially to that of Military Commissioner (*jiedu shi* 節度使). Ibid., 144 / 772.

39   Ibid., 518 / 6881.

40   Ibid., 104 / 18.

41   *Tongjian*, 49.7b; *Xiaoyao xujing*, 2.33a. The teachings recieved by Zhang are referred to in both of these texts by the phrase "the fire phase of the golden fluid returned elixir" (*jinyi huandan huohou* 金液還丹火侯).

42   *Sansheng biyao*, 15a.

and to Chang Po-tuan in the South. A claim such as this was no doubt extremely useful to textual codifiers who sought to find a common origin for syncretic traditions of diverse provenance.[43]

Following Lu's death (no date is provided) Zhang moved north to Shanxi province where he became associated with one Chuhou (處厚) in Hedong. After an undetermined period of time Chuhou received a summons and just before he departed Zhang gave him a copy of the *Wuzhen pian* asking him to disseminate the work.[44] According to the *Tongjian*,[45] Zhang then embarked upon his return journey and died in 1082, during the *yuanfeng* (元豐) reign of emperor Shen Zong.

The above details exhaust the information found in the four canonical biographies describing the life of Zhang Boduan. There is, however, one story found in the *Gujin tushu jicheng* (The Imperial Encyclopedia) (see note 35 below) concerning Zhang's entry into the Tao which bears mentioning. The details are very vague: It seems that, after having achieved official status, Zhang one day saw a servant girl taking a fish and mistakenly believed her to be stealing it. He reported the incident and the girl was flogged. While in a state of anger and indignation, and presumably shame, she killed herself. Somehow Zhang came to realize his error and as a result felt deep regret and was compelled to enter the Tao. The following poem is added to describe Zhang's realization of the inequities associated with his official status:

> Carrying the official's pen for forty years,
> right, right, wrong, wrong countless [times over].
> A single household well fed and clothed, a thousand households of resentment;

---

[43] Boltz, *Taoist Literature.*, 173. There is an obvious difficulty involved in asserting this line of transmission. The dates for Wangzhe are 1112-1170 while those of Zhang Boduan are 903-1082.

[44] *Xujing*, 2.34a; *Tongjian*, 49.10a.

[45] *Tongjian*, 49.10a.

half a generation honoured and esteemed, one hundred generations at fault.
Purple tassels and gold insignias, now are all gone;
straw sandals and bamboo cane, naturally wandering afar.
People ask me the way to Penglai;
[it is] clouds in the green mountains, the moon in the sky.[46]

According to the first line of this poem, Zhang must have been at least in his early sixties before he

entered the Tao. The story goes on to describe Zhang's banishment to the frontier.[47] It is said that

Zhang was banished because he committed the crime of intentionally burning official documents

(*huofen wenshu lü* 火焚文書律).[48] Presumably this is where the biographies begin their account

of his stationing in the garrisons at Guilin and Chengdu.

II. Zhang's Place within Taoism

a. The Southern Lineage

Zhang Boduan is traditionally considered the second patriarch of the Southern Lineage

(*Nanzong* 南宗) of Taoism.[49] The Southern Lineage refers to a form of Taoism in which inner

alchemy plays a central role in (or perhaps constitutes) the spiritual cultivation of the practitioner.

Zhang's teachings, and the lineage with which he is associated, are defined in relation to (that is

---

[46] This poem and the story can be found in section 18 (*Shenyi*) of the *Gujin tushu jicheng* (Imperial Catalogue) under Arts and Sciences (*Bowu*).

[47] Zhang's banishment to the frontier is also mentioned in the the *Tongjian*, 49.13a.

[48] Ibid.

[49] The Southern Lineage is also designated the Quanzhen Nanzong (全眞南宗) though when and how this came to be is not clear. It appears to have occurred after the Mongols conquered China and the practitioners from the Northern and Southern lineages began to interact. These observations are taken from comments on the first draft of this chapter made by Stephen Eskildsen.

differentiated from) the Northern School (*Beizong* 北宗) which is identified with the Complete Reality (*Quanzhen* 全眞) movement founded by Wang Zhongyang (王重陽) (1112-1170). The designation "Southern Lineage" seems to be one which was applied some time after the death of Zhang Boduan. Nowhere in his writings does Zhang refer to his teachings using the term *Nanzong*. Judith Boltz refers to this designation of Zhang's teaching as the "ex post facto Nan-tsung."[50] There is good reason to suppose that the Southern Lineage is indeed ex post facto. The lineage associated with the teachings of Zhang Boduan appears to be a response to, and an imitation of, the lineage associated with the Complete Reality school with its Five Patriarchs (*wu zu* 五祖) and Seven Perfected (*qi zhenren* 七眞人). The Southern Lineage also claimed five patriarchs: Zhang Boduan, Shi Tai (石泰) (fl. 1106), Xue Daoguang (薛道光) (fl. 1120), Chen Nan (陳楠) (fl. 1212), and Bai Yuchan (白玉蟾) (fl. 1216). The seven masters of the Southern Lineage are constituted through the addition of Liu Yongnian (劉永年), a disciple of Zhang Boduan and Peng Si (彭耜), a disciple of Bai Yuchan[51] to the above list of five patriarchs. Commenting on the Nanzong "school" associated with Zhang Boduan, Isabelle Robinet states:

> Unlike the Quanzhen school, this group established no contact with centers of power. Most of its masters wandered around the country, and despite the group's claims to go back to Zhang Boduan, nothing that could be called a real school developed before the time of Chen Nan and Bo Yuchan (fl. 1209-1224), especially after the latter became a grand master of the thunder ritual.[52]

---

[50] Boltz, *Taoist Literature*, 173.

[51] Tao-chung Yao, *Ch'uan-chen: A New Taoist Sect in North China During the Twelfth and Thirteenth Centuries* (Ph.D. diss., University of Arizona, 1980), 178-179.

[52] Robinet, *Taoism*, 224-225.

In addition to the influence brought to bear by the awareness of the Quan Zhen school, it would be reasonable to suppose that the importance of lineage to the Chan tradition may also have had some impact on those who deemed it necessary to provide a more stable representation of the teachings associated with Zhang Boduan. At various times throughout the history of Taoism there have been examples of responses to Buddhism which have given shape to various aspects of Taoist tradition. Examples of this are discussed by Ōfuchi Ninji in his well known paper on the formation and organization of the Taoist Canon, "The Formation of the Taoist Canon."[53]

b. Sources of Zhang's Thought

Looking past the "ex post facto" establishment of Zhang Boduan as a patriarch within a lineage it is evident that he drew upon a broad cross section of ideas. Zhang's place within Taoism can, to some extent, be determined by considering the various streams of thought which he drew upon in formulating his inner alchemical theory. The ideas employed by Zhang go back to the Warring States period (403-222) and end with the thoughts expressed in the Tang and Song dynasties by teachers in the Chan Buddhist tradition.

The *Wuzhen pian* contains many allusions to and direct quotations from the *Daode jing*. There are at least seventeen obvious references to this early Taoist work. It is apparent that the *Zhuangzi* is also a significant influence, especially in the later sections of the text. The manner in which Zhang employs the references to the *Daode jing* and the *Zhuangzi* are quite different. The quotations and allusions to the *Daode jing* are always tied very directly to the various aspects of

---

[53] Ninji Ōfuchi, "The Formation of the Taoist Canon," in *Facets of Taoism: Essays in Chinese Religion*, ed. Holmes Welch and Anna Seidel (New Haven: Yale University Press, 1979), 253-261.

inner alchemical theory being described. It is entirely likely that Zhang was aware of how such references would add authority to his own ideas and also that they would serve to emphasize the long history of the inner alchemical way of cultivation. This obviously does not negate the likelihood that Zhang believed in all sincerity that the *Daode jing* did indeed contain references to a kind of inner alchemical cultivation.[54] The influence of *Zhuangzi*, on the otherhand, is brought to bear in a more subtle way. Subtle for at least two reasons: Firstly, because much of the thought expressed in the *Zhuangzi* resonates strongly with ideas found in Chan texts, and thus it becomes difficult to detect where the *Zhuangzi* ends and Chan doctrine begins. Ideas which come to mind here are those of spontaneity or non-intentionality and also of the strong tendency to dispense with all oppositions such as right and wrong. Secondly, the statements which echo the *Zhuangzi* are not used to shed light on the more technical dimensions of inner alchemy in the way that those from the *Daode jing* are. Instead they serve to inform the underlying attitude of the adept, an attitude which assumes the place of a necessary foundation. Some examples of references taken from the *Daode jing* and the *Zhuangzi* should help to illustrate the different role played by each of these texts in the *Wuzhen pian*.

---

[54] Kristofer Schipper has argued that there are grounds for considering references to the governance of the state in the *Daode jing* as a metaphor for the governance of the body. He draws attention to the existence of many early commentaries which read the text in this way and which provide analyses of its meaning which resonate with ideas found in the fully developed inner alchemical texts of the Song dynasty. He is critical of the exclusive attention garnered by the more "philosophical" commentaries most famously represented by that of Wang Bi (226-249) whom he notes was not a Taoist. Kristofer Schipper, *The Taoist Body*, trans. Karen Duval (Berkeley: University of California Press, 1993), 187-195. Isabelle Robinet also warns against disregarding commentarial traditions which view the *Daode jing* as containing references to longevity practices. Robinet, *Taoism*, 29-30.

A typical example of how the *Daode jing* is employed to describe the technical aspects of inner alchemical theory is found in the following passage from the *Wuzhen pian* which includes phrases taken from two separate chapters in the *Daode jing*:

> Empty the mind and fill the belly; the meaning of this is truly profound;
> simply put, to make the mind empty [you] must understand the mind.
> There is nothing better than filling the belly before refining the lead;
> [this] causes [one] to preserve and gather gold which fills the hall.[55]

The first line in the above passage contains the phrase "Empty the mind and fill the belly;" which is an exact quotation taken from chapter 3 of the *Daode jing*.In its original context the phrase, which appears to be a reference to one of the methods employed by the sage-ruler in governing the people, reads as follows:

> Therefore in governing the people the sage empties their minds but fills their bellies,
> weakens their wills but strengthens their bones. He always keeps them innocent of
> knowledge and free from desire, and ensures that the clever never dare to act.
> Do that which consists in taking no action, and order will prevail.[56]

Here Zhang employs the line "empty the mind and fill the belly" to describe the gathering of the requisite ingredients within the body as a nececessary precursor to the next stage of cultivation. The primary "ingredients" of the inner alchemist are circulate within the body of the adept and each must be stored and refined to a more pure state. These ingredients are: essence (*jing* 精), *qi* (氣), and spirit (*shen* 神).[57] The commentary of Ye Shibiao (in the *Wuzhen pian*) equates emptying the mind with

---

[55] *Wuzhen pian*, 27.7a. Additional, more technical footnotes, have not been included here but can be found in the translation of the full text which comprises Chapter Two.

[56] D.C. Lau, trans., *Tao Te Ching* (Hong Kong: The Chinese University Press, 1963), 7.

[57] Details concerning this process are included in the following two chapters.

nourishing the *qi* (*yang qi* 養氣), and filling the belly with nourishing the elixir (*yang dan* 養丹).[58]

The final phrase in the above passage, "gather gold which fills the hall" is an allusion to chapter 9

of the *Daode jing* which reads:

> There may be gold and jade to fill a hall
> But there is none who can keep them.
> To be overbearing when one has wealth and position
> Is to bring calamity upon oneself.
> To retire when the task is accomplished
> Is the way of heaven.[59]

This verse is apparently concerned with the appropriate conduct of one who occupies a high social

position, Zhang, however, brings out a causal relationship which he understands to obtain between

the phrase contained in the first line of chapter 3 ("empty the mind and fill the belly") and the first

line of chapter nine ("there may be gold and jade to fill a hall"). Zhang links these lines, taken from

different parts of the *Daode jing*, by perceiving them as representing closely associated stages in the

inner alchemical process; a process in which a close relationship exists between filling the belly,

refining the lead, and gathering the gold. In this context lead is the *qi* of true unity (*zhen yi zhi qi* 眞

一之氣)[60] which has to be gathered in the belly prior to being refined. A final example of phrases

taken directly from the *Daode jing* is provided in the following stanza from the *Wuzhen pian*:

> In employing the general [you] must divide the armies of left and right;
> permit the other to act as host and oneself as guest.
> [As a] general [rule], [when] the ranks approach, do not take the enemy lightly,
> [lest you] lose your own home and priceless treasure.[61]

---

58   *Wuzhen pian*, 27.7a.

59   Lau, *Tao Te Ching*, 13.

60   *Wuzhen pian*, 27.6b. See the commentary of Wu Mingzi.

61   Ibid., 27.16a.

Chaper sixty nine of the *Daode jing* contains the following lines:

> The strategists have a saying,
> I dare not play the host but play the guest . . .
> There is no disaster greater than taking the enemy too easily.
> So doing nearly cost me my treasure . . .[62]

For Zhang the terms 'host' (*zhu* 主) and 'guest' (*bin* 賓) refer to the interaction of the trigrams *kan* (坎) [water] and *li* (離) [fire]or, more specifically, to the central line of these trigrams. *Kan* is comprised of two *yang* (solid) lines on the outside and one *yin* (broken) line in the centre while *li* is composed of two *yin* lines on the outside and one *yang* line on the inside. Part of the inner alchemical process is symbolized by the exchanging of the central lines in these two trigrams in order to complete two new trigrams which are pure *yang* (*qian* 乾) and pure *yin* (*kun* 坤). In order for this to happen the natural state of affairs must be inverted: the central *yang* line (fire) must be made to fall rather than rise and the *yin* central line (water) must be made to rise rather than fall.[63] The commentaries do not provide a clear account of the significance of the second line inspired by the *Daode jing* ("[lest you] lose your own home and priceless treasure"). Wang Mu explains that the "treasure" (*bao* 寶) is a reference to the "mother of the elixir" (*danmu* 丹母).[64] *Danmu* is an inner

---

[62] Lau, *Tao Te Ching*, 102-103.

[63] Wang Mu, *Qianjie*, 66, n.4. The relationship of the terms 'host' and 'guest' to the inversion of the trigrams is explained in some detail in Joseph Needham, *Science and Civilization In China*, vol. 5.5, *Spagyrical Discovery and Invention:Physiological Alchemy* (Cambridge: Cambridge University Press, 1983), 61-63. He provides two charts which are also helpful: see 53, 60. An additional symbolic parallel is given in the commentary of Wuming zi who associates the "host" and "guest" with the cycling of the fire within the adept's body. This is known as the fire phase (*huohou* 火候) and refers to the fire which rises up the back and then sinks down the front of the body. *Wuzhen pian*, 27.16a.

[64] Wang Mu, *Qianjie*, 67, n.7.

alchemical technical term which refers to the raw ingredient (*yuan liao* 原 料) comprising the

internal medicine[65] which in turn is needed to enable the adept to form a foetus of immortality within

his or her body.

In each of the above examples Zhang employs the passages from the *Daode jing* in a way that

ties them very closely to specific inner alchemical events. The phrases used are indistinguishable

from any of the other poetic allusions to the various phases of the alchemical process. In this way

Zhang establishes, or perhaps recognizes, a link between the most important foundational text for

the various traditions of Taoism and the innovations represented more than a millenium later by the

inner alchemical texts of the Tang and Song dynasties.

The *Wuzhen pian* appears to contain no direct references to the *Zhuangzi*[66] although certain

themes are strongly reminiscent of this early Taoist work. Zhang teaches, for example, that those

interested in his method of cultivation should be indifferent to status and wealth.

> Simply coveting profit and favour, seeking honour and fame,
> not caring for the body and suffering the distress and decay of ignorance.
> Let me ask, if [you] piled up gold as high as a mountain peak,
> at the end of [your] life[67] could [you] pay enough to prevent death from coming?[68]

---

[65] *Daojiao da cidian*, 297, s.v. 丹母.

[66] A possible exception to this is a reference to the "well frog" in describing the ignorance of those who are unaware of the raw ingredients within their own bodies which can confer longevity if cultivated in the correct way. *Wuzhen pian*, 26.16a. A passage in the *Zhuangzi* states, "Jo of the North Sea said, 'You can't discuss the ocean with a well frog—he's limited by the space he lives in.'" Watson, *Chuang Tzu*, 175.

[67] This reading of *wuchang* (無常) is taken from Wang Mu, *Qianjie*, 2, n.10. *Wuchang* can also be employed as a Buddhist term referring to the doctrine of impermanence. William E. Soothill and Lewis Hodous, comps., *A Dictionary of Chinese Buddhist Terms*, 6th ed. (Gaoxiong, Taiwan: Foguang chuban she, 1990), 378, s.v. 無常.

[68] *Wuzhen pian*, 26.8b.

Here Zhang appears to link the seeking of advancement in society with a state of "distress and ignorance" which demonstrates a lack of care for the body. These two notions are also closely associated in the *Zhuangzi*,

> People who are rich wear themselves out rushing around on business, piling up more wealth than they could ever use—this is a superficial way to treat the body. People who are eminent spend night and day scheming and wondering if they are doing right—this is a shoddy way to treat the body. Man lives his life in company with worry, and if he lives a long while, till he's dull and doddering, then he has spent that much time worrying instead of dying, a bitter lot indeed! This is a callous way to treat the body.[69]

While striving for wealth and official status is not considered desirable in the *Zhuangzi*, neither is escape from the world of everyday affairs considered necessary. Like Zhuangzi, Zhang is not an advocate for abandoning society and hiding in a mountain retreat.[70] Instead he advises that one "must be able to understand this great mystery [while] dwelling in the chaotic market place."[71]

The later sections of the *Wuzhen pian*, which contain predominantly Buddhist material, also resonate strongly with relativistic and mystical tendencies found in the *Zhuangzi*. In the *Wuzhen pian* one reads:

> As for [the idea that there is] a permanent lord within which rules completely over life,
> [this is] preferring to divide that and this, high and low.
> . . . Seeing the right; when has [one] seen the right?
> Hearing the wrong; [one] has not necessarily heard the wrong.[72]

---

[69] Burton Watson, trans., *The Complete Works of Chuang Tzu* (New York: Columbia University Press, 1968), 190.

[70] See for example Burton Watson, *Chuang Tzu*, 167-168.

[71] *Wuzhen pian*, 26.15a.

[72] *Wuzhen pian*, 30.11a.

In chapter two of the *Zhuangzi* one reads:

> Therefore the sage does not proceed in such a way, but illumines all in the light of Heaven. He too recognizes a "this," but a "this" which is also "that," a "that" which is also "this." His "that" has both a right and a wrong in it; his "this" too has both a right and a wrong in it. . . . A state in which "this" and "that" no longer find their opposites is called the hinge of the Way.[73]

One more passage from the *Wuzhen pian* reads:

> Grief and joy, gain and loss; respect and insult, danger and ease.
> [My] mind does not see in a dual way; peaceful, it is unified in its considerations.
> Not considering the start of fortune nor the beginning of calamity.
>
> [When] influenced, [I] respond; [when] compelled [I] begin [to act].
> [Since I] do not fear sharp knives; why dread the tiger and rhinoceros?[74]

In the *Zhuangzi* one finds the following, strikingly similar, recommendation which advises acting like grazing animals that are able to overlook a change in pasture or fish who are unconcerned with a change of stream:

> [Be like them] and joy, anger, grief, and happiness can never enter your breast. In this world, the ten thousand things come together in One, and if you can find that One and become identical with it, then your four limbs and hundred joints will become dust and sweepings; life and death, beginning and end will be mere day and night, and nothing whatever can confound you—certainly not the trifles of gain or loss, good or bad fortune![75]

In both of these passages a state of internal peace is achieved through cleaving to unity. One's mind must be "unified in its considerations" and must recognize that all the apparent multiplicity, which acts as a ground for one's anxieties, comes "together in One."

---

[73]   Watson, *Chuang Tzu*, 40.

[74]   *Wuzhen pian*, 30.9b.

[75]   Watson, *Zhuangzi*, 225-226.

Zhang Boduan looks to seated meditation as a means for realizing this underlying unity and its attendant state of internal quietude, and it is also evident in the *Zhuangzi* that some form of meditation is involved in the cultivation practice of the sage. In the *Zhuangzi* the term used to refer to meditation is *zuowang* (坐忘), literally, sitting and forgetting. Near the end of chapter six Confucius has a conversation with Yan Hui (顏回) concerning the nature of meditation. Confucius is curious about something that Yan Hui has been practicing. Yan Hui refers to his practice as sitting down and forgetting everything:

> Confucius looked very startled and said, "What do you mean, sit down and forget everything?"
> Yan Hui said, "I smash up my limbs and body, drive out perception and intellect, cast off form, do away with understanding, and make myself identical with the Great Thoroughfare. This is what I mean by sitting down and forgetting everything."[76]

Another description, provided in chapter eleven, is a response by Master Guang Cheng (廣成子) to a question posed by the Yellow Emperor who wants to know how to go about cultivating longevity. Guang Cheng suggests the following approach:

> Let there be no seeing, no hearing; enfold the spirit [*shen* 神] in quietude and the body will right itself. Be still, be pure do not labour your body, do not churn up your essence [*jing* 精], and then you can live a long life. When the eye does not see, the ear does not hear, and the mind does not know, then your spirit [*shen* 神] will protect the body, and the body will enjoy long life.[77]

The close association of the need to maintain inner stillness and purity with the function of the "spirit" as the preserver of life is a central notion in the inner alchemy of Zhang Boduan as is the assumption that the preservation of the "essence" is, in some important way, foundational to the preservation and extention of life itself.

---

[76] Ibid., 90.

[77] Ibid., 119.

In addition to the *Daode jing* and the *Zhuangzi*, Zhang Boduan drew upon the symbols of the *Yijing* and the eight trigrams of the *bagua* (八挂) as well as the system of the five phases *(wu xing* 五行) and the dynamic interaction between *yin* (陰) and *yang* (陽), all of which were employed during the Han dynasty to formulate various cosmogonic and cosmological accounts. While the theories of the five phases and the symbols of the *Yijing* and the *bagua* predate the Han, it was during the former Han that the machinations of the *fangshi* (方士), literally, the masters or scholars of prescriptions, brought these various strains of thought together in a way which would provide some of the key conceptual devices to be employed centuries later by the developers of inner alchemy. The *fangshi* were certainly preoccupied with the quest for longevity and even material immortality as the famous account of Li Shaojun (fl. -133) and his advice to the first emperor of the Han attests:

> Li Shao-ch'ün then advised the emperor, "If you sacrifice to the fireplace you can call the spirits to you, and if the spirits come you can transform cinnabar into gold. Using this gold, you may make drinking and eating vessels which will prolong the years of your life. With prolonged life you may visit the immortals who live on the island of P'eng-lai in the middle of the sea. If you visit them and perform the Feng and Shan sacrifices, you will never die. This is what the Yellow Emperor did.[78]

In this brief passage the currents of religious activity, practical operative alchemy, and the health of the human body all converge. Whether or not this was the very first example of such a confluence, it demonstrates the early existence of a foundation which was a precursor to the evolution of methods of external alchemy (*waidan* 外丹), many of which were described in the *Baopuzi* of Ge Hong (284-364). It was these methods of external alchemy which provided the metaphorical

---

[78] Burton Watson, *Records of the Grand Historian of China: The Shih chi of Ssu-Ma Ch'ien*, vol. 2 *The Age of Emperor Wu 140 to circa 100 B.C.* (New York: Columbia University Press, 1961), 39.

language employed by the inner alchemists of the Tang and Song dynasties. The operative alchemist's stove (*lu* 爐) and tripod (*ding* 鼎) became associated with various regions of the body while the herbs, base metals, and chemicals which were used to generate an elixir for ingestion became equated with various forms of *qi* in the adept's body. The three forms of medicine (*san yao* 三藥), the three jewels (*san bao* 三寶), or the three primes (*san yuan* 三元) became equated with essence (*jing* 精), *qi* (氣), and spirit (*shen* 神) all of which are permutations of the basic *qi*, each one being in a more rarefied and and therefore more celestial or holy state.

In Sima Qian's account of the *fangshi*, Li Shaojun, part of the mystique associated with this individual was his abilities at prognostication. An important part of the *fangshi's* repertoire was an understanding of divinatory methods and the calendrical cycles which underlay the passage of time. A natural extension of such concerns was a knowledge of astronomy. The result of the *fangshi's* interest in prognostication was an intersection of theories concerning both space and time. This merging of interests provided a second conceptual schema for the external and later the internal alchemist. The hexagrams and trigrams of the *Yijing* provide both the basic syntax for the expression of alchemical ideas and a schema for mapping and regulating the process. The alchemical process involves knowing the appropriate time for movement or for stillness, for emerging or retiring. The alchemist must also be fully apprised of the various regions of the inner universe and the ways in which they are inter-related. Much more discussion of these ideas will be included in Chapter Two.

The next significant source of influence on the *Wuzhen pian* is a text entitled the *Zhouyi cantongqi* (Hereafter *Cantong qi*) TY996, DZ623. This text is attributed to Wei Boyang whom

Robinet describes as "a legendary immortal who supposedly lived in the second century A.D."[79]

While there are references to a work of the same title which date back to the Han dynasty it is

considered very unlikely that this is the same text which is today preserved in a number of editions

in the Taoist Canon.[80] The *Cantong qi*, which has been interpreted as a work on both inner and outer

alchemy, is full of symbolism found in later inner alchemical texts including the *Wuzhen pian*. The

outer alchemist, the alchemist who was preoccupied with the manufacture of a substance which

would confer longevity or even immortality, employed heat to change basic ingredients into an elixir

of immortality. With the use of fire came the need to regulate the intensity of the heat which was

generated. Throughout twelve double hours of the day the intensity of the heat had to be carefully

increased until the peak was reached at the hour of *si* (巳) (9am-11am) then, through the rest of the

day, the heat was gradually lowered until the hour of *hai* (亥) (9pm-11pm). These fluctuations of

heat through the day can be mapped onto twelve hexagrams which describe the sine-like fluctuations

in the intensity of the heat by means of the movement of the broken and solid lines through the

hexagrams. These hexagrams are: *fu* (復), *lin* (臨), *tai* (泰), *dazhuang* (大壯), *guai* (夬), *qian* (乾),

gou (姤), *dun* (遯), *pi* (否), *guan* (觀), *bo* (剝), and *kun* (坤). Starting with *fu*, which corresponds

with the hour *zi* (子) (11pm-1am), there is one solid line at the bottom of the hexagram. Through

the following hours one solid line is added (always from the bottom up) until the hexagram becomes

pure *yang* at the hour of *si* (巳). During the noon hours of *wu* (午) (11am-1pm) *yin* returns with one

---

[79] Robinet, *Taoism*, 220. Fabrizio Pregadio agrees with Robinet on this point. Fabrizio Pregadio, "The Representations of Time in the Zhouyi Cantong qi," *Cahiers d'Extrême-Asie* 8 (1995): 168.

[80] Further details concerning the various recensions of the *Cantong qi* can be found in the appendix to entitled Historical notes on the *Cantong qi* included at the end of the following article: Pregadio, "Time in the Zhouyi Cantong qi,": 168-171.

broken line appearing at the bottom of the *fu* (復) hexagram. The cycle then moves to completion as the *yin* lines gradually build from the bottom up until the hexagram becomes pure *yin* during the hours of *hai* (亥) after which the whole cycle begins anew. The *Cantong qi* employs this correlation of the above twelve hexagrams with the hours of the day to describe the regulation of the alchemists fire.[81] In the *Wuzhen pian* this system of correspondences is employed for the purpose of describing the fluctuations of *yin* and *yang* within the body of the adept. The last two lines of following passage is a typical example of how the twelve hexagrams are used to describe the alchemical process:

> The red dragon and the black tiger [belong to] the west and east [respectively];[82]
> the four signs coalesce at the centre which is *wu ji*;
>
> [The process of] *fu* and *gou* is able, from this point, to be carried out;
> [as for] the golden elixir who says its work cannot be completed.[83]

Fu and *gou* mentioned above represent the re-emergence of *yang* and the re-emergence of *yin* respectively and these stages are related directly to the formation of the golden elixir which is being created inside the adept and which will confer on him or her a state of transcendence and awakening as well as robust health.

The cycle described above corresponds directly with the movement of the sun through the day but the *Cantong qi* also made use of the moon's movement to describe fluctuations in terms of

---

[81] The *Cantong qi* is comprised of 90 *zhang* (章) and the sections dealing specifically with these correlations include *zhang* 49-60.

[82] Details concerning the symolism in this line can be found in footnote 183.

[83] *Wuzhen pian*, 27.12b. Many more examples can be found in the text and have been described in the annotation to the translation which follows.

months rather than hours.[84] It is important to note that the two systems (monthly and hourly) are based on twelve divisions. This allows the alchemist to view his work as a way of compressing time. What the alchemist did with his stove (*lu* 鑪) and cauldron or reaction vessel (*ding* 鼎) was essentially to reproduce a pure substance out of base ingredients which would normally take centuries to form in the earth. Then, by ingesting the final product the alchemist would reap the benefit of the thousands of years which inhered in the elixir.[85] References to the cycles of the moon abound in the *Wuzhen pian* and are used in a manner parallel to that of the diurnal cycle.

Other features which *neidan* language has have been borrowed from the *Cantong qi* are summarised as follows by Robinet:

> The basic trigrams are personalized: the father, the mother, the sons, and the daughters and are then associated with the Five Agents and their various characteristics. They are also the basic materials that provide the authors of inner alchemy with their rich font of images and symbols: the toad of the sun, the hare of the moon, the cauldron and the furnace in the shape of a crescent moon, the yellow sprout, the chariot of the river, the black mercury that contains the golden flower, and so on.[86]

With the exception of the last two terms all of these symbols from the *Cantong qi* have been incorporated into the description of the inner alchemical process found in the *Wuzhen pian*. In addition the *Cantong qi* also makes use of references to the dragon and the tiger which, in the *Wuzhen pian*, are used to symbolize the interaction between the trigrams *kan* and *li*. It is within these

---

[84] The sections dealing with the phases of the moon and their correspondence with the hexagrams are found in *zhang* 13-15 and 46-48 of the *Cantong qi*.

[85] These ideas are detailed in Nathan Sivin, "The Theoretical background of Elixir Alchemy," *Isis* 67 (1976) 513-527.

[86] Isabelle Robinet,"Original Contributions of Neidan" in *Taoist Meditation and Longevity Techniques*, ed. Livia Kohn (Ann Arbor: Center for Chinese Studies The University of Michigan, 1989), 303.

trigrams that pure *yang* and pure *yin* are to be found. The coming together of the dragon and tiger

are employed as a symbol of reunion, a reunion which represents a movement back through the

cosmogonic unfolding described in chapter 42 of the *Daode jing* to the time when there was unity

rather than division:

> The white tiger of the western mountain goes mad;
> the green dragon of the eastern sea cannot stand it.
> The two animals grasp [each other in a] battle to the death,
> [and thus] are transmuted into a single lump of purple-gold frost.[87]

Examples of references to the dragon and the tiger are found in *zhang* 29 and 40 of the *Cantong qi*

however, not having made a close study of this difficult text, it would be premature to attempt an

account of how they function within the *Cantong qi*. In general terms, the *Wuzhen pian* is indebted

to the *Cantong qi* for much of its symbolic vocabulary including the terms of external alchemy and

the system of mutual dependence and influence represented by the Five Phases and also for the

manner in which different time-scales are correlated and then paired with the movement of *yin* and

yang through the hexagrams of the *Yijing*.

The final major stream of thought evident in the *Wuzhen pian* is that of Chan Buddhism. The

function of Chan doctrine within the text is, in part, comparable to that of the *Zhuangzi* insofar as

one of its primary purposes is to describe the attitude of non-attachment required by the adept who

undertakes the process of inner alchemy. On the other hand the presence of Buddhist thought within

the text is far from being merely allusory in nature as appears to be the case with the *Zhuangzi*. The

Buddhist material constitutes roughly one third of the text and is explicitly Chan Buddhist. There

is also a very clear line of division between the more technical alchemical material comprising the

---

[87] *Wuzhen pian*, 27.13b.

first two thirds of the text and the Buddhist material in the remaining third. The alchemical section

of the text contains only scattered examples of Buddhist terminology and there is little evidence of

any attempt on the part of Zhang Boduan to integrate the two. In addition to its passive, descriptive

function, the Buddhist material provides a means by which the adept can free his or her mind from

the confines of conventional assumptions regarding a fixed, personal identity existing relative to an

objective, essentially real world as it is experienced through the senses:

> But alas, deluded people are detained in pursuit of [their] surroundings;
> still [they] take hold of words and appearances seeking to name and enumerate.
> [But the] true thusness underlying reality is fundamentally without words;
> without low, without high, [completely] boundless;
> Without form [yet] not empty, no duality of substance;
> the field of qualities [which extends] through the ten directions is a single complete
> mandala.[88]

A definite link is understood to obtain between the realization of these non-conventional truths and

the adept's ability to enter into a state of deep concentration in meditation. The next few lines of the

same verse continue as follows:

> Has true concentration ever distinguished between speech and silence?
> [It] cannot be attained by grasping [and it] cannot be attained by rejecting.
> Simply do not restrain the mind in all the differentiating characteristics [of things];
> accordingly this is the true guiding rule of the Tathāgata.
> Do away with illusory appearances and hold to the true response;
> [if the idea of] illusion is not produced [then] truth also remains obscured.
> [If you] are able to realize that neither truth nor illusion exist,
> then [you will] attain the true mind which is without hindrances.[89]

For the purposes of inner alchemy it is the unhindered true mind which allows the adept to gain

access to the depth of concentration required to set in motion the events described in the first two

---

[88] Ibid., 30.4a.

[89] Ibid., 30.4a-b.

thirds of the text. While it is obvious to the reader that the Buddhist section of the text is clearly

separated from that containing the alchemical theory, they do share this common purpose. Both parts

contribute in their own way to shake the adept's faith in both conventional truths, and the usefulness

of language to provide the kind of insight needed to propel the subject through the course of

internally generated alchemical events. The difference lies not so much in function as in form.

The language of inner alchemy serves both to communicate and to frustrate. By combining

these functions the reader or listener is drawn into a universe of discourse which, on the surface,

appears to contain its own internal integrity and meaning only to find that there is no explicit

resolution to the story being told. After having become hopelessly ensnared the adept is perhaps

pushed over the linguistic edge into a more intuitive mode of comprehension. Isabelle Robinet

paraphrases the explanation of the *Quanzhen* master and second patriarch Danyangzi (丹陽子)

(1123-1183) who sheds light on this function of inner alchemical discourse:

> He [Danyang zi] went on to emphasize that alchemy is nothing but metaphors. In
> summary he said that *neidan* is nothing really new except that it uses a special
> language that aims at disrupting ordinary thinking by tearing apart the hardened
> knots, the solid barriers. Eventually this language will soften the mind in exactly the
> same way as the body has been relaxed previously by the various techniques of
> respiration.[90]

What one comes to see is that while the language of inner alchemy appears very different from that

of Chan Buddhism they do indeed share a common purpose. The difference lies only in the approach:

The language of Chan attempts the inspiration of revolution from without. An attempt is made to

disclose the adept's circumstances and to shock him out of complacent, conventional modes of

---

[90] Robinet,"Original Contributions of Neidan," 302. Unfortunately Robinet does not provide
a reference for this paraphrasing of Danyang zi's thoughts.

thought. Inner alchemical language is less obvious about its aim. A more subtle and perhaps subversively oriented force is brought to bear on the subject.

In concluding this section it should be mentioned that there are many other texts within the vast corpus of *neidan* material which have, no doubt, contributed to the shaping of ideas found in the *Wuzhen pian* which Judith Boltz describes as a "watershed in Taoist contemplative literature."[91] There are many important texts from the Tang dynasty through the Five Dynasties period (907-960) which must have had a strong influence on Zhang Boduan's thoughts. The list of texts would have to include works such as the *Yinfujing* TY121, DZ57, of which ther are several editions in the Taoist Canon, the *Jiuyao xinyinjing* TY224, DZ112, and the *Ruyao jing* which is found in chapter 37 of the *Xiuzhen shishu*. A project which is long overdue would be the writing of a history which traces the development of *neidan* from its earliest phases represented perhaps in the *Cantong qi* through to the present.

III. Outline of the Text

There are several editions of the *Wuzhen pian* included in the Taoist Canon and they vary considerably in length. The edition chosen for study here is the longest and includes a substantial section of Chan Buddhist material. It is found in the anonymously compiled collectaneum, *Xiuzhen shishu* (Ten Compilations on the Cultivation of Perfection) (TY262, DZ122-131).[92] The date of compilation for this work has not been determined; however Judith Boltz notes that the latest

---

91 Boltz, *Taoist Literature*, 174.

92 This is Judth Boltz' translation of the title. Boltz, *Taoist Literature*, 234.

collections of writings included date to the mid thirteenth century.[93] The *Wuzhen pien* comprises chapters (*juan* 卷) 26 through 30 of the *Xiuzhen shishu*. The text is broken down into a number of distict sections.

The opening section, which is untitled, contains sixteen heptasyllabic verses which exhort readers to cultivate themselves according to the way of the golden elixir (*jindan* 金 丹). The significance of the number sixteen is explained by a brief note placed under the section title in another edition of the text.[94] It states (employing a metaphor from operative alchemy) that this is done in order to represent the mixing together of two equal quantities of eight "ounces" each to make a total of sixteen "ounces" or one pound (*jin* 斤).[95] The emphasis is not on the specifics of this method but rather on compelling the reader to wake up to his circumstances and to the potential for change which the text offers. The reader is also alerted to the fact that everyone has the necessary ingredients for effecting the changes of inner alchemy within their own body. Thus there is no need to go in search of herbs or minerals. The second concern is the establishment of an identity for the way of the golden elixir which "among all the marvels of perfection is the most true."[96] The author describes a number of specific practices which are not the way of the golden elixir. These include techniques for regulating respiration, fasting, operative alchemy, and celibacy.[97]

---

[93] Ibid., 236.

[94] *Ziyang zhenren wuzhen pian zhushu*[hereafter *Zhushu*] (TY141, DZ61-62), 1.1a.

[95] One *jin*, comprised of sixteen "ounces," is equal to 1.3 pounds or 0.5897 kilograms.

[96] *Wuzhen pian*, 26.11b.

[97] These "other" ways of cultivation are listed in verses eight and fifteen. Ibid., 26.20a-21a; 26.30a-32a. Concerning celibacy, a practice advocated by the *Quanzhen* sect, the text actually refers only to divorcing one's wife, which is seen as unproductive. All it achieves

Next is the largest section of the *Wuzhen pian*. It contains sixty-four heptasyllabic verses in imitation of the sixty-four hexagrams of the *Yijing*. It is here that one finds the core of Zhang's alchemical theorizing. Almost every verse is dense with metaphors from the language of external or operative alchemy and with descriptions of complex interconnections between images and ideas generated by the five phases, the eight trigrams, astronomy, Taoist ideas concerning the inner landscape, ancient medical theory and even folktales. The opening of this section gives hope to the reader that a linear unfolding of the alchemical process is about to be described. All such hope is extinguished in fairly short order.

The third part of the text contains five heptasyllabic verses. The number of verses is said to represent the five phases although the usual material representations of the phases (wood, fire, earth, metal, and water) are replaced with a second set: lead, mercury, cinnabar, silver and earth.[98] Despite this claimed symbolic representation the verses actually place considerable focus on Buddhist ideas in addition to those of Taoist inner alchemy. The reader is cautioned against being satisfied with merely understanding the teachings of inner alchemy and is urged instead to actually put them into practice. Failure to do so will consign the adept to the endless round of birth, death and rebirth. Following this section is a single thirty character, pentasyllabic verse representing the Supreme Unity (*Taiyi* 太一)[99] which contains the marvel of the true *qi* (以象太一 含真氣之妙). *Taiyi* has functioned in several different ways throughout the history of Taoism. It has, for example, been used as a synonym for the Tao and has represented the most important deity within the body. One of the

---

is the separation of *yin* and *yang*. Ibid., 26.30b.

[98] *Sanzhu*, 5.19b.

[99] *Zhushu*, 3.15b; *Sanzhu*, 5.1a.

famous Nine Songs (Jiu ge 九哥) includes the name of this deity in its title.[100] The role of *Taiyi* in this context is difficult to determine with any precision as no additional information is provided.

The next set of twelve verses is titled "The West River Moon" and follows the pattern of two sets of six characters followed by one of seven and concludes with another six character line. This sequence is repeated twice for each verse. The choice of twelve as the number of verses corresponds with the twelve months of the year.[101] Most of these verses provide descriptions of the alchemical process although there is also emphasis placed on the need to cultivate good conduct and to practice meritorious deeds which, to be effective, must be performed secretly. In addition to performing good works one must also treat others with equanimity.

The twelve months of the year having been represented by the previous twelve verses, one extra verse is added and correlated with the intercalary month which has to be added seven times in nineteen years to compensate for the fact that the lunar month has fewer days than a solar month. It is remarkable that even the number of verses is carefully considered so that the reader will understand that the movement through the alchemical process within the universe of the body is a movement closely tied to cycles of time in the larger universe. The verse equates successful cultivation of the inner elixir with comprehending the way of no rebirth. The result of this success will be the attainment of the supernatural powers of a Buddha within one's present lifetime.

The numerous verses concerned with inner alchemy conclude with an ode to the *Zhouyi cantong qi* described earlier in this chapter. This verse in the *Wuzhen pian* asserts the parallel that exists between the cycles of change described by the hexagrams of the *Yijing* and the development

---

[100] David Hawkes, *Ch'u Tz'u: The Songs of the South* (Boston: Beacon Press, 1962), 36.

[101] *Sanzhu*, 5.2a.

of the inner elixir. It states that Wei Boyang, being aware of this affinity, chose to look deeply into

the hexagrams in order to provide insight into the inner alchemical process.[102] The verse ends by

cautioning the reader that once the words of the text have achieved their end of illuminating the

significance of the hexagrams, they should then be forgotten. Additionally, once the hexagrams have

made clear the underlying idea they also should be abandoned.[103]

  The Buddhist section of the text is entitled "Song in Praise of the Chan School" (*Chanzong*

gesong 禪宗歌頌) and is comprised of sixteen subsections all of which, unlike the alchemical

verses, include titles which provide some insight in to the content of the various verses. The chart

below provides a list of their Chinese titles and English translation. Also included is the length in

characters of each section and the length of the phrases which consitute the verses. In some cases the

number of characters per phrase is almost consistent throughout a verse with one or two exceptions

as is the case, for example, with the verse entitled "Ode to the Mind Indeed Being Buddha" which

includes a single six character phrase while the remainder of the verse is comprised entirely of seven

character phrases.

---

[102] *Wuzhen pian,* 29.16b. See also the commentary of Weng Baoguang concerning the employment of the hexagrams to shed light on the inner alchemical process. *Wuzhen pian zhushi* [hereafter *Zhushi*], TY145, DZ66, *xia,* 5b.

[103] Ibid., 29.19a.

Table 1: Buddhist Verses in the Wuzhen pian

English Title	Chinese Title	No. of Characters	Characters Per Phrase
Ode to the Ground of Buddha Nature	性地 頌	176	5/7/6 [104]
No Sinfulness or Blessedness	無罪福	48	6
The Three Realms are Only Mind	三界惟心	24	6
If You See Things You See Mind	見物便見心	40	5
Universal Penetration	圓通	28	7
According with Others	隨他	28	7
The Precious Moon	寶月	28	7
Ode to the Heart Sutra	心經頌	24	6
Others and Myself	人我	48	4
On Studying Chan Master Xue Dou's Anthology on Eminent Adepts	讀雪寶禪師祖英集	251	7
An Explanation Concerning Discipline, Concentration, and Wisdom [105]	戒定慧解	180	prose
Ode to the Mind Indeed Being Buddha	即心是佛 頌	139	7
Ode to Picking up the Pearl	採球歌	294	prose
A Song on Meditative Concentration and Pointing Out Illusion [106]	禪定指迷歌	651	6/prose
The Song of Non-intentionality	無心歌	255	4
West River Moon	西江月	600	6-6-7-6

---

[104] The first is titled, "Ode to the Ground of Buddha Nature" consists of six brief stanzas, the first of which is forty characters in length. There are then four stanzas of twenty eight characters and a sixth of twenty four characters. The length of lines varies according to the chart above.

[105] *Ding* (定) is translated here as "concentration" which is a translation of the Sanskrit term *samādhi*. *Samādi* is a precondition for meditation (Sanskrit: *dhyāna*, Chinese: *Chan* 禪). Soothill and Hodous, *Chinese Buddhist Terms*, 254, s.v. 定.

[106] "Meditative concentration" is comprised of two characters: *chan* (禪) meaning meditation, thought, reflection, and especially profound and abstract religious contemplation and the second character *ding* (定) meaning to compose the mind, intent contemplation and perfect absorbtion of thought into one object of meditation. Ibid, 459, s.v. 禪; 254, s.v. 定.

It is remarkable that out of the almost three thousand characters comprising the Buddhist section of the *Wuzhen pian*, not a single inner alchemical term is ever mentioned. The verses focus instead on awakening the reader to the Buddha-nature within. Awareness of one's true nature is to be realized through transcending the world as it is represented through the senses: "[If,] in all things, one restrains hearing, seeing, apprehending, and knowing, then [the Buddha-nature], hidden within the dusty realm, will manifest its inner power."[107] The objects which constitute the conventional notion of what the universe is are all empty, "Objects of the senses and objects of the mind are all without substance."[108] Through the realization of the ultimately empty nature of all things the mind becomes freed from all attachments and, like Vairocana, one "understands the extinguishing of life with no residue."[109] In this way one will be assured of having broken the endless cycle of birth, death and rebirth.

---

[107] *Wuzhen pian*, 30.2a.

[108] Ibid. This belief in the immanence of Buddha-nature is parallel to the inner alchemical claim that the medicine which one seeks is already possessed by everyone. As the text states: "All people have within them the medicine of long life."

[109] Ibid., 30.7a-b. For information concerning Vairocana see footnote 395 in Chapter Two.

Chapter Two
Chapters on Awakening to the Real

1. [If you] do not seek the great way to leave the path of delusion,

   although [you] maintain virtue and ability are [you] a worthy man?

   One hundred years[110] is the flash of a spark;

   a whole lifetime is a fleeting bubble.

   Simply coveting profit and favour, seeking honour and fame,

   not caring for the body and suffering the distress and decay of ignorance.

   Let me ask, if [you] piled up gold as high as a mountain peak,

   at the end of [your] life[111] could [you] pay enough to prevent death from coming?

2. Although the [regular] span of human life is one hundred years,

   [one has] no foreknowledge concerning longevity or premature death, failure or success.

   Yesterday [you] rode [your] horse along the street,

   today [you are] already a sleeping corpse in a coffin.

   [Your] wife and property all abandoned, no [longer] your possessions;

   [your] sinful karma will go into effect; it will be difficult for you to cheat it.

---

[110] The period of one hundred years was widely held to be the limit of the normal span of life. See the second stanza below.

[111] This reading of *wu chang* (無常) is taken from Wang Mu, *Qianjie*, 2, n.10. *Wu chang* can also be employed as a Buddhist term referring to the doctrine of impermanence. Soothill and Hodous, *Chinese Buddhist Terms*, 378, s.v. 無常.

[If you] do not search for the great medicine how will [you] be able to encounter it?

To encounter it but fail to refine it is stupid and foolhardy.

3. [If you are going to] study immortality then it must be celestial immortality,[112]

[which] alone is the most superior doctrine of the golden elixir.

When the two things[113] come together [then the] emotions and inner nature coalesce,

the dragon and tiger[114] entwine where the five phases become complete.

From the beginning rely upon *jueji*[115] to be the matchmaker;

then cause the husband and wife to be calm and joyous.

---

[112] There are a number of classes of immortals such as, for example: celestial immortals (*tian xian* 天仙), earthly immortals (*di xian* 地仙), spirit immortals (*shen xian* 神仙), human immortals (*ren xian* 人仙), and ghostly immortals (*gui shen* 鬼仙). The celestial immortal being the highest among them. *Daojiao da cidian*, 182, s.v. 天仙. An alternative classification including three types can be found in the *Discussions of Immortals* (*Lun xian* 論仙) section of the *Baopu zi neipian* TY 1175, DZ 868.

[113] The commentary alludes to the the two trigrams *kan* (坎) and *li* (離) of the eight trigrams (*ba gua* 八卦) as the "two things." *Kan* is said to be water while *li* is fire. A central motif in inner alchemy is the union of opposites and these two trigrams are frequently used to describe this union within the alchemist's body. *Wuzhen pian*, 26.10b-11a. In all cases the hexagrams will be referred to in *Hanyu Pinyin* and will not be translated. Translating the term may cause a second reading or allusion to be ignored. Instead, explanations concerning the use of each hexagram in its specific context will be provided in the footnotes.

[114] The tiger and dragon are refered to frequently in this text. The tiger represents true *yang* (*zhen yang* 眞陽) while the dragon represents true *yin* (*zhen yin* 眞陰). They also represent the trigrams *kan* and *li*. These mythical animals are often described as being brought together which is another way of describing the exchange of the central lines of *kan* and *li* in order to generate the trigrams *qian* and *kun*.

[115] *Jue* (戊) and *ji* (己) refer to the fifth and sixth of the ten celestial stems (*tian gan* 天干) which, in combination, correspond to the earth phase which occupies the central position. The centre is the place where *kan* (坎) and *li* (離) are joined.

Simply wait until the work is completed [then] pay court to the Northern Palace;[116]

amidst the brightness in nine rose-coloured clouds [you will] ride the auspicious *luan* bird.

4. This method, among all the marvels of perfection, is the most true;

everything accords with me alone being different from others.[117]

I am aware of inversion [which] proceeds from *li* and *kan*;

who recognizes that [their] floating and sinking[118] establish host and guest?[119]

[If one] wishes to retain the mercury within the vermilion[120] in the golden cauldron,

---

[116] No mention of the "northern palace" is made in the commentary, however, the *Ziyang zhenren wuzhen pian jiangyi* [hereafter *Jiangyi*] TY146, DZ66, renders "northern palace" (*bei yue* 北闕) as "jade palace" (*yu que* 玉闕). This term is defined as the dwelling of an immortal in the *Daojiao wenhua cidian* (Shanghai: Jiangsu Guji Chubanshe, 1992), 1205, s.v.玉闕. Isabelle Robinet has translated this term as "Northern Gate" (Porte du Nord) see Isabelle Robinet, *Introduction à l'alchimie intérieure taoïste De l'unite et de la multiplicité* (Paris: Les Éditions du Cerf, 1995), 206.

[117] This phrase appears to echo the end of chapter 20 of the *Daode jing* as found in Lau, *Tao Te Ching*, 31: "I alone am foolish and uncouth. / I alone am different from others / and value being fed by the mother."

[118] This line is describing the interchange between the trigrams *kan* and *li* in the later heaven eight trigrams. *Kan*, which is paired with water and true lead, normally sinks while *li*, which is paired with fire and true mercury, would normally rise. This describes the natural state of affairs which leads to aging and death. The alchemist seeks to invert this process (*dian dao* 顛倒); hence fire must sink and water must rise which can also be understood as the exchange between *kan* and *li*. *Zhushi, shang*, 9b-10a.

[119] Ordinarily, *kan* would be the guest, by virtue of its being associated with sinking, while *li* would be the host because it is associated with rising or floating. This is the constant or ordinary way (*chang dao* 常道). The alchemist seeks to reverse these appellations, making *li* the guest by causing it to sink and making *kan* the host by causing it to rise. *Zhushi, shang*, 9b-10a; *Wuzhen pian*, 26.11b-12a. See also the very clear explanation provided by Wang Mu in *Qianjie*, 6, n.6.

[120] In this context vermilion (*zhu* 朱) refers to vermilion sand (*zhu sha* 朱砂), an outer

then the silver in the water of the jade pool[121] [must first be caused to] descend.

The work of the spirit and the circulation of the fire does not require a whole evening [before the] single orb of the sun manifests, emerging from the deep pool.[122]

5. The tiger dances; the dragon mounts the wind and waves; the principal seat of the true centre[123] generates the mysterious pearl.[124]

---

alchemical term synonymous with elixir-sand or cinnabar (*dan sha* 丹砂), which in more coventional chemical nomenclature signifies red mercuric sulfide. Wong Shiu Hon, Comp., *Daozang danyao yiming suoyin* (Taipei: Xuesheng shuju, 1989), 50. (Note: *The Concise Oxford Dictionary*, 7th ed., s.v. cinnabar, lists the term 'vermilion' as a synonym for cinnabar.)

[121] The jade pool (*yu chi* 玉池) has a number of possible meanings. For example the *Xiu zhen shi shu jin dan da cheng ji* [hereafter *Dacheng ji*] TY262, DZ123 (see the section entitled *Questions and Answers on the Golden Elixir, Jin dan wen da* 金丹問答) states clearly that "jade pool" refers to the mouth. Wang Mu disagrees, stating firmly that in this context jade pool should not be understood as referring to the mouth but rather to the trigram *kan*. Wang Mu, *Qian Jie*, 7, n.9. The commentary of Weng Baoguang in *Zhushu*, 2.10b-11a, which pairs the trigram *li* with the cauldron and *kan* with the jade pool appears to support Wang's observation. Furthermore, within this couplet the cauldron and the jade pool do appear to be functioning as a mutually dependent pair.

[122] "Deep pool" (*shen dan* 深潭) does not refer to the jade pool described above. Rather it refers to the upper elixir field (*shang dantian* 上丹田). The *Daojiao da cidian*, 893, s.v. 深潭, lists sixty six synonyms for this term including mud-ball palace (*ni wan gong* 泥丸宮), flowing pearl palace (*liu qiu gong* 流球宮), and mysterious palace (*xuan gong* 玄宮).

[123] This four character phrase (*zhong yang zheng wei* 中央正位) refers to the lower elixir field (*xia dantian* 下丹田). The commentary describes the lower elixir field as being three inches below the umbilicus. *Wuzhen pian*, 26.13b. Ye Shibiao uses the synonym, "Central Palace" (*zhong gong* 中宮) to refer to the lower elixir field. Ibid., 13a. A discussion of the elixir fields (translated by Joseph Needham as "regions of vital heat") can be found in Needham, *Science and Civilization*, vol. 5.5, 38-39.

[124] The mysterious pearl is a synonym for the "baby boy" (*yinger* 嬰兒) or the the "golden fluid recycled elixir" (*Jinyi huandan* 金液還丹).

Fruit produced on the branch will, in time, ripen;

could the baby in the womb[125] be any different?

South and north accord with the Source [through]inversion of the signs of the trigrams;[126]

at daybreak and dusk the fire phases [of the adept's body] accord with the celestial axis.[127]

[You]must be able to understand this great mystery [while] dwelling in the chaotic market place;

what need is there [to retreat] deep into the mountains to preserve peaceful solitude?

6. All people have [within them] the medicine of long life;

[yet,] self assured, stupid, and deluded, [they] vainly toss it away.

When the sweet dew descends[128] heaven and earth unite;

---

[125] This phrase refers back to the "mysterious pearl" mentioned above, employing the metaphor of the baby boy which has been conceived internally by the alchemical adept through a process of the reunion or copulation of opposites.

[126] North and south are the directions of the trigrams *kan* and *li* in the later heaven (*houtian* 後天) arrangement of the eight trigrams and *kun* and *qian* in the earlier heaven (*xiantian* 先天) arrangement. Through the inversion or exchange of the centre lines of *kan* and *li* these two trigrams are transformed into *qian* in the south and and *kun* in the north which "accords with" the earlier heaven configuration and thus, with the original state of being.

[127] This term almost certainly refers to the first of the seven stars in the Northern Bushel (*bei dou* 北斗) which is part of the circumpolar constellation, Ursa Major. This term is intended to emphasise the importance of matching the microcosmic rhythms within the adept's body with those of the macrocosm. The waxing and waning of the moon and the transition from day to night, both of which were conceived of as as fluctuations if *yin* and *yang*, appear frequently in inner alchemical literature as macrocosmic parallels to fluctuations of *yin* and *yang* in the human body. The Northern Bushel appears to the observer to rotate diurnally and annually. Its rotation was taken as a parallel to the circulation of *qi* in the body. Needham, *Science and Civilization,* vol. 5.5, 59, n.b.

[128] According to the commentary of Xue daoguang "sweet dew" (*ganlu* 甘露) and "yellow sprouts" (*huang ya* 黃芽), which appears in the next line of the text, both refer to the golden elixir. The commentary of Ziye Lu found in the same text agrees that both terms are names

[at the] place where the yellow sprouts[129] grow, *kan* and *li* interact.

The well frog[130] responds saying there is no dragon's lair;

how can the quail on the fence know that there is a phoenix nest?

[Once the] elixir is cooked, the room[131] is filled with gold;

why bother seeking herbs and learning how to cook water mallows.

7. It is important to be aware of the place which is the well-spring of the medicine;

    simply put, its home place is in the southwest.[132]

    When it happens that lead is produced from *gui*[133] [you] must quickly gather it up;

---

for the medicine (*yao* 藥), which is, of course, a common synonym for the golden elixir. *Sanzhu*, 1.20a-21a.

[129] References to yellow recur frequently in the text. Yellow is paired with the earth phase and the centre, the place at which opposites are brought together to form a unity. In this couplet the union of heaven and earth is mentioned as is the interaction of the trigrams *kan* and *li*. The connection between these two lines is that, due to their interaction, the central lines of *kan* and *li* (pure *yin* and pure *yang*) are exchanged and the resulting trigrams are *qian* and *kun* known as heaven and earth.

[130] This may be an allusion to a famous phrase in the *Zhuangzi*: "Jo of the North Sea said, 'You can't discuss the ocean with a well frog—he's limited by the space he lives in.'" Watson, *Chuang Tzu*, 175.

[131] Wang Mu, *Qianjie*, 12, n.15 claims that this term refers to the elixir cavity (*dankong* 丹穴), however Yuan Gongfu states that "room" (屋) refers to the body (體) as does Ye Shibiao. *Wuzhen pian*, 26.16b.

[132] In the later heaven arrangement of the eight trigrams the direction southwest is occupied by the trigram *kun* which corresponds with the earth phase. An illustration of both the early and later heaven arrangements of the eight trigrams and their various correlates is provided in Needham, *Science and Civilization*, vol. 5.5, 50-51.

[133] *Gui* (癸) is the tenth of the celestial stems (*tian gan* 天干) and corresponds to the direction north and, when paired with *ren* (壬), corresponds with the water phase. The *Daojiao da*

whenever the moon is full[134] gold will be far away and [you will] not be able to taste it.

[You must] send it back to the earth cauldron[135] and securely seal it up;

next put in the flowing pearl;[136] together they are a suitable match.

---

cidian, 815, s.v. 鉛遇癸生, includes an entry describing the relationship between these two terms and the four character phrase, *qian yu gui sheng* (鉛遇癸生), which occurs in this line of the *Wuzhen pian*. A partial translation of the entry follows: "Lead is a term representing the water of the kidneys. This water can be divided into two kinds: The kidney water of the earlier heaven inner nature known as *ren* (壬) water; this water is clear and light. The kidney water of the later heaven known as *gui* (癸) water; this water is murky and heavy. *Ren* water is stored within *gui* water; without the production of *gui* water *ren* water will not manifest and true lead will not be seen." The entry goes on to explain that half a pound (*ban jin* 半斤) of each type of water is necessary. It is at the time that both types of water are in balance within the body that earlier and later heaven are said to interact. (One *jin*, comprised of sixteen "ounces," is equal to 1.3 pounds or 0.5897 kilograms.)

[134] The waxing and waning of the moon is an image used to describe the rising and falling or advancing and retreating of *yin* and *yang* within the body throughout the diurnal cycle. The full moon represents the peak of *yang* and would correspond to noon (*wu* 午) (11am-1pm). This might, at first glance, appear to be a positive moment in the cycle. Needham points out, however, that the hours of *zi* (子) and *wu* mark "moments of instabiltiy and change-over." Needham, *Science and Civilization*, vol. 5.5, 70. Thus, the passage warns that this would be an inopportune time to take advantage of the precious gold which has been generated.

[135] "Earth cauldron" (*tufu* 土釜) refers to the lower elixir field (*xia dantian* 下丹田). *Daojiao wenhua cidian*, 751, s.v. 土釜. This accords with the commentary of Weng Baoguang in which "elixir field" is used to refer to the earth cauldron. *Wuzhen pian*, 26.19a. [Note: in the *Wuzhen pian* Weng Baoguang is referred to as Wu Mingzi. For the sake of simplicity, I refer to him only by the name Weng Baoguang in this thesis.]

[136] Xue Daoguang equates the flowing pearl (*liu qiu* 流球) with mercury. *Sanzhu*, 1.23a, 24a. "Flowing pearl" is one of 42 synonyms for mercury listed in *Daozang danyao yiming suoyin* [hereafter *Daozang danyao*] (Taiwan : Taiwan Xuesheng Shuju, 1989), 275-280/2346.

The weight of the medicine is one *jin* [which] must [be comprised of] two times eight[137] [ounces];[138]

adjust the fire phases [in order to] support *yin* and *yang*.

8. Stop refining the three yellows and the four spirits;[139]

[even] if [you] search through the multitude of medicines, still none are real.

When *yin* and *yang* obtain their proper categories, they return to mutual interaction;

the two eights being properly suited are naturally harmoniously joined.

The sun glows red at the bottom of the pool and *yin* mysteriously disappears;

the moon over the mountain top is white and the medicine flourishes anew.[140]

---

[137] The two eights refer to the ingredients lead and mercury which must be used in equal portions by the inner alchemist. The two eights also refer to the lunar quarters when the moon is half in darkness and half in light and *yin* and *yang* are momentarily balanced. Needham, *Science and Civilization,* vol. 5.5, 57-59.

[138] This line echoes the equal amounts (half a pound each) of the two types of water described in footnote 133.

[139] The "three yellow" (*san huang* 三黃) and the "four spirits" (*si shen* 四神) refer to various chemical agents and raw materials employed by outer elixir (*waidan* 外丹) practitioners. The three yellows are orpiment (*cihuang* 雌黃), disulphide of arsenic also known as realgar (*xiong huang* 雄黃) which is arsenic disulphide, and sulphur (*liuhuang* 硫黃). *Daozang danyao*, 42/0373, 349/2896, 174/1514. The four spirits are cinnabar (*zhusha* 朱砂), mercury (*shuiyin* 水銀) (also a synonym for cinnabar), lead (*qian* 鉛), and potassium nitrate also known as saltpetre (*xiao* 硝). Ibid., 50/0437, 277/2362, 219/1915, 341/2846.

[140] Weng Baoguang explains that the imagery in these two lines describes the two principal ingredients of the inner alchemist: lead and mercury. The commentary explains that the redness of the sun at the bottom of the pool is *yang* within *yin* and the whiteness of the moon over the mountain top is *yin* within *yang*. *Zhushu*, 3.5b.

[My] contemporaries must recognize true lead and mercury;

[these] are not ordinary sand and mercury.

9. Do not take hold of the solitary *yin* in order to have *yang*

to simply cultivate the one thing only perpetuates weakness.[141]

Labouring the body [by practising] massage and gymnastics,[142] these are not the way;

refining the *qi*[143] and swallowing morning clouds,[144] both are madness.

[Even if they] search [their] whole lives for the secret of lead and mercury;

when [will they] be able to witness the descent of the dragon and tiger?

[I] exhort you to carefully ascertain the place where the self is born;

reverting to the root, returning to the origin, this is the superior medicine.

---

[141] The commentaries provide no specific explanation for these two lines of text. It seems reasonable to conclude that they are an amplification of the point made in the previous stanza that two ingredients, lead and mercury, are necessary. Lead and mercury are paired with two of the eight trigrams, *kan* and *li* respectively; the alchemist must facilitate the exchange of the two central lines of these two trigrams which are pure *yin* and pure *yang*. By doing this the alchemist is able to reconfigure the later heaven arrangement of the eight trigrams to generate the earlier heaven arrangement. This can only be accomplished if both the single *yin* line and the single *yang* line are removed from each trigram and replaced in the other. This view of the text is in agreement with the explanation found in Wang Mu, *Qianjie*, 16, n.1.

[142] "Massage" and "gymnastics" are represented here by the paired characters (*an* 按) and (*yin* 引) which here stand for massage (*anmo* 按摩) and gymnastics (*taoyin* 道引).

[143] A variety of practices associated with breathing exercises and the consumption of medicinal substances are refered to by "refining the *qi*" (煉氣). *Daojiao wenhua cidian*, 818, s.v. 煉氣法.

[144] This refers to a method of directing the *qi*. *Xia* (霞) could perhaps be translated simply as mist or vapour, however this practice involves specifically inhaling the dawn mists. It is at this time that the red and yellow *qi* of the sun begins to emerge. Ibid., 823, s.v.餐霞.

10. Grasp well the true lead[145] and search attentively;

do not allow time to slip by.

Instead make the earthly *po* soul seize the vermilion mercury;

so the heavenly *hun* soul spontaneously governs watery gold.[146]

It may be said that when the Tao is exalted the dragon and tiger will yield;

[one] can say that [when] virtue is taken seriously the ghosts and spirits [will be] respectful.

[If you] yourself comprehend [this way of achieving] long life equal to heaven and earth;

[then] annoyance and grief will have no way to continue stirring up the mind.

11. It is not difficult to search for the yellow sprouts and white snow;[147]

those who have ability must rely upon the profundity of virtuous conduct.

---

[145] "True lead" represents *yang* within *yin* and according to the five phases is treferred to as metal within water. *Daojiao da cidian*, 792-793, s.v. 眞鉛. "True lead" (*zhen qian* 眞鉛) is also listed as one of thirty six synonyms for the outer medicine (*waiyao* 外 藥) listed in Weng Baoguang's detailed study of the *Wuzhen pian*, *Ziyang zhenren wuzhen pian zhizhi xiangshuo sancheng biyao* [hereafter *Sancheng biyao*], DZ64, TY143, 31b-32a.

[146] Yuan Gongfu explains that these phrases are describing *yin* searching for *yang* and *yang* searching for *yin*. *Wuzhen pian*, 26.15a. This is consistent with Weng Baoguang's categorization of inner alchemical terminology according to *yin* and *yang*. He classifies the *po* souls as *yin* and mercury as *yang* and the *hun* souls as *yang* and gold as *yin*. *Sancheng biyao*, 25b-27a. A more detailed explanation of these two lines is provided by Weng Baoguang. *Zhushu*, 3.4a-5a.

[147] Yellow sprouts (*huang ya* 黃芽) and white snow (*bai xue* 白雪) are different names for lead and mercury. Wang Mu, *Qianjie*, 20, n.1. Wang cites the *Xiuzhen shishu* as his source and provides a quotation. Unfortunately he does not provided a more specific reference. The *Daojiao da cidian*, 397, s.v. 白雪, is in agreement with Wang's observation. There is also an entry in the *Jindan wenda* section of the *Dacheng ji*, 10.7a which lists "horse teeth" and "white snow" among the terms used to refer to lead and mercury. "Horse teeth" is a "cover name" for "yellow sprouts." Needham, *Science and Civilization*, vol. 5.5, 213.

The four signs[148] and the five phases completely rely upon earth;[149]

the three primes[150] and the eight trigrams, are they far from *ren*?[151]

It is difficult for people to recognize the completely refined noumenal substance;

[once] all of the malignant *yin* spirits are dispersed the ghosts will not invade.

[Though I] desire to pass on to others these explanations of the mysterious,

[I] have not yet heard a sound from a single person who understands this.

---

[148] Ye Shibiao explains that the "four signs" (*si xiang* 四象) refer to the green dragon, white tiger, and two sets of constellations: *zhuqiao* (朱雀) (vermilion bird) and *xuanwu* (玄武) (dark warrior). *Wuzhen pian*, 26.25a. Yuan Gongfu is in agreement with this explanation. Ibid., 25b. Robinet has chosen to translate "four signs" as the "four hexagrams" and adds in her annotation that the four hexagrams are *qian*, *kun*, *kan* and *li*. Robinet, *Introduction à l'alchimie*, 214. The four terms refered to by the above commentators correspond to the cardinal directions and to the fourth, eighth, eighteenth and twenty fifth lunar mansions (*xiu* 宿). These four positions also corresond exactly with the four hexagrams described by Robinet. A picture entitled *An Illustration of the Bright Mirror* (*Ming jing zhi tu* 明鏡之圖) provides a very helpful graphic representation of much of the correlated spacio-temporal terms employed in inner alchemy. See *Jindan dayao*, TY1056, DZ736-738, also see Needham, *Science and Civilization*, vol. 5.5, 56-57. A detailed discussion of the system of lunar mansions can be found in Needham, *Science and Civilization in China, Mathematics and the Sciences of the Heavens and the Earth*, vol. 3, 242-252.

[149] Earth is one of the five phases but it plays a role of great importance as it represents the centre. Thus, it is the cite of interaction for the remaining four phases, which are paired with the cardinal directions and the four hexagrams mentioned above.

[150] Yuan Gongfu equates the "three primes" (*san yuan* 三元) with heaven, earth and humanity. *Wuzhen pian*, 26.25b. It is difficult to understand how this interpretation fits into the present context. "Three originals" is also often used in inner alchemical texts to refer to essence (*jing* 精), *qi* (氣) and *spirit* (shen 神). These are the three "ingredients" of the inner alchemist in their pure, or original form prior to their degradation after birth. Needham, *Science and Civilization*, vol. 5.5, 26. Robinet believes that this term is alluding to visualization practices employed during meditation. Robinet, *Introduction à l'alchimie*, 215.

[151] Weng Baoguang, (*Zhushu*, 3.1b), and Xue daoguang, (*Sanzhu*, 2.8b) both equate *ren* (壬) with water. *Ren* is also the ninth of the celestial stems, it is paired with the element water and refers to the direction north. See footnote 133.

12. The *yin* and *yang* of grasses and trees are indeed paired equally;

if one is lacking, [they] will not [become] fragrant.

[When] green leaves begin to open *yang* first leads;

next, [when] red flowers bloom, *yin* later follows.

[As for] the constant Tao, it is simply this which is used in daily life;

who understands reversion of the true source?

All of the gentlemen who declare that they study the Tao

[and yet] do not recognize *yin* and *yang* should not laugh at [this].

13. [If you] do not recognize the turning over of inversion within the mysterious,

how [can you] understand the careful cultivation of the lotus within fire?[152]

Drag the white tiger back home for nourishment;

produce a bright pearl like the orb of the moon.

Gradually guard the medicine stove and observe the fire phases;

attentively observe the spirit and the breath and let them be natural.

[When] all *yin* has been entirely stripped away and the elixir has been completely prepared;

[Thus you] leap from the cage of the mundane and live a long life of ten thousand years!

---

[152] Needham offers the following explanation for this phrase: "This graphic phrase is yet one more example of the paradoxes of Yin-Yang theory, equivalent to saying that a male adept can produce a baby boy within himself." Needham, *Science and Civilization,* vol. 5.5, 92. This observation appears to accord with the commentary of Weng Baoguang. *Wuzhen pian,* 26.27a.

14. Three, five, one, all of these three numbers;[153]

from ancient times to the present, those who understand [them] are truly rare.

East is three, south is two and together they make five;

north is one , the direction west being four, completes it.[154]

The natural dwelling of *wuji* gives rise to the number five;

the mutual recognition of these three households[155] forms the baby boy.

[Thus] the baby boy is unified and embodies the true *qi*;

in ten months the foetus is complete; it is the foundation for entering the sacred.

15. If you do not recognize the true lead genuine ancestor;

employing the ten thousand kinds [of false methods will cause you to] employ effort in vain.

---

[153] Yuan Gongfu provides a list of terms which are correlated with the three numbers mentioned. Three corresponds with wood, the *li* woman (*li nu* 離女), and vermilion mercury (*zhu gong* 朱汞). One corresponds with water, the *kan* man (*kan nan* 坎男) and white metal (*bai jin* 白金). Five corresponds with earth, the central palace (*zhong gong* 中宮) and the seat of *wu ji* (*wu ji wei* 戊己位) (Note: *wu* and *ji* are the fifth and sixth of the celestial stems which when paired represent earth.). *Wuzhen pian*, 26.29a. This information provided by Yuan Gongfu establishes a clear correlation between the numbers mentioned in the text and those of the *River Diagram* (*he tu* 河圖). Thus, the result is a description of *yin* and *yang's* union at the centre.

[154] The numbers and their corresponding directions match those pictured in the *River Diagram* and the sum of each line (five) represents the earth phase, the centre and unity.

[155] "Households" (*jia* 家) refers to pairs of correlated numbers in the *River Diagram*.

Divorcing [your] wife, [who is] dishonoured and banished,[156] [will merely cause] *yin* and *yang* to separate;

follow the vain teaching of cutting off grains and [your] stomach will be empty.

Grasses, trees, gold and silver, all are dregs;

things such as morning clouds, and sun and moon[157] are deceptions.

Furthermore, [you should] overlook spitting out and drawing in and concentrating the thoughts;

all of these various techniques are not the same as golden elixir activities.

16. The words of the ten thousand scrolls and scriptures of the immortals are all the same;

the golden elixir, only this is the foundational teaching.

Rely upon that position of *kun* to enliven and complete the body;

plant it in the house of *qian*, the palace of mutual interaction.

Do not blame the intelligence bestowed by heaven for complete leaking out and exhaustion;

all this is due to the complete delusion of students.

If people understand the meaning within these verses,

then [they] will immediately see the Three Pure Ones, the Most High Elders.[158]

---

[156] Wang Mu notes that this line probably contains an error in the fourth character which should be "way" or "path" (*dao* 道) rather than "to banish" (*qian* 遣). Written this way the line would read: "the false way of divorcing your wife . . ." Wang Mu, *Qianjie*, 27, n.4. Wang Mu's observation is based on a Qing dynasty commentary entitled *Wuzhen pian zhengyi*.

[157] Robinet's translation of this passage refers to the practice of absorbing the light of the sun and moon. Robinet, *Introduction à l'alchimie*, 218. Wang Mu accounts for this reference to the sun and moon in the same way. Wang Mu, *Qianjie*, 28, n.9. A fairly detailed discussion of this technique is found in Needham, *Science and Civilization*, vol. 5.5, 181-184.

[158] The Three Pure Ones (*san qing* 三清) are Celestial Precious Lord (*Tian bao jun* 天寶君)

The First Section of Four Stanza Verses[159]

1. First take *qian* and *kun* as the reaction vessel;

   next lead the medicine of the raven and hare[160] [to the reaction vessel] for cooking.

   Once these two things have been urged to return to the yellow path

   how could the golden elixir not be produced?

2. Arrange the stove and set up the cauldron in imitation of *qian* and *kun*;

   forge and refine the essence flower[161] and regulate the *po* and *hun* souls.[162]

---

also know as Celestial Lord of the Promordial Beginning (*Yuan shi tian jun* 元始天尊); Numinous Precious Lord (*Ling bao jun* 靈寶君) also known as Most High Lord Dao (*Tai shang dao jun* 太上道君) and Divine Precious Lord (*Shen bao jun* 神寶君) also known as Most High Lord Lao (*Tai shang lao jun* 太上老君). *Daojiao da cidian*, 74, s.v. 三清. Further discussion of these figures and their correlation with the three primary vitalities of the body (essence, qi and spirit) can be found in Kristofer Schipper, *The Taoist Body* (Berkeley: University of California Press, 1993), 118-119.

[159] The title of this section in the *Zhushu* indicates that the sixty four stanzas contained in this section are intended to represent the sixty four hexagrams of the *Yijing*.

[160] The raven and the hare, also called the golden raven and the jade hare, represent *yang* and *yin* and are paired with the sun and moon. If one assumes that this passage is describing the state of affairs prior to cultivation of the golden elixir then a further set of correspondences based on the later heaven arrangement of the eight trigrams would abtain: the raven would be paired with mercury and the heart, while the hare would be paired with lead and the reins (*shen* 腎). *Dacheng ji*, 10.10a. See also the table of correspondences in Needham, *Science and Civilization*, vol. 5.5, 55.

[161] The "essence flower" (*jing hua* 精華) is one of a set of three flowers which also includes the "qi flower" (*qi hua* 氣華) and the "spirit flower" (*shen hua* 神華). *Daojiao da cidian*, 76, s.v. 三華. Of the three ingredients located inside the practitioner, essence is the first to be transformed at the start of the inner alchemical process.

[162] The *po* and *hun* souls number seven and three repsectively. During one's lifetime they inhabit the body but at the moment of death they depart and scatter. Maspero, *Taoism*, 266-267.

Gather and disperse the enshrouding mists[163] to bring about transformation;

[now I] presume to discuss the wonderful and mysterious, and so on in a leisurly fashion.

3. Do not waste effort constructing a clay elixir oven;

to refine the medicine you must seek out the crescent moon stove.[164]

[You] yourself have a natural true fire [which can be] used;

it is not necessary to blow on firewood and coals.[165]

4. Within the crescent moon stove jade flowers are produced;

within the vermillion sand reaction vessel the mercury is level.[166]

---

[163] "*Yin yun*"(氤氲) could also be translated as "generative forces of heaven and earth." Ye Shibiao uses the term "*xun zheng*" (熏烝), steam or hot vapour, to describe the "true *qi*" which he takes to be the referent in this passage. *Wuzhen pian*, 27.2b.

[164] Needham explains that "crescent moon" (*yan yue* 偃月) refers to the interior shape of the alchemist's stove. Needham, *Science and Civilization,* vol. V.4, 12. He also states that the crescent moon shape was an allusion to cycles of the *qi* which are frequently described in terms of the waxing and waning of the moon. Needham, *Science and Civilization*, vol. 5.5, 99. Needham's observations are in agreement with the commentary of Weng Baoguang. *Wuzhen pian*, 27.3a.

[165] Livia Kohn reads the character *zhai* (柴) as *zi* (紫) and thus translates this line as, "There is no need for purple coal or blowing bellows." Livia Kohn, *The Taoist Experience*, 314. Thomas Cleary reads this line in the same way. Thomas Cleary, trans., *Understanding Reality: A Taoist Alchemical Classic* (Honolulu: University of Hawaii Press, 1987), 62. The use of *zhai* (柴) is consistent in all of the *Daozang* versions. Also, none of the commentators indicate that this character is written in error therefore I have chosen to translate the character as it is written in the text.

[166] Weng Baoguang explains that the crescent moon stove (*yan yue lu* 偃月爐) is *yin* and the jade flowers (*yu rui* 玉蕊) are *yang*. Thus, this image represents *yang* within *yin*. The second line represents *yin* within *yang*; the red sand reaction vessel (*zhu sha ding* 朱砂鼎) is *yang* and the mercury (*shuiyin* 水銀) contained within it is *yin*. *Wuzhen pian*, 27.4a. This idea of

Only after the power of fire has blended and harmonized

[will] seeds will become yellow sprouts, gradually growing to completion.

5. Swallowing saliva and taking in *qi*; these are things people do;

    [but] there are prescriptions which are able to create and transform life.

    If, within the reaction vessel, [you] lack the true seed,

    [this would be] like taking water and fire and boiling an empty vessel.

6. Blending and harmonizing lead and mercury will complete the elixir;

    great or small it does not matter; the two kingdoms are completed.[167]

    [You] ask what sort of thing true lead is;

    it is the brightness of the toad[168] shining on the western river the whole day long.[169]

---

    yang within *yin* and *yin* within *yang* also aludes to the two key trigrams *kan* and *li* respectively.

[167] Ye Shibiao explains that mercury is *yin* while lead is *yang* (in the later heaven configuration of the eight trigrams). *Yang* is considered honoured (*zun* 尊) while *yin* is lowly (*bei* 卑) hence the metaphor of two kingdoms: one great and one small. He goes on to state that the student of the elixir must not commit the error of leaning too much toward *yin* or *yang*. *Wuzhen pian*, 27.4b.

[168] The brightness of the toad (*chan guang* 蟾光) is moonlight. *Ciyuan* (Beijing: Shangwuyin Shuguan, 1987), 1515, s.v. 蟾.

[169] This description of moonlight shining during the day is a metaphor for the blending and harmo-nizing of *yin* and *yang*. West is the direction of metal according to the five phases. Weng Baoguang explains that the coalescing of metal and water (the river) completes true lead which is one of the two principle ingredients (the second is true mercury). *Zhushi, zhong*, 8a. The commentaries in *Zhushu*, 4.11b-12b provide further details.

7. [If you] have not yet refined and reverted the elixir do not enter the mountains;

   amid the mountains, inside or outside, there is no lead.

   This material is most precious and all families have it;

   concerning this, the insight of stupid people is incomplete.

8. [If] bamboo is broken [then you] should take hold of bamboo to repair it;

   [in order to] hatch a fledgeling you ought to use an egg to do it.

   [Amid the] myriad kinds [to employ] the wrong kind is to vainly exert effort;

   how does doing this resemble combining the true lead with [one's] saintly power?

9. In using lead [one] should not use ordinary lead;

   [when you have] finished using true lead cast it aside.

   This is the truly marvellous secret for employing lead;

   use lead [but] do not use it; this is a trustworthy account.

10. Empty the mind and fill the belly;[170] the meaning of this is truly profound;

    simply put, to make the mind empty [you] must understand the mind.

    There is nothing better than filling the belly before refining the lead;

    [this] causes [one] to preserve and gather gold which fills the hall.[171]

---

[170] This is a quotation from chapter three of the *Daode jing*. Lau, *Tao Te Ching*, 1963, 7.

[171] "Hall" must designate the interior of the body though the precise region is unclear. The middle elixir field can be referred to as the yellow hall (*huang tang* 黃堂). *Daojiao da cidian*, 299, s.v. 丹田. It is also very possible that the precise location in the body is of less

11. In a dream I visited Xi Hua[172] and reached the ninth heaven;

[a] Realized Man gave me the *Chapters on Pointing to the Mysterious*.[173]

Its contents are simple and easy, with no superfluous words,

simply teaching people to refine the mercury and lead.

12. From empty non-being the Tao produces a single *qi*;

then from this single *qi*, *yin* and *yang* are produced.

Yin and *yang* then come together to give birth to the three substances;

these three substances further generate the splendour of the ten thousand things.[174]

---

importance in this case than the general idea of conserving the precious resources within the body, a long standing principle of Taoist longevity techniques. The clue to this reading is provided in the commentary of Yuan Gongfu (*Wuzhen pian*, 27.7a) who points to the parallel between the last line of the verse and chapter 9 of the *Daode jing* which reads: 金玉滿堂 莫之能守 "There may be gold and jade to fill a hall / But there is none who can keep them." Lau, *Tao Te Ching*, 12-13. In inner alchemy it is not uncommon for the essence, *qi* and spirit to be described in terms of precious treasures such as, for example, three treasures or jewels (*san bao* 三寶).

[172] This may be the name of a Tang dynasty Taoist associated with the School of Abstruse Learning (*Xuanxue pai* 玄學派). The complete name (*hao* 號) of this famous Taoist teacher is Xi Hua Fa Shi (西華法師). This title was confered upon Cheng Xuanying (成玄英) (fl. 631-650) by the Tang emperor Tai Zong (太宗) in the fifth year of his reign, 631CE. *Daojiao da cidian*, 445, s.v. 成玄英.

[173] Two texts bearing the title *Chapters on Pointing to the Mysterious* (*Zhixuan pian*) are known: One is attributed to Chen Tuan (d. 989 CE) and is no longer extant and the other is found in a collection entitled *Luzu chuanshu* attributed to Lu Yan (b. 798? CE). The latter work is not included in the Taoist Canon. Wang Mu, *Qianjie*, 47, n.4. Robinet also notes the possible reference here to the work of Chen Tuan. Robinet, *Introduction à l'alchimie*, 223.

[174] This stanza clearly echos chapter 42 of the *Daode jing*: "The way begets one; one begets two; two begets three; three begets the myriad creatures." Lau, *Tao Te Ching*, 1963, 63.

13. The lightning of *kan* boils and rumbles[175] in the region of metal and water;[176]

fire issues forth from the Kunlun mountains[177] and *yin* and *yang* are together.

If the two things are returned they will be harmoniously combined;

the elixir will [then be] thoroughly cooked and the whole body will be fragrant.

---

[175] *Kan* is water and the lightning represents fire. This symbolizes fire within water or *yang* within *yin*. See the commentaries of Yuan Gongfu (*Wuzhen pian*, 27.8b), Wu Mingzi (Ibid., 9a), and Xue Daoguang (*Sanzhu*, 3.10a). These commentaries also describe the lightning of *kan* (*kan dian* 坎電) as refering to the crescent moon *qi* of the tiger (*hu zhi xian qi* 虎之弦氣) which is another term used to describe *yang* within *yin*. A categorization of these terms (and many others) into two groups: *yin* within *yang* and *yang* within *yin* can be found in *Sancheng biyao*, 27b-30a. See Ibid, 29b for the reference to the "Crescent qi of the tiger".

[176] With one exception (Zi Ye, *San zhu*, 3.10a) the commentators agree that "metal and water" refers to the central palace (*zhong gong* 中宮), a term used to refer to the elixir field (*dan tian* 丹田). Both Wu Mingzi (*Wuzhen pian*, 27.9a) and Weng Yuanming (*Zhushi, zhong*, 19b) use the synonym "mysterious gate" (*xuan men* 玄門) to refer to the central palace. A list of synonyms for central palace is included in *Sancheng biyao*, 30a-b. See page 30b for the reference to "mysterious gate." Needham's translation of this passage does not agree with the conclusion reached here though surprisingly he provides no explanation for his translation. Needham, *Science and Civilization*, vol. 5.5, 95.

[177] Within the landscape of the body the Kunlun mountains represent the head. Two of the better known illustrations which show the Kunlun mountains as the head are the *Yuanqi tixiang tu* and the *Neijing tu*. The first can be found in the *Jindan dayao*, TY1056, DZ736-738 and the second is a carving preserved at the White Cloud Temple (*Baiyun guan* 白雲館) in Beijing. Both of these illustrations are included in Needham, *Science and Civilization*, vol. 5.5, 105, 115. The fire issuing forth from Kun Lun mountain represents *yin* within *yang*. This is stated most clearly by Yuan Gongfu. *Wuzhen pian*, 27.8b. Thus with *yang* having emerged from *yin* in the first line of the stanza and *yin* having emerged from *yang* in the second, the pair is completed and they may now be combined as is stated in the third line.

14. Suppose that *li* and *kan* are returned without *wuji*;

   although the four signs[178] are held together the elixir will not be completed.

   Just cause "that" and "this"[179] to embrace the true earth;

   then you will cause the golden elixir to be reverted and returned.

15. The sun dwells in the place of *li* and reverts, becoming female;

   kan is matched with the toad palace and converts to male.

   If [you] do not understand the idea of inversion;

   then stop [your] lofty discussions of narrow-minded[180] views.

---

[178] The four signs are the trigrams *qian, kun, kan* and *li*. See footnote 148.

[179] "That" (*pi* 彼) and "this" (*ci* 此) refer to the trigrams *kan* and *li* which are paired with *yin* and *yang* respectively. The commentators also employ the imagery of the moon and sun and the the crescent *qi* (*xian qi* 弦氣) associated with the dragon and tiger. It is tempting to explain this passage by saying that, through the interaction of *yin* and *yang* at the centre (earth/*wu ji*), a unity is realized. This assumes a pre-existent, stable centre towards which the symols of duality move. However, the centre is itself composed of two elements represented by the temporal symbols *wu* and *ji*. In a passage from the *Zhouyi cantong ji* which is quoted by the commentators Ye Shibiao, Yuan Gongfu, Xue Daoguang, and Weng Baoguang, *ji* is paired with *kan* (*yin*) and *wu* is paired with *li* (*yang*). Thus the aim of the alchemist is not merely to unite a pair in the centre but through that uniting to actually constitute the centre. The passage mentioned above is found in section nine of the *Zhouyi cantong qi fenzhang tong zhenyi* TY996, DZ624. It states: 坎戊月精離己日光. A very tentative translation of this phrase is: "The *ji* of *kan* is the essence of the moon, the *wu* of *li* is the brightness of the sun."

[180] *Guan jian* (管見) would literally be "tube view." "*Guan*" is used to illustrate narrow mindedness in the *Autumn Floods* section of the *Zhuangzi*: "To him there is no east or west—he begins in the Dark Obscurity and returns to the great thoroughfare. Now you come niggling along and try to spy him out or fix some name to him, but this is like using a tube to scan the sky or an awl to measure the depth of the earth . . ." Watson, *Chuang Tzu*, 187.

16. Take hold of the heart-substance at the centre of the seat of *kan*;

[use it to] transform the *yin* within the stomach of the palace of *li*.

Following this transformation, the strong form of *qian* will be completed;[181]

[the choice to] hide in retirement or to fly and skip [will then] proceed entirely from the mind.

17. Mercury of the zhen dragon proceeds from the district of li;

lead of the dui tiger is produced in the region of kan.[182]

These two things [conform to] the general principal of the baby boy producing the mother;

when the five phases are complete they must enter into the centre.

---

[181] The trigram *kan* consists of two *yin* lines outside and *yang* in the centre. *Li* is *yang* outside and *yin* in the middle. Thus the *yang* centre of *kan* is being removed and inserted into the centre (belly) of *li*. Thus *li* now has three solid *yang* lines and has become the trigram *qian*.

[182] These two lines are based on correlations described in the later heaven arrangement of the eight trigrams and make reference to the two axes: east/west and north/south. "Thunder" (*zhen* 震) is located in the east and is paired with the dragon; "lake" (*dui* 兌) is located in the west and is paired with the tiger (see stanza eighteen below). *Kan* and *li* correspond with north and south. Additionally, the reference to mercury in the east and lead in the west which are said to come from *li* in the south and *kan* in the north ties together the two axis and assumes the necessity of their interaction.

18. The red dragon and the black tiger are each west and east;[183]

    the four signs coalesce at the centre which is *wu ji*;

    [The process of] *fu* and *gou*[184] is able, from this point, to be carried out;

    [as for] the golden elixir who says its work cannot be completed.

19. The white tiger of the western mountain goes mad;

    the green dragon of the eastern sea cannot stand it.

    The two animals grasp [each other in a] battle to the death,

    [and thus] are transmuted into a single lump of purple-gold frost.[185]

---

[183] This line can appear perplexing as the dragon and tiger are always said to represent green and white respectively. The conundrum can be resolved by reading 'red' and 'dragon' and 'black' and 'tiger' as each having their own independent symbolic function. Thus read this line reiterates the need to bring together the axes of north and south and east and west in the later heaven configuration of the eight trigrams. Red is associated with the south and with fire while the dragon is associated with the east and with wood. Black is associated with the north and with water while the tiger is associated with the west and with metal. Thus, according to the five phases, these pairs of phases are bound together in a relationship of production: wood produces fire and metal produces water. A clear exposition of these ideas is given by Weng Baoguang in *Zhushi*, 6.5a. Wang Mu notes also that fire can designate mercury while water can designate lead. Wang Mu, *Qianjie*, 61, n.1. Unfortunately, the order of the directions at the end of the line remains puzzling. One would normally expect their order to be reversed.

[184] *Fu* (復) and *gou* (姤) are two of the set of twelve hexagrams employed to describe the fire phase through the twelve hours of the day. *Fu* contains a single *yang* line at the first position (bottom) of the hexagram while *gou* contains a single *yin* line at the first position of the hexagram. Thus they represent the start and completion of the fire phase. *Zhushi*, *xia*, 8a.

[185] This is a synonym for the golden elixir. See, for example, the commentary in *Zhushu*, 4.14a or *Wuzhen pian*, 27.14a.

20. On top of Flower Peak Mountain[186] the male tiger roars;

at the bottom of the Fusang[187] Sea the female dragon moans.

The yellow old woman naturally [knows how to] resolve the matter of making the match;

bringing them together she causes them to become husband and wife, together of one mind.

21. Just as the moon [reaches] the horizon with the brightness of the half moon,

at dawn there is the sound of the dragon's moan and the tiger's roar.[188]

Then make good use of [your] mind to cultivate the two eights;[189]

in the hour of zhen[190], internally control the completion of the elixir.

---

[186] Flower Peak Mountain is located in the west. *Wuzhen pian*, 27.14a and *Zhushu*, 4.10b.

[187] Fusang Sea is the place where the sun rises and thus is a metaphor for the east. *Zhushu*, 4.10b-11a. *Wuzhen pian*, 27,14a.

[188] When the moon has reached the half moon stage of its cycle, *yin* and *yang* are balanced momentarily. There are two half moons: one midway between the new and full moon and another midway between the full and new moon. In the first case *yang* is waxing and *yin* is waning; in the second *yin* is waxing and *yang* is waning. This is refered to in alchemical terms through reference to the tiger and the dragon: The tiger represents *yang* emerging from within *yin* (new moon to full moon) and the dragon represents *yin* emerging from within *yang* (full moon to new moon). Thus at each half moon one becomes dominant over the other hence the metaphor of impending struggle between the two animals.

[189] See footnote 133.

[190] The hour of *zhen* (辰) is from 7am - 9 am.

22. First, moreover, observe heaven[191] and understand the five thieves;[192]

next, [you] must carefully examine the territory in order to pacify the people.

[Once the] people are pacified, the kingdom prospers [and they can] look for battles;

[when the] battles are ended [you] will be able to have an audience with the sage-lord.[193]

---

[191] A passage from the *Yinfu jing* TY31, DZ27 is quoted in the commentary indicating that in this context heaven (*tian* 天) should be taken to refer to nature or to the natural order which the inner alchemist attempts to emulate in her own body. Zhang Boduan refers to the *Yinfu jing* in stanza fifty eight below.

[192] In accordance with the celestial/corporeal correlation just alluded to, heaven has five thieves (*wu ze* 五賊) and so does the body. The commentaries suggest that the celestial thieves are five stars however there is some disagreement concerning the thieves in the body. One commentator suggests they are the five phases (*Wuzhen pian*, 27.15b); another suggests that the five store-houses (internal organs) (*wu zang* 五臟) are the five thieves (*Zhushi, zhong*, 16a). The fact that the five phases and the five internal organs are corelated may nullify any apparent discrepancy here. A third explanation is that the thieves are: desire, lust, covetousness, anger and foolishness (*ai* 愛, *yu* 慾, *tan* 貪, *chen* 嗔, *chi* 癡) (*Sanzhu*, 3.18b). This is not necessarily a standard list. For an alternate see *Daojiao da cidian*, 222, s.v. 五賊.

[193] These two lines make reference to the interior of the body. Representation of the body's interior in terms of a miniature universe including celestial bodies, geographic features and people or spirits have a long history in Taoism and related spheres of thought such as medical theory. Medical terminology as early as the second century BCE included a host of analogies to various facets of state ecomomy which were employed to describe the inner workings of the body. Paul U. Unschuld, *Medicine in China: A History of Ideas* (Berkeley: University of California Press, 1985), 79-83. Later, Taoist texts such as the *Huangting jing* TY262, DZ122-131. *Taishang Laojun neiguan jing* TY636, DZ342, *Chongyang zhenren jinguan yusuo jue* TY1147, DZ796 are examples of texts which employ the notion that the world exists within the body to establish their respective systems of correspondence.

23. In employing the general [you] must divide the armies of left and right;[194]

permit the other to act as host and oneself as guest.[195]

[As a] general [rule], [when] the ranks approach, do not take the enemy lightly,

[lest you] lose your own home and priceless treasure.[196]

---

[194] The commenatries appear to agree that this stanza is alluding to the regulation of the fire phase within the body. Weng Baoguang explains that the general represents fire and the armies a subdivision of that fire into two types: "civil" (wen 文) (slow) and "miltary" (wu 武) (quick) fires. *Wuzhen pian*, 27.17a. This parallels the practice of regulating the inensity of the fire in operative or outer alchemy as the various elixir ingredients are being cooked. One might think of the innitial stage of cooking as requiring intense, quick heat to bring the concoction to a boil. Once the ingredients have been brought to the boil the fire may then be reduced in intensity to a slow and more gentle heat. In inner alchemical terms the quick fire is employed prior to the completion of the elixir while the slow fire is employed to sustain the elixir once it is complete. *Daojiao wenhuan cidian*, 763, s.v. 文火, 778, s.v. 武火.

[195] The terms "host" (zhu 主) and "guest" (bin 賓) are paired with the trigrams *kan* and *li* as are "other" (ta 他 or bi 彼) and "self" (wo 我). This verse draws on the following lines from chapter 69 of the *Daode jing*: "The strategists have a saying, / I dare not play the host but play the guest, / I dare not advance an inch but retreat a foot instead." "There is no disaster greater than taking on an enemy too easily. / So doing nearly cost me my treasure." Lau, *Tao Te Ching*, 103-104.

[196] The process of regulating the internal fire phases requires the utmost care and attention. This idea is developed further in the following stanza.

24. The production of fire from wood[197] originally conceals a sharp point;[198]

[if you] do not understand how to bore and rub,[199] do not apply great effort and work.

Calamity will arise and [you] will only cause injury to yourself;

it is essential that you be intent upon [self-]regulation and seek out the golden old man.[200]

25. Originally, the golden old man was the son of the eastern family;

[he was] sent to the western neighbour to lodge and grow up.

---

[197] This version of the text actually reads "The production of wood from fire . . ." This appears to be a mistaken reversal of "fire" and "wood." None of the other *Daozang* versions or their commentaries contain this apparently erroneous phrase. According to the productive cycle of the five phases fire produces earth; earth produces metal; metal produces water; water produces wood and wood produces fire.

[198] Perhaps this could be read as refering to hidden danger. Another possibility is that the reference to a sharp point might be similar to the idea of looking for a needle in a haystack as appears to be the case for example in an explanation provided by Ye Shibiao: "This [passage] explains the extraction of mercury from lead. The [fact that] we cannot see the form of the mercury concealed within lead is like not [being able] to see the brightness of fire [before] it is produced from wood." *Wuzhen pian*, 27.18a.

[199] This refers to the creation of fire through the use of a drilling stick. Wang Mu, *Qianjie*, 69, n.3.

[200] "Golden old man" (*jin weng* 金翁) is listed in the *Sancheng biyao*, 29a as representing *yang* within *yin*. It should be noted that all of the other *Daozang* versions of the text are slightly different as they use the term "golden gentleman" or "golden duke" (*jin gong* 金公). This term is listed in the *Wen da* section of the *Dacheng ji*, 10.4a. The explanation there is that if 'gold' and 'gentleman' or 'duke' are written next to each other they form the character for lead. Hence this is a way of refering to lead. To complicate matters further Ye Shibiao maintains that "golden old man" (*jin weng* 金翁) should also be understood as refering to lead. *Wuzhen pian*, 27.18b.

[Having been] recognized he is invited to return home to be nourished;

[He is then] matched with a young woman and they are brought together in intimacy.[201]

26. The young woman[202] wanders from her own place;

in advancing [she] must go a short [distance] in withdrawing [she] must go a long [way].

[Upon] returning [she] withdraws into the house of the yellow[203] old woman;

[where she] marries the golden old man [whom] she makes her husband.

27. Although [you may be] aware of the vermilion sand and black lead;[204]

[If you] do not understand the fire phase [you are] just like an idler.

Generally [you must] rely upon the force of [self-]regulation;

even the smallest mistake will destroy [any chance] of making the elixir.

---

[201] This appears to be another reference to the earlier heaven arrangement of the eight trigrams in which the trigrams *li* and *kan* are located in the east and west. The discussion of movement back and forth in this and the following stanza describe the exchange of the inner line of each of these trigrams which represent true lead and true mercury. Wang Mu, *Qianjie*, 69-70, n.2. See also *Science and Civilization*, vol. 5.5, 59-63 for a discussion of this process of exchange.

[202] All three of the commentaries in the *Wuzhen pian* indicate that the "young woman" (*cha nu* 姹女) is mercury. If the "golden old man" and the "young woman" are paired with lead and mercury then stanzas 25 and 26 make obvious sense as lead and mercury are also paired with *kan* and *li* which must interact if the later heaven (degenerative) configuration of the eight trigrams is to be transformed.

[203] Yellow is the colour associated with the centre. It is the site where opposites are united. In this case the pure *yin* (female) and pure *yang* (male) lines in the middle of *kan* and *li*.

[204] "Red sand" (*zhu sha* 朱砂) and "black lead" (*hei qian* 黑鉛) are the true mercury and true lead described in terms of the "yellow old man" and the "young woman" in the previous two stanzas.

28. Various records, essays, scriptures and songs [profess to] explain the highest truth,

[but you] cannot grasp the fire phase if it is [merely] set down in words.

[You] must understand oral instructions [in order to] penetrate the mysterious place;

[thus you] should [enter into] careful discussions with spirit immortals.

29. On the fifteenth day of the eighth month[205] play with the brightness of the toad;[206]

it is precisely at this [time] that the essence of metal[207] is robust and strong.

If you arrive at the time when the single *yang* arises [signaling] return,[208]

then [you should] sustain the advance of the fire without delay.[209]

---

[205] The fifteenth day of the eighth month is the autumn equinox at which time *yang* has waxed and *yin* has waned to a point of momentary balance at the midpoint between mid-autumn and mid-winter.

[206] This is a reference to the moon. Because the Chinese based their calendar on the lunar cycle the moon would indeed be bright as it would be full on the fifteenth day of the month. This is mentioned by Ye Shibiao. *Wuzhen pian*, 27.22a.

[207] The fifteenth day of the eighth month corresponds with the eighth terrestrial branch (*you* 酉) which aligns with the west. In the later heaven arrangement of the eight trigrams this would be the direction of metal. This second line serves to reiterate the point on the annual cycle which is being refered to in the first line.

[208] This line anticipates the next stanza by referring to the time at which a single *yang* line returns. The word 'return' (*fu* 復) is the name of one of the sixty four hexagrams which is comprised of a single *yang* (solid) line at the bottom and five *yin* (broken) lines above. The hexagram *fu* is paired with the eleventh terrestrial branch *zi* (子) located just after the winter solstice in the yearly calendar and the two midnight hours within a single day. It is at this time that *yang* has just returned and is gaining ascendence. In the hexagrams this is represented by the addition of one *yang* line at a time, rising from the bottom up until the hexagram *qian* is complete.

[209] The advancing of the fire refers to the movement of the quick fire (*wuhuo* 武火) from a point corresponding roughly with the perineum (*weilu* 尾閭) through the passes or gates (*guan* 關) along the spine up to mud ball (*niwan* 泥丸), which may correspond with the brain. The

30. [When] the single *yang* has just begun to move, that is the time for making the elixir;

the lead cauldron[210] gradually warms up illuminating the curtains.[211]

It is easy to recognize when you begin to receive the *qi*;

[while] carrying out the process of drawing out and augmenting[212] you ought to guard against

dangers.

31. The mysterious pearl has a form following the production of *yang*;[213]

as *yang* peaks and *yin* has dissipated,[214] gradually the form of *bo*[215] [emerges].

---

weilu is also correlated with the hour *zi* mentioned in the previous footnote.

[210] "Lead cauldron" (*qian ding* 鉛 鼎) refers to one of the three elixir fields though it is difficult to determine which of them is being referred to in this passage.

[211] There is no specific explanation for this term in any of the *Daozang* commentaries. Wang Mu, *Qianjie*, 77, n.5. suggests that "curtains" (*huang wei* 幌帷) refers to the eyes. If this is correct then it would seem likely that the upper elixir field is being refered to in the second line of this stanza.

[212] This is another reference to the movement of the fire up towards the head.

[213] This is once again a reference to the emergence of *yang* lines through the six hexagrams starting with *fu* and reaching completion with *qian*. These coincide with the first to the sixth month of the yearly cycle and with the hours from midnight to noon. This line is describing the connection between the gestation of the mysterious pearl and the gradual building of *yang* though the first half of the cycle or fire phase which is also known as the fire phase of advancing *yang* (*jinyang huohou* 進陽火候).

[214] "*Yang* peaks and *yin* has dissipated" is a translation of the stock alchemical phrase which is used to refer to the second half of the fire phase known as the fire phase of retreating *yin* (*duiyin huohou* 退陰火候). A brief description of this phrase can be found in *Daojiao da cidian*, 505, s.v. 陽機陰消.

[215] "*Bo*" (剝), refers to one of the twelve hexagrams used to describe the waxing and waning of *yin* and *yang*. This particular hexagram is eleventh in the sequence and is immediately prior to the hexagram *kun* at the end of the cycle.

In the tenth month the frost flies and the elixir starts to cook;

at this time the spirits and ghosts will certainly be frightened.

32. After the first quarter of the moon and prior to the last quarter of the moon

the taste of the medicine is even and the form of the *qi* is complete.

Once [the medicine] is gathered put it back into the stove and refine it;

[once] the refining is complete warm it and nourish it in the same way that you would cook fresh

food.[216]

33. The eldest son, for the first time, drinks the water of the west;

the young daughter[217] for the first time opens the flower of the northern region.[218]

---

[216] Yuan Gongfu explains that in advancing the fire one has to employ the same kind of care as one would in cooking a small fish. *Wuzhen pian*, 27.24b.

[217] The commentaries unanimously agree that the "eldest son" (*changnan* 長男) refers to the hexagram *zhen* (震) while "young woman" (*shaonu* 少女) refers to the hexagram *dui* (兌). These hexagrams are paired with the directions east and west, the dragon and tiger, and with the phases water and metal .

[218] The references to west and north allude to the system of correspondences which obtains between the River Diagram (*hetu* 河圖) and the five phases; west corresponds to metal and north corresponds to water. "Metal-water" is one of the "households" of the River Diagram and represents the stage of inner alchemy at which the original essence (referred to as water in the first line) merges with the original spirit (possibly the flower mentioned in the second line) and then descends into the lower elixir field. The *Zhushi*, *Sanzhu* and *Zhushu* all include the term "metal-wine" (*jin jiu* 金酒) rather than "metal-water." The entry in the *Daojiao da cidian* explains, however, that wine should be understood as referring to water. *Daojiao da cidian*, 369, s.v. 北地華, 438, s.v. 西方酒.

After causing the green and the beautiful[219] to meet each other

immediately lock them up in the yellow house.

34. When the moon of the rabbit and chicken reach their seasons;[220]

punishment and virtue[221] approach the door and the medicine resembles it.[222]

---

[219] Here the characters *jing* (青) and *e* (娥) could be translated together as "young woman" however, in this case, the occurrence of the character *xiang* (相) meaning "mutual," and the dictates of the context urge the reader to see these as two distinct terms. The word "green" is a reference to the elder son (east) and "beautiful" refers to the young woman (west). Consistent with the rest of the stanza this is another layer of allusion to the reunion of opposites at the centre (the yellow house). This is in agreement with suggestions made by Wang Mu, *Qianjie*, 84, n.7.

[220] The "moon" and the "chicken" are names of two of the earthly branches. The first is *mao* (卯) (5am -7am), the fourth earthly branch, and the second is *you* (酉) (5pm - 7pm), the tenth earthly branch. The months, or more literally the moons, which correspond to these two daily periods are the second (mid-spring) and the eighth (mid-autumn). Weng Baoguang provides a clear account of this, *Wuzhen pian*, 28.3a-b. These moments in the daily and yearly cycles are moments of balance between *yin* and *yang*. In the first case *yin* is waxing and *yang* is waning in the second *yang* is waxing and *yin* is waning. It is important to keep in mind that the use of diurnal symbols to indicate points on the annual cycle reiterates the microcosmic cyclical parallel of the *qi* circulating within the adept's body.

[221] "Punishment" (*xing* 刑) and "virtue" (*de* 德) refer to the second and eighth months mentioned above and also to specific moments of the internal fire phase which moves through a daily cycle within the body. These stages are graphically represented by the hexagrams *fou* (否) and *tai* (泰). Weng Baoguang, Dai Qizong, *Zhushu*, 5.5a.

[222] Presumably, the formation of the medicine within the body can be likened to the fluctuations of *yin* and *yang* which occur through the annual seasons as well as in the bodily fire phase.

When it comes to this golden sand[223] [you] must bathe in it;[224]

if [at this time you] continue to add to the fire [this is] certainly dangerous.

35. During each thirty day period the sun and moon meet once;[225]

use the exchange of hours for days to regulate the efforts of the spirit.[226]

Guard the city, do battle [in the] countryside[227] and be aware of fortune and misfortune;

add numinous sand[228] [until] the whole cauldron is red.

---

[223] "Golden sand" (*jin sha* 金砂) is a synonym for "golden elixir." *Sancheng biyao*, 31b-32a.

[224] In accord with the rest of this stanza "bathe" (*mu yu* 沐浴) refers to the fire phase in the body. The first character (*mu* 沐) is paired with the (*jinyang huo* 進陽火) which moves up the spine to the top of the head while the second character (*yu* 浴) is paired with the second half of the fire phase in which the retreating *yin* fire (*tuiyin huo* 退陰火) moves down the front of the body to the lower elixir field. It is worth noting here that this binary term is also known as *mao ji* bathing (*mao ji mu yu* 卯酉沐浴). *Daojiao da cidian*, 567, s.v. 沐浴.

[225] That is, the new moon occurs at the moment that the moon is interposed between the earth and the sun.

[226] The translation of this line remains tentative. Robinet suggests that the fluctuations of the sun and moon or *yin* and *yang* which are observed in the macrocosm, are to be reflected and accorded with in the spirirtual work of inner alchemy taking place within the body. Robinet, *Introduction à l'alchimie*, 233. As it is presently translated this line is taken to refer to the cycling of the body's fire phase which must be subject to the same rhythm of waxing and waning of *yin* and *yang* as is found in the cycles of the sun and moon both through the diurnal cycle and through the monthly and yearly cycles. In this line *fa* (法) has been translated as "regulate" in order to reflect the need for careful monitoring of the inner fire so that it comes to accord with the macrocosmic fluctuations of *yin* and *yang*.

[227] The clearest description of the significance of this phrase is found in the commentary of Ye Shibiao. He explains that "guarding the city" (*shou cheng* 守城) refers to the retreating *yin* fire and the guarding of the medicine while doing "battle in the [surrounding] countryside" refers to the advancing *yang* fire. *Wuzhen pian*, 28.3b-4a.

[228] Numinous sand (*ling sha* 靈砂) is the medicine which is accumulating in the adept. *Daojiao da cidian*, 593, s.v. 靈砂. In this context the cauldron is almost certainly the lower elixir

36. The myriad things overflow after *pi* and *tai* come together;[229]

the two hexagrams *tun* and *meng*[230] receive life and [are made] complete.

Here-in [you can] attain [your] intention [but] stop searching the diagrams [for truth];

if you examine into the many lines [of the hexagrams you will be] employing your emotions in

deception.

37. The establishing of the trigrams within a hexagram is based on fixed forms;

in understanding the trigrams forget words and the meaning will be illuminated of itself.

Later generations follow along in delusion merely mired in the trigrams;

this notwithstanding, [they] proceed according to the *qi* of the hexagrams hoping to ascend.

---

field.

[229] The two hexagrams, *pi* and *tai,* perform a number of symbolic functions: *pi* and *tai* (the third and fourth of the sixty four hexagrams) are composed of the trigrams *qian* and *kun* or heaven and earth. *Qian* represents the top of the head while *kun* represents the *huiyin* (會陰), a point at the base of the *renmai* (任脈) central channel which runs down the front of the body and corresponds anatomically with the perineum. *Dictionary of Traditional Chinese Medicine* (Taipei: Southern Materials Center, Inc., 1984), 30. This channel would coincide with the retreating (*yinfu* 陰符)fire which moves down the front of the body during the second half of the day. This pair of hexagrams also represent the central theme of inversion; *pi* is composed of *qian* on top and *kun* below while *tai* is composed of *kun* on top and *qian* below. *Pi* and *tai* also correspond with the hours 5am - 7am (*mao* 卯) and 5pm - 7pm (*you* 酉) during the day and with the spring and autumn equinoxes. Finally each of these hexagrams also represent moments of balance between *yin* and *yang* and also of impending transition. The hexagram pi (否) is comprised of the trigrams *qian* above and *kun* below while *tai* (泰) has *qian* below and *kun* above.

[230] The commentaries indicate that the hexagrams *tun* (屯) and *meng* (蒙) represent the commence-ment of the fire phase. *Wuzhen pian*, 29.11b-12a; *Zhushu*, 7.12b-13a; *Sanzhu*, 5.13a-b. Wang Mu explains that *tun* represents the advancing *yang* fire while *meng* represents the retreating *yin* fire. Wang Mu, *Qianjie*, 89, n.4.

38. Heaven and earth fill and then empty [according to] their own seasonal [rhythms];

[Only when you] examine into the ebb and flow [will you] begin to understand the inner power.

Proceeding from *geng* and *jia*[231] give a clear command;

kill all three corpses[232] and the Tao can be hoped for.

39. [If you] want to attain the long life without death of the valley spirit,

[you] must rely upon the mysterious female to establish the root and foundation.[233]

The true essence having returned to the room of yellow gold,[234]

a kernel of numinous brightness endures and does not depart.

---

[231] *Geng* (庚) is the seventh of the celestial stems and *jia* (甲) is the first. They correspond to the directions east and west which have figured so prominently throughout this text.

[232] The three corpses (*san shi* 三 尸), also known as the three worms (*san qong* 三 蟲) are parasitic spirits which reside in the body's three elixir fields. They are intent upon escape from the body and so seek to bring about the death of their host as quickly as possible. This is achieved by attacking the three elixir fields in order to bring on a variety of maladies and also by reporting any moral transgressions of the host to the Director of Destiny (*si ming* 司 命) in heaven who then deducts an appropriate number of days from the lifespan of the host. Henri Maspero, *Taoism and Chinese and Religion*, trans. Frank A Kierman, Jr. (Amherst: The University of Massachusetts Press, 1981), 331-333.

[233] This stanza echos chapter six of the *Daode jing* which reads: The spirit of the valley never dies./ This is called the mysterious female./ The gateway of the mysterious female/ Is called the root of heaven and earth./ Dimly visible, it seems as if it were there,/ Yet use will never drain it. Lau, *Tao Te Ching*, 1963, 9.

[234] This line appears to be repeating an earlier reference to the middle elixir field (see stanza ten on page 59).

40. Few in the world understand the gateway of the mysterious female;[235]

do not engage in the foolish practices of the mouth and nose.

[Though] wealthy gentlemen practice spitting out and drawing in for a thousand years;[236]

how can they obtain the golden raven and the hare child.[237]

41. [They have] different names [yet] share the same origin;[238] few people understand [this];

---

[235] Ye Shibiao (echoing chapter six of the *Daode jing* as mentioned in footnote 233) explains that the mysterious female ought to be taken as the foundation if one does not wish to cut off the true *qi*. He adds that the mysterious female is the doorway of *yin* and *yang*, and the root of heaven and earth. *Wuzhen pian*, 28.6b.

[236] This stanza is warning against practicing an ancient method of nourishing the life (*yang sheng* 養生). Mention of this technique is made as early as the 4th C. BCE in the *Zhuangzi*. This well known reference can be found in the section entitled *Constrained in Will* (*ke yi* 刻意) where a description of one who feels it necessary to withdraw from the world is provided: "To pant, to puff, to hail, to sip, to spit out the old breath and draw in the new, practicing bear-hangings and bird-stretchings, longevity his only concern..." Watson, *Chuang Tzu*, 167. It is interesting that in this inner alchemical work Zhang Boduan is in agreement with Zhuangzi's disdain for such preoccupations.

[237] Reference to the raven and the hair was made in the first of the sixty-four stanzas. They represent *yang*/mercury and *yin*/lead respectively (see footnote 160 for details).

[238] It is likely that the two things being referred to are the raven and the hare mentioned in the preceding stanza. If one considers the *yin* and *yang* correlates to this pair then the passage becomes a reiteration of stanza twelve on page 60 which describes how *yin* and *yang* emerge from the unified *qi* which the Tao produces after arising out of empty non-being. Thus, the assertion that the two things, the raven and the hare, share the same origin. Weng Baoguang's commentary is consistent with this reading: He draws an explicit parallel between the cosmological text found in chapter 1 of the *Daode jing* and the generation of *yin* and *yang* within the body: "The nameless was the beginning of heaven and earth; / The named was the mother of the myriad creatures." Lau, *Tao Te Ching*, 1963, 3. He then expands on this idea referring to the correlations of heaven and earth, the hexagrams *kan* and *li*, and lead and mercury and then moves straight into a paraphrase taken from the same chapter: Being unified in their emergence [they] then differ; being the same, call it a mystery; mystery upon mystery. *Zhushu*, 4.16a-b. The commentary of Ye Shibiao focuses on lead and mercury, though his account of the origin of these constituents seems to differ. He explains that lead

as for these two, mystery upon mystery,[239] they are the important inner power.

To protect life and complete the form [you] must understand increase and decrease;

the medicine of the purple gold elixir is most numinous and marvellous.

42. In the beginning there is action [but] nobody sees it;

when it comes to non-interference everyone begins to understand.

But, seeing non-interference as the most important way;

how can [you] know that acting is the foundation?

43. In the midst of black there is white[240] which is the mother of the elixir;

within the male is hidden the female and this is the sacred foetus.

---

and mercury produce each other and therefore share the same origin. It should be noted, however, that he relies upon precisely the same passage from the *Daode jing* as Weng Baoguang. *Wuzhen pian*, 28.8b.

[239] The reference to "mystery upon mystery" continues the allusion to chapter 1 of the *Daode jing* which contains the following lines: "These two are the same / But diverge in name as they issue forth. / Being the same they are called mysteries, / Mystery upon mystery / The gateway of the manifold secrets." Lau, *Tao Te Ching*, 3.

[240] This refers to *yang* within *yin* or silver within lead, and *yin* within *yang* or mercury within cinnabar (the commentaries use "vermillion" (*zhu* 朱)). Lead is the mother of the elixir while mercury is the sacred foetus. All of the commentaries appear to be in agreement on this but Ye Shibiao states the point most clearly. *Wuzhen pian*, 28.9a-b. These two principal ingredients are brought together to form the unified *qi* mentioned in the third line of the stanza.

Supreme unity [241] resides in the stove; [you] ought to guard it carefully;

the three [elixir] fields gather what is precious[242] and correspond to Three Terraces.[243]

44. Amid the indistinct and blurred, seek out [that which] has form;

within the vague and obscure search for the true essence.

Being and non-being: follow their natural interpenetration;

[if you] have not yet seen, how can [you] think [you will] succeed?

45. When the four signs assemble the mysterious form is completed;

at the place where the five phases become complete the purple gold shines.

---

[241] Weng Baoguang appears equate the "*qi* of true unity" with "Supreme Unity" (*Tai Yi* 太一). *Zhushu*, 4.17b-18a.

[242] Ye Shibiao describes the gathering of what is precious (*ju bao* 聚寶) as the gathering of the medicine by each each of the three elixir fields, each of which he names. It appears that he is implying that each of the elixir fields gathers its own respective medicine. Unfortunately he provides no further detail to indicate with certainty that three distinct medicines are involved here. *Wuzhen pian*, 28.9b-10a. Xue Daoguang provides some clarification by explaining that what is being gathered is the three inner natures (*san xing* 三性). *Sanzhu*, 4.12a. No further comment is given on the possible identity of these three inner natures. Wang Mu claims that this is a reference to the three treasures (*san bao* 三寶) though he offers no justification for this conclusion.

[243] The "three terraces" (*san tai* 三台) refer to a group of six stars which are arranged in a line in the constellation Ursa Major which includes the Northern Bushel (*beidou* 北斗). The location of these stars in the Northern Bushel is mentioned by Yuan Gongfu. *Wuzhen pian*, 28.10a. The *Daojiao da cidian*, 72, s.v. 三台, lists the names of the three terraces of the Northern Bushel: (*xu jing* 虛精), (*liu chun* 六淳), and (*qu sheng* 曲生).

The foetus which has been released[244] enters the mouth and pervades the sacred [spirits] of the body;[245]

the innumerable dragon spirits are all overcome with fear.[246]

46. When you have finished drinking from the flower pool[247] the moon is clear and bright;[248]

astride the Golden Dragon you visit the [constellation] Purple Mystery.[249]

Henceforth, after the host of immortals recognize each other,

[amid] the tides, hills and valleys [they] move about as they please.[250]

---

[244] See footnote 252 for a discussion of the "foetus" which is released.

[245] "The sacred spirits of the body" (*shen sheng* 身聖) is a reference to the spirits which dwell in the body. *Wuzhen pian*, 28.11a.

[246] I have used Robinet's translation of this line. Robinet, *Introduction à l'alchimie*, 237.

[247] "Flower pool" (*hua chi* 華池) usually refers to the mouth or the area just below the tongue where saliva collects during meditation. See for example entries in the *Daojiao da cidian*, 468, s.v. 華池 and *Daojiao wenhua cidian*, 770, s.v. 華池. However, the commentators all associate the flower pool in this verse with the elixir (*Zhushu*, 6.4a; *Zhushi, zhong*, 29b) or with the place where the elixir is produced (*Wuzhen pian*, 28.11a; *Zi Ye, Sanzhu*, 4.14a). To confuse matters further there is a passage in Zhang Boduan's *Jindan sibai zi* which provides a functional account of the flower pool rather than describing it in terms of a specific location: "Move the true water in the lead stove; cycle the true fire in the mercury cauldron; thereby, lead's meeting (見) with mercury is called the flower pool." *Jindan sibai zi*, in *Xiuzhen shishu zazhu jixuan pian* (book one of the *Xiuzhen shishu*), 5.4a.

[248] The moon alludes to the brightness of the medicine which is being gathered in the cauldron. *Wuzhen pian*, 28.11a; *zhushi, zhong*, 29b.

[249] "Purple Mystery" (*Ziwei* 紫微) is the name of a constellation. Wang Mu claims that it is a metaphor for the cauldron of the central palace. Wang Mu, *Qianjie*, 106, n.5. Robinet describes it as a paradise (Robinet, *Introduction à l'alchimie*, 237) which is consistent with the commentary of Ye Shibiao which describes the "Purple Mystery" as the place to which the newly completed foetus ascends. *Wuzhen pian*, 28.11a.

[250] Ye Shibiao says simply that this couplet refers to the sages or saints (*sheng* 聖) which

47. [If you] want to know the method of the golden fluid returned elixir;

[you] must plant the seed in the family garden.[251]

Do not mistakenly blow and sigh and thus expend your strength;

naturally the elixir will be cooked [and you will] shed the true foetus.[252]

---

pervade the body. *Wuzhen pian*, 28.11b. The other commentators provide only general descriptions of the physical transformations which the adept undergoes at this stage. *Zhushi, zhong*, 29b; *Zhushu*, 6.4a. The descriptions of the transformed adept found in the above commentaries are taken directly from a description of the spirit-immortal found in chapter one of the *Zhuangzi*: ". . . there is a Holy Man living on faraway Ku-she Mountain, with skin like ice and snow, and gentle and shy like a young girl. He doesn't eat the five grains, but sucks the wind, drinks the dew, climbs up on the clouds and mist, rides a flying dragon, and wanders beyond the four seas." Watson, *Chuang Tzu*, 33. The mention of tides, hills and valleys is almost certainly a reference to the interior landscape of the body.

[251] The commentaries consistently emphasise that the ingredients for generating the foetus of immortality are close at hand. The family garden should be taken to refer to the adept's own body. See, for example, the comments of Ye Shibiao and and Yuan Gongfu, *Wuzhen pian*, 28.11b-12a.

[252] The last line of this stanza is somewhat problematic. It reads as follows: 自然丹熟脫眞胎 . It is possible to render this line line as: "Naturally the elixir will be cooked [and you] will escape the true foetus." This, though, is inconsistent with the notion that the foetus must be carefully nurtured within the body and with the idea of the immortal foetus (or foetus) leaving the adept's body upon completion of the inner alchemical process. The required care and attentiveness is described in the following passage: Cherish and protect the numinous root like the dragon nourishing the pearl or the chicken brooding over her eggs; cautiously guard and support without causing any mistake; even the slightest error [will cause] all former merit to be wasted. When the *Yang* Spirit goes out from the husk (the body) this is called the escaping foetus (*tuotai*). *Daojiao da cidian*, 880, s.v. 脫胎. The *Daojiao da cidian*, 880, s.v. 脫靈胎 quotes this line from the *Wuzhen pian* to support its description of this term as the completion of the form of the great medicine. (Note: the *Zhushu* has *tuo lingtai* (脫靈 胎) rather than *tuo zhentai* (脫眞胎).) *Zhushu*, 5.4a. Yuan Gongfu describes the *tuotai* as follows: "As for the escaping foetus, it is the foetus going out from the womb at the tenth month." *Wuzhen pian*, 28.11a.

48. Instead of labouring in artful and contrived ways,

recognize and take advantage of the methods of avoiding death employed by others.

Within the pot[253] the wine which retains life is then added;

within the cauldron[254] is received the broth which returns the *hun* soul.[255]

49. The consistently delicious butter liquor of the Snowy Mountains,[256]

is poured into the eastern *yang* stove of creative transformation.

---

[253] Weng Baoguang equates the "pot" (*hu* 壺) with the belly or abdomen (*fu* 腹). *Zhushi, zhong,* 38b. The term *hunei* (壺內), found in this line of the text, is also an inner alchemical term refering to the lower elixir field, located in the abdomen. *Daojiao da cidian,* 800, 壺內.

[254] The cauldron, which can refer to the lower elixir field, is not described by any of the commentators. In discussing this line of the text Wang Mu says that at the time when the refined *qi* is transformed into spirit the cauldron is located in the yellow court (*huang ting* 黃庭). Wang Mu, *Qianjie,* 108, n. 5. The yellow court is associated with the *niwan* palace in the head and the *Jindan wenda* section of the *Dacheng ji,* 10.2b does state that the cauldron is located near the yellow court. Unfortunately the same text also gives a fairly precise description of the yellow court's location which provides an alternative possibility: "[The yellow court] is located above the bladder, below the spleen, infront of the kidneys, to the left of the liver and the the right of the [left] lung." Ibid., 10a.

[255] Two ingredients are being described in these two lines, though the nature of those ingredients is not clear. Weng Baoguang equates the "pot" (*hu* 壺) with the stomach (*fu* 腹) and the "wine which retains life" (*liuming jiu* 留命酒) with "the mercurial fire which extends life" (*yanming zhi gonghuo* 延命之汞火). He appears to associate the "*hun* broth" (*hunjiang* 魂漿) with "the *yang*-elixir which [brings about] return to the root" (*fan ben zhi yangdan* 返本之陽丹), *Zhushi, zhong,* 38a-38b or the slight variant "the *yang*-elixir which [brings about] the return of the *hun* (soul)" (*fan hun zhi yang dan* 返魂之陽丹). *Zhushu,* 8.14a. Shang Yangzi equates the *hun* soul with the true *qi* (*zhenqi* 眞氣) and the "wine which retains life" with the true essence (*zhenjing* 眞精). S*anzhu,* 4.15a-15b.

[256] The "Snowy Mountains" (*xue shan* 雪山) refers to the Himālayas. Soothill and Hodous, *A Dictionary of Chinese Buddhist Terms,* 366, s.v. 雪.

If [he] goes northwest past the Kunlun mountains,

Zhang Qian[257] will then gain an audience with the Hemp[258] Maiden.[259]

50. Not recognizing the essence of *yang* and [the idea of] host and guest,[260]

and knowing those other [methods, makes] distant what is close at hand.

In [your] room vainly shutting up the *weilu*[261] opening;

how many people in Jambudvīpa[262] have been inadvertently killed [in this way].

---

[257] Zhang Qian (張騫) (? - 114 BCE) was a famous emissary during the reign of emperor Wu (武帝) at a time when the policy of pacifying the Xiongnu (匈奴) was being reconsidered. Zhang Qian sought, through his extensive travels, to locate potential allies and trading partners to help bolster the position of the Chinese *vis-à-vis* the Xiongnu.

[258] The Hemp Maiden (Ma Gu 麻故) is a Taoist immortal who is described in a section of Ge Hong's *Baopu zi* entitled *Chronicals of the Spirit-immortals* (*Shenxian chuan*). A passage from the above work, which describes a kitchen ritual in which the Hemp Maiden is a participant, is translated by Henri Maspero: "She is a pretty girl of eighteen years, with her hair dressed in a coil twisted on top of her head, the rest of her hair falling to her waist." Maspero, *Taoism and Chinese Religion*, 291.

[259] This passage refers to the exchange of the central lines of the trigrams *kan* and *li*. In the first line "snow" is an allusion to the colour white which, in the five phases, corresponds to metal and to the direction west. In the earlier heaven *bagua* this is the position of *kan*, the water trigram (*yin* outside, *yang* in the centre). The "eastern yang stove" refers to the direction of the fire trigram, *li* (*yang* outside, *yin* in the centre). The meeting of the central lines, *yin* and *yang* is represented by the meeting of the male (Zhang Qian) with the female (Hemp Maiden). *Wuzhen pian*, 28.12b-13a.

[260] See footnote 195 concerning the ideas of "host" and "guest."

[261] See footnote 209 on the location of the *weilu*.

[262] The term found in the text is *yan fu* / (閻浮). This is a phonetic rendering of the Sanskrit term *jambu*, the name of the rose-apple tree which gives its name to Jambudvīpa one of the great Buddhist continents or islands which surround Mount Meru and upon which a preponderance of Jambu trees are to be found. Soothill and Hodous, *Chinese Buddhist Terms*, 451-452, s.v. 閻.

51. The ten thousand things flourish and revert to the root;

by reverting to the root and restoring life[263] [you will] lengthen [your years].[264]

To know the constant and revert to the root, people find difficult to understand;

[but] reckless practices which bring misfortune are known to everyone.

52. Ou Ye[265] personally passed down the method for casting swords;

[In] Mo Ye[266] [the combining of] metal and water, matched soft with hard.

Once the smelting was completed [it was] then [possible] to know peoples' intentions;

for ten thousand *li* [they] slew demons in an instant.

---

[263] The use of the term 'life' to translate *ming* (命) is tentative. Robinet leaves the term untranslated, Robinet, *Introduction à l'alchimie*, 239. The range of meaning which applies to the term '*ming*' within the context of inner alchemy warrants considerable further study.

[264] These two lines are inspired by chapter 16 of the *Daode jing*: "The myriad creatures all rise together / And I watch their return. / The teeming creatures / all return to their separate roots. / Returning to one's roots is known as stillness. / This is what is meant by returning to one's destiny." Lau, Tao Te Ching, 23.

[265] Ou Ye (歐冶) was a great sword smith of the Spring and Autum period (*Qun Qiu* 春秋) (722-484 BCE). He is famous for having made five swords for the king of Yue (越王) with another famous sword maker named Yu Jiang (于將). *Ciyuan*, 897, s.v. 歐冶子.

[266] Mo Ye (莫耶) is the name of a famous sword of the Spring and Autumn period. Legend states that He Lu (闔閭), king of Chu (楚王), commanded Yu Jiang (于將) to make him a sword. Before Yu Jiang had added the molten iron to the smelting stove, his wife, Mo Ye, threw herself into the stove. Yu Jiang made two swords one male, which he named Yu Jiang and the other female, which he called Mo Ye. The first sword was presented to the king while Yu Jiang hid the second sword. It seems that ever after the female sword missed her male counterpart and wept continuously. *Ciyuan*, 1443, s.v. 莫邪.

53　Strike the bamboo,[267] summoning the tortoise[268] to swallow the jade mushroom;[269]

Sound the lute[270] calling the phoenix to drink a measure.[271]

---

[267] The striking of the bamboo (*qiao zhu* 敲竹) is, according to Weng Baoguang, a reference to the mind which is empty, without emotions. *Zhushi, zhong*, 39a. He also explains that the "striking" is an allusion to the "mutual striking" (*xiang ji* 相擊) of the two creatures (*liang wu* 兩物), which are the dragon and tiger. *Zhushu*, 8.15b. An exception to this account is provided by Ye Shibiao who describes the bamboo as what will be tentatively translated here as "vaporous *qi*" (*xiqi* 息氣). I cannot locate this as an inner alchemical technical term which may indicate that it should be read as translated above or that it should be understood as a conjunction of "breath" and "*qi*." *Wuzhen pian*, 28.15a.

[268] The commentators take the tortoise and the phoenix (mentioned in the second line) to represent the hexagrams *kan* and *li*, though they choose a number of varying but corresponding symbols in place of the hexagrams. Ye Shibiao, for example, describes the two as fire and water (*Wuzhen pian*, 28.15a) while Weng Baoguang, in two different commentaries, refers to them as lead and mercury, two constellations (*bei fang zhi xuanwu* 北方之玄武 and *nan fang zhi zhuqiao* 南方之朱) (*Zhushu*, 8.15b), and as the black tiger and the red dragon (*Zhushi, zhong*, 39a). In all of these cases the chosen symbols correspond with the later heaven eight trigrams.

[269] The jade mushroom (*yu zhi* 玉芝) is also known as the white mushroom (*bai zhi* 白芝). *Daozang danyao*, 1989, 17/0127. Most of the commentaries equate the "jade mushroom" and the "measure" (*dao gui* 刀圭) with the crescent moon *qi* of the tiger (*hu zhi xianqi* 虎之弦氣) and the crescent moon *qi* of the dragon (*long zhi xianqi* 龍之弦氣). *Wuzhen pian*, 28.15a, *Zhushi, zhong*, 39a, *Zhushu*, 8.15b, *Sanzhu*, 4.20b. These terms which are correlated with the lunar cycle are intended to denote the emergence of *yang* from within *yin* and of *yin* from within *yang*. Needham, *Science and Civilisation*, vol. 5.5, 57-58.

[270] The sounding of the lute is described as evoking the need for internal harmony, a necessary prerequisite for the regulation of the internal process of alchemy. This harmony is described in terms of the relationship which exists between a husband and wife. *Zhushu*, 8.15b, *Sanzhu*, 4.20b. This mention of harmony is consistent with Weng Baoguang's general comment on the meaning of this passage: "This [stanza] is an explanation of the work of cycling the fire." 此言運火之功也. *Zhushu*, 8.15a. The fire can damage or help the adept depending on his or her ability to regulate it. See footnote 194 for a discussion of the need to regulate the internal fire.

[271] The term *daogui* (刀圭) refers to an ancient vessel employed for measuring medicine. *Daojiao wenhuan cidian*, 746, s.v. 刀圭. An interesting description of the significance of this term is provided by Ye Shibiao who notes that the character *gui* (圭), is composed of two "earths" (*tu* 土), which, he claims, represents the union of the two hexagrams *kan* and *li*.

Recently the whole body manifests a golden light;

do not discuss these rules with ordinary people.

54. The form is complete when the medicine encounters the [*yin* and *yang*] categories of *qi*;[272]

Tao spontaneously brings together that which cannot be seen and that which cannot be heard.[273]

When one grain of golden elixir is swallowed and enters the stomach,

you will begin to understand: my fate does not depend on heaven.

55. In one day the luminous red golden elixir can be completed;

the words handed down by the ancient immortals are truly worthy of being listened to.

As for those who speak of nine years or three years,

all of these are [merely] delaying and extending the daily practice.

56. Cultivation of the great medicine has difficult [points] and easy [ones];

furthermore, understanding comes from oneself as well as from heaven.

Wuzhen pian, 28.15a.

[272] This line includes the inner alchemical technical term *qilei* (氣類) which refers to the mutual influencing and joining of *yin* and *yang qi.* These two foms of *qi* are mutually attracted at which point they become unified. *Daojiao da cidian,* 287, 氣類.

[273] "... that which cannot be seen and that which cannot be heard." is said to refer to the *qi* of true unity of the chaotic beginning (*hunyuan zhenyi zhi qi* 混元眞一之氣). *Sanzhu,* 4.22b, *Zhushi, zhong,* 10b, *Zhushu,* 4.13b. This passage echoes chapter fourteen of the *Daode jing,* the first two lines of which state: "What cannot be seen is called evanescent; / What cannot be heard is called rarefied;" Lau, *Tao Te Ching,* 19.

If [you] do not accumulate [good] conduct and exhibit merit,

[you will] stir up crowds of demons, and create obstructive karma.

57. The three powers[274] rob each other, eating at the [appropriate] time;[275]

this is the inner power of the spirit immortals' Tao and Virtue.

Once the myriad transformations have been settled all anxiety will cease;

[thus] the [abiltity to] regulate the whole body is evidence of non-purposive action.

---

[274] The three powers (*san cai* 三才) are heaven, earth and humanity.

[275] This line reads as follows: 三才相盜食其時 and has been translated in a way which includes the word 'eating' (*shi* 食). Cleary and Robinet avoid translating this term. Cleary, *Understanding Reality*, 116; Robinet, *Introduction à l'alchimie*, 241. A clue to the possible meaning of this phrase is found a passage from the *Yinfu jing* (*The Yin Convergence Scripture*) TY31, DZ27 which is quoted as a commentary to the passage (*Wuzhen pian*, 28.17b). It describes a system of mutual dependence or, more literally, pillaging or robbing (consumption) which exists on a cosmological scale between heaven and earth, humanity and the myriad creatures. Robinet (ibid) points out that chapter 1 of the *Liezi* alludes to this state of affairs. (See A.C. Graham, trans., *The Book of Lieh-tzu: A Classic of Tao*, Morningside Edition, 1990 (Columbia University Press: New York, 1960), 30-31. For the purposes of inner alchemical exposition this would have to be understood as a description of the body's internal workings. Weng Baoguang provides a detailed account of this cosmological process in which he points out that the natural course of things involves a system of relationships between heaven and earth, the myriad creatures, and humanity which results in a state of gradual decay and specifically, and most importantly for the practitioner of inner alchemy, it results in death for human beings. He goes on to explain that "If [you] can blend these three forms of robbery (presumably within the body) and unify them, reverse this mechanism and control it, reverse its time (or perhaps its "seasons") and eat it, then the whole body will be entirely regulated and the myriad transformations will be settled. The myriad transformations having been settled, all anxieties will completely cease." *Zhushi, zhong*, 22a. The references to "eating" in both the original text and the commentary are obscure and the precise meaning is difficult to assertain however this commentary does shed some light on the general meaning of this line and on the stanza as a whole.

58. The precious words of the *Yin Convergence* [Scripture][276] exceed three hundred in number;

the numinous text of the *Dao and Virtue*[277] stops at five thousand.

The high immortals of present and past, of limitless number,

all [of them] understand the true explanation [found] in this place.

59. Allowing that you have intelligence surpassing that of Yan and Min;[278]

[if you] do not encounter the transmission of a teacher do not insist upon mere guesswork.

Simply writing elixir scriptures without oral instruction,

where will you be able to form the spiritual foetus?

60. [If you] understand the mind monkey, the inner workings of the heart,

[and, as the result of] three thousand meritorious achievements become equal with heaven,

[you] will naturally have the vessel with which to cook the dragon and tiger.

Why assume the burden of family and being attached to wife and children?[279]

---

[276] The text referred to here is the the *Huangdi yinfu jing* (The Yellow Emperor's Yin Convergence Scripture), often refered to as the *Yinfujing* and also know as the *Tianji jing* (*Scripiture of the Celestial Mechanism*). The Taoist Canon contains numerous versions with their respective commentaries. The text is attributed to Li Quan (李筌), who is said to have received it in 718 CE.

[277] The *Daode jing*.

[278] Yan (顏) and Min (閔) were two disciples of Confucius both of whom are mentioned in the *Lunyu*.

[279] Compare this question with the contents of stanza 15 on page 62 where one finds that divorce is listed among a variety of useless methods to be avoided by the inner alchemist.

61. [If you have] not yet refined the returned elixir [you] must quickly refine it;

having refined and returned it, [you] must then know [when to] stop at sufficiency.

If restraint from excess is not already [practised in your] own mind,

[you will] not avoid one morning encountering danger and shame.

62. [You] must take the door of death and make it the door of life;

do not cling to the gate of life and call it the gate of death.

If you comprehend the moving force of destruction and understand return,

only then will [you] begin to be aware that, [even] within suffering, compassion arises.

63. The sources of misfortune and fortune are mutually dependent;

following each other like shadows and echos follow form and sound.

If [you are] able to turn around this moving power of production and destruction,

[then], in the time it takes to turn your palm, calamity will be transformed into good fortune.

64. [In] cultivating conduct, mix with ordinary people and soften [your] brightness;[280]

[if circumstances require] roundness, be round; [if they require] squareness be square.

---

[280] This phrase appears to be inspired by chapter four of the *Daode jing* which includes the following phrase: "soften the glare" (*he qi guang* 和其光). Lau, *Tao Te Ching*, 7. This notion of the accomplished adept muting his or her inner radiance is consistent with the rest of the stanza.

[Thus, whether] manifest or hidden, [whether] opposing or following, people will not fathom [you];

how will people be able to discern [your] actions or concealment?

Additional Four Line Stanzas

Five Stanzas

1. Even though you sir may understand truly eternal inner nature,[281]

   [you will] not yet escape throwing away [this] body and then entering another body.[282]

   What could be better than also cultivating the great medicine?

   suddenly you will transcend, [and] being without leaks,[283] [you will] become a Realized Man.

---

[281] This line contains the Buddhist term "thusness" *zhenru* (眞如). *Zhen* (眞) is interpreted as "the real" (*zhen shi* 眞實) while *ru* (如) is understood as *ruchang* (如常), "thus always" or "eternally so." This term designates that which is eternal and unchanging in contrast to the forms and phenomena observed through conventional perception. This term is fundamental to Mahāyana philosophy and is synonymous with Buddha-nature (*foxing* 佛性) and the *Dharma*-body (*fashen* 法身). Soothill and Hodous, *Chinese Buddhist Terms*, 331, s.v. 眞如.

[282] This is a reference to rebirth, a central doctrine of Mahāyana Buddhism.

[283] This is a translation of the Buddhist term *wulou* (無漏) which literally means "no drip, leak or flow." It refers to a passionless state which leads "away from the downward flow into lower forms of rebirth." Soothill and Hodous, *Chinese Buddhist Terms*, 380, s.v. 無漏. This bears a strong resemblance to the Taoist notion of the five thieves which rob the body of its vitality. These thieves are also described in psychological terms by Shangyang zi. *Sanzhu*, 3.19a-b. Of course Taoism is also well known for its concern with avoiding leakage of the body's *qi* or essence (*jing* 精) in the interest of preserving health. See footnote 192 for further details concerning the various classes of "thieves."

2. [Those who] project [themselves] into an foetus, snatch residences, change [their] abode,

    [and, dwell in] old lodgings are called followers of the four fruits.[284]

    If [you] understand [how to] defeat dragon and [make] the tiger submit,

    and build a house with true gold, when will it decay?

---

[284] The "four fruits" (*si guo* 四果) is a Buddhist term which refers to the four *phala* or rewards which take the form of four grades of sainthood conferred upon the subject. Soothill and Hodous, *Chinese Buddhist Terms*, 177, s.v. 四果. The "four fruits" can also refer to an inner alchemical technical term, *xianjia si guo* (仙家四果) which might be translated (unhelpfully) as "the four fruits of immortal houses." It refers to four scenarios designated by the following four terms which are listed in the first two lines of this stanza: projecting into a foetus (*tou tai* 投胎) is subdivided into three types but they all involve the entry of a foreign sprit into the womb prior to the secure establishment of the proper spirit within the foetus; snatching a residence (*duo she* 奪舍) means that the foreign spirit actually takes over the newly conceived foetus from the rightful occupant; changing abode (*ji zhu* 移居) means that after death a spirit wanders about looking for a fresh corpse; upon finding one which has not suffered extensive injury from weapons, fire, or drowning it then takes up residence in the corpse; old lodgings (*jiu zhu* 舊住) refers to human immortals (*ren xian* 人仙) who are able to live indefinitely in the same body. Thus, over extended years their body is considered an old lodging. *Daojiao da cidian*, 389, s.v 仙家四果. The goal of the inner alchemist is to fashion a golden residence rather than to adopt the above four inferior methods.

3. The methods of mirror forms,[285] stopping the breath[286] and contemplating the [bodily] spirits[287]

   are difficult when you first set out, but later the road is smooth.

   Suddenly, although [you may be] able to roam a myriad kingdoms,

   what remedy is there [for having to] change your dwelling once it is decrepit and old?

4. Śākyamuni taught people to cultivate the [Realm of] Utmost Bliss;[288]

   furthermore, associated with the [Realm of] Utmost Bliss is the direction of metal.

---

[285] A commentary states: 鑒形者懸鑒于屋存神於中而出 As for mirror forms, [this term refers to] hanging a mirror in [your] room and, preserving the spirit within, [it] emerges. *Zhushu*, 6.17a. Wang Mu appears to say that by staring into a mirror one is able to forget one's body and enter the mirror. He does not state clearly whether he means that the spirit enters the mirror. Wang Mu, *Qianjie*, 161, n.1.

[286] Restraining the breath (*bi qi* 閉氣) refers to the practice of foetal respiration (*taixi* 胎息). The assumption underlying this practice is that if one can retain inhaled air within the body for an extended period of time, it becomes possible, with great concentration, to direct the flow of air to various regions of the body. The longer the breath can be held the longer the adept has to channel the breath within the body. An excellent description of this process is given in Maspero, *Taoism and Chinese Religion*, 342-343. The explanation provided by Maspero accords closely with the one given in *Zhushu*, 6.17a-17b.

[287] The commentary defines the practice of contemplating the spirit (*si shen* 思神) as preserving or keeping the spirit in a single place within the body. Two of the places mentioned are the Yellow Court and a place located above the space between the eybrows. *Sanzhu*, 6.17a.

[288] "Utmost Bliss" (*jile* 機樂) is the name of the Buddhist Pure Land of Amitābha in the West. Soothill and Hodous, *Chinese Buddhist Terms*, 403, s.v. 機. Hence the mention of metal in the next line which, in the early and later heaven configurations of the eight trigrams is located in the west.

Of all appearances and forms[289] it alone is real;

the remaining two are not real, [amounting to self] deceptive deliberations.

5. Common sayings often accord with the way of the sages;

[you] should focus on their centre to carefully investigate and study [them].

[If you are] able daily to employ the [principle of] inversion [in your] seeking,

the dust and sand of heaven and earth will all become jewels.

The woman wears green robes;

the husband puts on white silk.[290]

What is seen cannot be used;

what is used cannot be seen.[291]

---

[289] I have chosen to translate "appearances" (se 色) and "forms" (xiang 相) seperately so that the reference to "the remaining two" in the last line makes sense. Soothill and Hodous, *Chinese Buddhist Terms*, 220, s.v. 色; 309, s.v. 相.

[290] These two lines are refering to the trigrams *li* and *kan*. The woman wearing green robes represents the trigram *li* which, in the ealrlier heaven arrangment of the eight trigams, corresponds with the colour green. The man in the white robes represents the trigram *kan* which, in the ealrlier heaven arrangment of the eight trigams corresponds with the colour white. *Wuzhen pian*, 28.22b-23a. An error exists in the commentary of Yuan Gongfu who explains that the green robe represents *yang* while the women herself represents *yin*. He then goes on to state that therefore this is *yang* within *yin* (*yin zhong zhi yang* 陰中之陽). He makes the same mistake in describing the male counterpart. Ibid. Other commentaries which provide the same kind of explanation do not make this error. *Zhushu*, 3.16a; *Zhushi, shang*, 28a.

[291] This appears to be a critique of techniques employing gross substances rather than the rarefied ingredients of inner alchemy (original essence, *qi* and spirit). This could obviously apply to the external or laboratory alchemists but could also be directed at those who employed various sexual techniques. Weng Baoguang describes the gross substances as "the

Within chaotic obscurity they meet each other;

within dark abstruseness there is transformation.

In an instant the fire's flames[292] fly up,

and the Realized Man[293] is naturally manifest.

The West River Moon

1. The inner medicine is also like the outer medicine;[294]

    the inner [medicine] circulates and the outer [medicine] also must be circulated.

    In matters concerning the elixir, the kinds of [ingredients] which are harmonized and blended

    are the same;[295]

---

dregs of later heaven . . ." which are distinguished from the rarefied and pure ingredients of earlier heaven. These two lines are reproduced exactly in Zhang Boduan's much shorter work entitled *Jindan sibai zi* (TY1070, DZ341), 5.2a. This division of ingredients into baser and more refined forms is also stated on the previous page of the same work. Ibid, 5.1b.

[292] This is another reference to the fire phases which must be controled throughout the process of inner alchemy. *Wuzhen pian*, 28.23b. Xue Daoguang explains that once the work of the fire has stopped the Realized Man appears. *Sanzhu*, 5.1b.

[293] Here, "Realized Man" is intended as a synonym for the "golden elixir." *Zhushi, zhong*, 29a, *Zhushu*, 3.16b.

[294] The concepts of the inner medinine (*neiyao* 內藥) and outer medicine (*waiyao* 外藥) in inner alchemy do not correspond with the classifications of inner alchemy (*neidan* 內丹) and outer alchemy (*waidan* 外丹); rather they refer to dual processes within the body which complement each other. In terms of the trigrams this can be explained as a reference to the extracted pure *yin* line within the trigram *li* and the extraction of the pure *yang* line within the trigram *kan*. A section of the *Jindan da yao* TY1056, DZ736-738, which offers an explanation (albeit not terribly transparent) of the inner and outer medicines, is translated in Needham, *Science and Civilisation*, vol. 5.5, 40-41.

[295] The translation of this line follows the suggestion made by Wang Mu that this line is refering to the fact that the ingredients, which are being blended (lead and mercury), originally share

a myriad types of medicine are used for warming and nourishing.[296]

Within [the body] there is the natural true fire;

in the furnace it is fiery and red for a long time.

You must employ diligence and skill in increasing and decreasing the fire of the outer stove,[297]

[in order to produce] the true seed that is wonderful and unsurpassed.

2. This Tao is most spiritual and most holy;

sadly, [if] your lot in life is poor, it will be difficult [for you to] understand.[298]

The mixing and harmonizing of the lead and cauldron[299] does not require a whole day;

[you will] soon gaze at the portentous form of the mysterious pearl.

If the determined scholar is able to [engage in] cultivation and refinement

---

the same form. Wang Mu, *Qianjie*, 137, n.5.

[296] The myriad conventional medicines are mentioned and then contrasted with the medicine inside the body.

[297] Weng Baoguang explains that, just as the body has an inner and an outer medicine, it also possesses an inner and an outer fire, both of which must be carefully regulated to bring about the desired transformations. *Wuzhen pian,* 29.2a-2b.

[298] Yuan Gongfu states that, lacking the requisite good karma (*fu* 福) and karmic affinity (*yüan* 緣) one is unable to carry out the alchemical process. *Wuzhen pian,* 29.4a. In accordance with this commentary the character *xiao* (消) has been translated as "understand" rather than as "melt," "thaw," or "dissipate." *Ciyuan*, 971, s.v. 消. Robinet has elected to translate *xiao* (消) as "decoction." Robinet, *Introduction à l'alchimie*, 245. Cleary translates it as "digesting." Cleary, *Understanding Reality*, 132.

[299] There appears to be an error in the text here. All other version of the *Wuzhen pian* in the *Daozang* refer to the harmonization of lead and mercury rather than lead and cauldron.

why [should he] be held back by dwelling in the midst of ordinary society.[300]

The labour is easy and the medicine is not far off;

[if I] revealed [this fact], people would surely burst into laughter.

3. The first passing through of the white tiger is most precious;[301]

the divine water of the flower pool[302] is true metal.[303]

Therefore [if you] understand the highest virtue [you] will profit from the source of profundity;

[this does] not compare with ordinary medicines.

---

[300] This line includes the three character phrase 在市居朝 which, translated litrerally would read "in the market dwelling at court." This phrase has been translated in accordance with a suggestion made by Daniel Overmyer which is consistent with Zhang Boduan's suggestion that it is not neccessary for the adept to retire to the quiet of the mountains. The bustle of the city need not be a deterrent to cultivation.

[301] The reference to the white tiger is related to the preceeding discussion of the inner and outer medicines. The tiger represents the outer medicine (*yang* withing *yin*) or the central line of the trigram *kan*. The reference to "the first passing through (*shou jing* 首經) of the white tiger" describes the beginning (*chu* 初) of the crescent *qi* of the tiger. *Zhushu*, 7.5b; *Sanzhu*, 5.6a. See also Robinet, *Introduction à l'alchimie*, 245.

[302] Ye Shibiao explains that the flower pool should not be taken to refer to the mouth and provides a rough description its location which he says is in the elixir cauldron (*danding* 丹鼎) and is also known as the "spirit-room of the golden foetus" (*jintai shenshi* 金胎神室) and the "palace of the elixir field's chaotic beginning" (*dantian hunyuan zhi gong* 丹田混元之宮). *Wuzhen pian*, 29.4b-5a. Commentaries in three other versions of the text appear to equate the crescent *qi* of the tiger with the spirit water (*shenshui* 神水) which is refined in the flower pool. Thus, the tiger in the first line and the flower pool in the second line seem to be different ways of alluding to the same thing. *Zhushu*, 7.6a; *Zhushi, zhong*, 45a, *Sanzhu*, 5.6b. See footnote 247 for additional comments on the flower pool.

[303] True metal is also known as the essence of true unity (*zhen yi zhi jing* 眞一之精). *Wuzhen pian*, 29.5a.

If [you] want to regulate and complete the nine circulations;[304]

[then] first [you] must discipline yourself and restrain the mind.

Gather and select at the appropriate time and settle the floating and sinking;

in advancing the fire you must guard against dangerous excesses.

4. Seven times reverted red sand returns to the root;

nine times returned golden fluid returns to the real.[305]

Stop clinging to *yin* and *zi* and counting *kun* and *shen*;[306]

---

[304] The "nine circulations" is a reference to the cycling of the internal fire also known as the fire phase. The commentaries suggest that the completion of the nine cycles is the culmination of nine years of disciplined meditation, self cultivation, and training or restraining of the mind (*chi xin* 持心). These afforts are likened to the nine years of meditative cultivation (*mian bi* 面壁) said to have been undertaken by Bodhidharma and to the moment of release experienced by the foetus after ten months of gestation. *Zhushu*, 7.6a-6b; *Zhushi, zhong*, 45b, *Sanzhu*, 5.6b-7a.

[305] The commentaries generally agree that these two opening phrases are alluding to a complex correlation between the River Diagram (*he tu* 河圖), the later heaven eight trigrams, and the five phases. Ye Shibiao explains that these two lines refer to the reuniting of lead and mercury which return to the sea of the origin (*yuanhai* 元海). *Wuzhen pian*, 29.5b-6a. This account is consistent with the more explicit reference to the same idea in lines three and four of the next stanza. A very different account of the terms "nine times returned" and "seven times reverted" is offered in the *Xiuzhen bijue* probably written before 1136CE by an unknown author. This text is not found in the Taoist Canon but is included in the *Leishuo*, a collection of excerpts from Song and pre-Song works edited by Ceng Cao. many of the texts included in this work are no longer extant. Needham provides a translated section from this text in which the first of the above terms is described as refering to a series of dependent raltionships in which, for example, "nourishment of the spirit" first requires "nourishing the *qi*" and "nourishing the *qi*" first requires "nourishing the essence" and so on. Needham, *Science and Civilisation*, vol. 5.5, 44. The second term is explained by reference to the twelve hours of the diurnal cycle. It should be noted that Zhang Boduan appears to explicitly reject this account in the third line of this verse.

[306] *Yin* (寅), *zi* (子), and *shen* (申) are three hours in the diurnal cycle, a cycle which is super-imposed on the human body. They refer respectively to: 3am-5am, 11pm-1am, and 3pm-

simply watch that the five phases are perfectly adjusted.

The root is in the flavour of mercury,

circulating all around through all time periods.[307]

[When] the *qi* of *yin* and *yang* is sufficient,

naturally the numinous[308] can go out and enter;

how could the mysterious female[309] be far away?

5pm.

[307] Once again reference is made to the twelve hours of the day which are represented in the body of the adept.

[308] Ye Shibiao assumes that this term is synonymous with the medicinal substance which is being formed in the adept's body. *Wuzhen pian,* 29.6b.

[309] It is very difficult, based on Zhang Boduan's writing or that of his commenators, to establish the meaning of the term "mysterious female" (*xuan pin* 玄牝). The term is described in chapter six of the *Daode jing* but has probably been reinterpreted in this text for the purpose of conveying internal alchemical ideas. As Wang Mu observes there is little agreement on where precisely it lies. Wang Mu, *Qianjie,* 147, n.9. A vague account of the term states that "myserious" (*xuan* 玄) is above while "female" (*pin* 牝) is below. The explanation continues, stating that the "mysterious pass" or "gate" is called "mysterious on the left" and "female on the right." *Dacheng ji,* 10.5b. A second, related, explanation of the term "gate of the mysterious female" (*xuan pin zhi men* 玄牝之門), states that "the heavenly air (*qi*) which passes through the nose is called the mysterious gate while the earthly air which passes throught the mouth is called the door of the female. [Thus], the mouth and nose are the gate and door of the mysterious female." It is very clear in this account that it is the air (*qi*) in both forms which constitute the gate of the mysterious female and not the nose and mouth. Ibid. A section of commentary in the *Jindan sibai zi* provides a more abstract account which explains that, prior to having a body, there exists the opening of the mysterious female. Furthermore it cannot be located in space as the text says: it is not located above, it is not located below and it is not located in the centre. *Jindan sibai zi,* 5.7a-b. This last account appears to be plainly opposed to the more spacially oriented descriptions cited above.

5. If [you] want true lead to retain mercury,

[when] among relatives do not depart from the household servants.[310]

Wood and metal[311] are divided with no way to meet;

[you] must borrow [the services of the] yellow old woman as matchmaker [to arrange the] betrothal.

The wood-nature[312] loves metal's according with righteousness;

the metal-emotions hanker after wood's concern for benevolence.

Swallowing each other and consuming each other [they] withdraw from their relatives;

[thus you] begin to be aware that the male baby boy has been conceived.

---

[310] Robinet translates this line as follows: "If you want the true lead to retain the mercury keep to the centre without leaving the domestic home." Robinet, *Introduction à l'alchimie*, 246. Cleary renders the same line as "keep near the center and do not leave the servant." I have chosen to follow the suggestion of Yuan Gongfu who notes that lead can be symbolized by the "gentleman" or "lord" (*jun* 君) and the "mother"(*mu* 母) while mercury can be represented by the "servant" (*chen* 臣) and the "child" (*zi* 子). *Wuzhen pian*, 29.7a. Precisely the same correspondence of terms is also described by Weng Baoguang. *Sancheng biyao*, 28a-29a. What appears to be of pivotal importance in this line is the notion of separation; in alchemical terms, a separation represented by lead and mercury but here also metaphorcally expressed as the division within a houshold of the family (including the lord of the house) and the servants.

[311] Wood and metal are, of course, representative of east and west, dragon and tiger, and mercury and lead in the later heaven eight trigrams.

[312] The approach taken to translating the terms *muxing* (木性) and *jinqing* (金情) follows that of Robinet who observes that, grammatically, one could translate them as the nature of wood, and the emotional nature of metal but that would not preserve the idea of a one to one correlation between these two terms and "rightiousness" and "benevolence." Robinet, *Introduction à l'alchimie*, 247.

6. Two and eight; the young woman of whose family? [313]

Nine and three; the young gentleman at which place?[314]

[They] call themselves wood sap and metal essence;[315]

Upon encountering the direction of earth the three names[316] are completed.

Continue to avail yourself of the forging and refining [power] of Duke Ding,[317]

[and] husband and wife [will] joyfully join together.

Do not dare let the water-wheel stop for a moment;

[continually] transport [the water] into the summit of the Kunlun mountains.

---

[313] Even numbers are *yin* and here two and eight are paired with the young girl (*chanu* 姹女) who represents mercury or *yin* within *yang*. *Wuzhen pian,* 29.8b; *Zhushu,* 7.7a.

[314] Odd numbers are *yang* and here three and nine are paired with the baby boy (*ying er* 嬰兒) who represents lead or *yang* within *yin*. Ibid.

[315] Wood sap (*mu yi* 木液) represents mercury and metal essence (*jin jing* 金精) represents lead.

[316] The three names (*san xing* 三姓) refer to the three directions: east/wood, west/metal and centre/earth. *Wuzhen pian,* 29.8b. Shang Yanzi describes these three in terms of the trigrams and their union: "The young girl refers to the mercury [within] the palace of *li*; the young gentleman is the lead [within] *kan,* and earth is the blending of [these] two into one substance." *Sanzhu,* 5.11a.

[317] The character *ding* (丁), is one of two celestial stems which is paired with the fire phase. The reference to forging (*duan* 煅) is also an allusion to fire. This is a reminder to the alchemist that it is essential to continue the work of the fire phase, pushing the *yang* fire up to the top of the head (the Kunlun Mountain) in much the same way as a water-wheel raises water. Xue Daoguang explains that once the lead and mercury are in the earth-pot, one must rely upon the work of the fire to complete the elixir. *Sanzhu,* 5.10b-11a.

7. [The constellations of the] Herdboy and the Weaving Girl[318] share feelings of affinity [and their] paths meet;

the classes of tortoise and snake[319] exist [according to their] natural endowments.

The toad and the raven[320] merge their beauties during the new moon;

[so, these] two kinds of *qi* support each other to circulate.

All [of these] are the marvellous functions of *qian* and *kun*;

who is able to comprehend this deep abyss?

---

[318] The Herdboy (*niu lang* 牛郎) and Weaving Girl (*jian nu* 織女) are names of the constellations Vega and Altair. Their exact locations are provided on a chart of the twenty eight luner mansions in Needham, *Science and Civilisation*, vol. 3, 250. A myth associated with these two constel-lations is recounted in Edward T.C. Werner, *Ancient Tales and Folklore of China* (1922; London: Bracken Books, 1986), 189-191.

[319] Line five of this stanza appears to indicate that each of the three pairs of symbols mentioned here, should be understood as ways of describing the interaction between the trigrams *kan* in the north and *li* in the south. Wang Mu certainly believes this is the case, identifying the tortoise with the water of the north and with the trigram *kan*, and identifying the snake with the fire of the south and the trigram *li*. Wang Mu, *Qianjie*, 156, n. 3. See also *Zhushi, zhong*, 46b. Robinet, on the other hand, believes that both animals represent the water in the north, and the trigrams *kan* and *kun*. She also concludes though, that all three sets of symbols (the constellations, tortoise and snake, and the toad and raven) actually all symbolize the interaction of *qian* and *kun* which occupy the postions of south and north in the earlier heaven arrangement of the eight trigrams. Robinet, *Introduction à l'alchimie*, 246. Her explanation is very puzzling and regretably she provides no documentation which would help shed light on her conclusions which, doubtless, are well thought out. Needham also makes a brief reference to the place of the tortoise and the snake, which he asserts are symbols of the "black north" Needham, *Science and Civilisation*, vol. 5.5, 102 (also see the illustration on 103). Unfortunately, the commentaries provide little help in resolving this conundrum, as they dwell almost exclusively on the fact that the two animals represent the two forms of *qi*: *yin* and *yang*. *Zhushu*, 7.8b; *Sanzhu*, 5.8b; *Wuzhen pian*, 29.9b. One notable exception is provided by Ye Shibiao who states that the tortoise and the snake are "the substance of the true *qi* of the north." *Wuzhen pian*, 29.9a. This is one of the rare occasions when the text itself is quite explicit on the meaning of the symbols and perhaps it would be best to simply accept what it states.

[320] The toad, symbolizing the moon, is frequently interchanged with the hare of the moon.

[If,] on the contrary, *yin* and *yang* separated, this would be completely erroneous;

how [could you] attain the longevity of heaven and the lifespan of earth?

8. Within the male is contained the substance of female;

sustaining *yin* embraces the essence of *yang*.

[When these] two kinds harmonize and combine the medicinal recipe is complete;

transform the meekness of the *po* soul and the overbearing [qualities] of the *hun* soul.

Truly it is said of a single grain of golden elixir,

[if] a snake swallows it [then it will] immediately transform into the form of a dragon;

if a chicken eats it then it will transform into a fabulous Peng bird

and fly into the perfect region of green-blue *yang*.[321]

9. Heaven and earth having passed through [the periods of] *pi* and *tai*,[322]

at dawn and dusk it is well to observe *tun* and *meng*.[323]

---

[321] The closing line of this verse is rendered differently in other versions of the text. Rather than "Green-blue *yang*" (*qingyang* 青陽) both the *Sanzhu*, 5.12b and the *Zhishi, zhong*, 48b, include "true *yang*" (*zhenyang* 眞陽) while the *Zhushu*, 7.12a says "empty *yang*"(*kongyang* 空陽).

[322] The periods of *pi* (否) and *tai* (泰) refer to the hours 5am-7am (*mao* 卯) and 5pm-7pm (*you* 酉) during the day. At these times during the fire phase *yin* and *yang* are balanced. Further details on the symbolic fuctions of *pi* and *tai* are provided in footnote 229.

[323] The commentaries indicate that the hexagrams *tun* (屯) and *meng* (蒙) represent the commence-ment of the fire phase while *pi* and *tai* represent the halting or pausing of the fire phase. *Wuzhen pian*, 29.11b-12a; *Zhushu*, 7.12b-13a; *Sanzhu*, 5.13a-b.

The blades of the water wheel[324] come together at the hub and the water returns to its source;

marvellous is the practice of alternately taking out and augmenting.

[If you] attain unity the ten thousand kinds will all be completed;

[then you should] stop dividing south and north and west and east.[325]

Decrease upon decrease;[326] be careful concerning former achievements;

the jewel of life should not be taken lightly.

10. When winter reaches its peak, a single *yang* returns;

[after] thirty days it increases by one *yang* line.

Within the period of one month *fu* arises at daybreak of the first day of the month,

[and when the] full moon is finished *qian* ends and *gou* is manifest.

[The period of a single] day also has wintry cold and summer heat;

yang is produced and thus *fu* arises at midnight.

---

[324] The blades of the water wheel (*fu* 輻) converging at the hub are intended to represent the movement of the fire during the *yin* phase when it returns down the front of the body to the cauldron (lower elixir field) just as the waters of the hundred rivers return to the sea. *Wuzhen pian*, 29.12a. The metaphor also is an allusion to the function of the water wheel which forces water upwards against gravity; again, this is a symbol of reversal.

[325] The task of unifying, once completed, makes it unnecessary to continue being concerned with the divisions of the five phases represented by the five directions. With the forming of the elixir in the centre, the four directions all merge into the centre. *Wuzhen pian*, 29.12a-b; *Zhushu*, 7.12b-13a; *Sanzhu*, 5.14a. This return to simplicity is perhaps the reason for including the quotation from the *Daode jing* mentioned in footnote 326.

[326] This may be a quotation of a phrase from chapter 48 of the *Daode jing* (損之又損). Both Robinet, *Introduction à l'alchimie*, 249, and Wang Mu, *Qianjie*, 151, n. 8 believe that this phrase is a quotation.

At the hour of *wu*[327] the single *yin* [line] of the sign *gou* begins [the waning of *yang*];

[if you want to] refine the medicine [you] must understand dusk and dawn.[328]

11. [After] cultivating over eight hundred deeds of virtuous conduct,

storing up fully three thousand secret merits,

[by treating] others and yourself equally, both friends and [those who have] wronged you,

[you will then] begin to accord with the original resolve of the spirit immortals.

[If you do this] the tiger, rhinoceros, sword and weapons will not injure [you];[329]

it will be difficult for the burning house of impermanence[330] to lead [you] along.

---

[327] *Wu* (午) denotes the hours from 11am-1pm.

[328] This verse is describing the fluctuations of *yin* and *yang* which occur throughout the year in the form of seasonal transitions delineated by the lunar cycle which parallels the waxing and waning of *yin* and *yang* through the twelve hours of a single day according to the movement of the sun. The final line of the verse emphasizes the need to understand these cycles within the body so that the internal medicine of immortality can be compounded. Weng Baoguang provides a very helpful explanation of this verse which pairs the names of the various hexagrams mentioned with a graphic representation of the hexagram. *Zhushi, zhong,* 50a-b.

[329] This line echoes a section of chapter fifty of the *Daode jing*: "I have heard it said that one who excels in safe-guarding his own life does not meet with the rinoceros or tiger when travelling on land nor is he touched by weapons when charging into an army." Lau, *Tao Te Ching,* 73.

[330] This is an allusion to a parable found in the *Miaofa lianhua jing* T9 (The Lotus Flower of the Wonderful Law). [Note: The first reference to Buddhist texts will include its number in the 1924-1929 edition of the *Dazheng xinxiu dazang jing* (*Taishō-shinshū daizōkyō*) indicated by a "T" after the title.] The parable describes the plight of a father whose children are caught in a burning house and, unaware of the immanent danger, continue with their play. The fire of the burning house is described as the suffering which is brought on by desires and attachments. Bunnō Katō, Yoshirō Tamura, and Kōjiro Miyasaka, trans., *The Threefold Lotus Sutra: Innumerable Meanings, The Lotus Flower of the Wonderful Law, and Meditation on the Bodhisattva Universal Virtue* (1975; reprint, Tokyo: Kosei Publishing Co., 1986), 85-89.

After the precious talisman[331] has descended go and pay court to heaven;

safely riding the phoenix-drawn carriage of the immortals.[332]

12. [If you] do not discriminate between the five phases and the four signs,

how [can you] distinguish the vermillion [cinnabar], mercury, lead and silver?

[If you] have not yet heard about cultivating the elixir and the firing phase,

it is [too] early to call [yourself] a hermit.

[If you are] not willing to contemplate your own mistakes

and even take erroneous ways and instruct others,

[you] hinder them by [causing them to be stranded] on the ford of delusion.[333]

A deceiving mind such as this—how can it be endured?

An Additional Verse

The elixir is the body's[334] most precious [part];

---

[331] The talsiman (*fu* 符) can be used like a password to gain entry into heaven. In the last two lines of this verse the successful alchemist is able to ascend to heaven for an audience. The bestowing of the precious talisman may be seen as a form of permission and a means of entry. On the function of the talisman see Isabelle Robinet, *Taoist Meditation: The Mao Shan Tradition of Great Purity*, trans. Julian F. Pas and Norman J. Girardot (Albany: State University of New York Press, 1993), 24-25; Schipper, *The Taoist Body*, 8, 225, n.7.

[332] "Carriage of the immortals" is a translation of *luan che* (鸞車). *Ciyuan*, 1933, s.v. 鸞車.

[333] "Ford of delusion" (lit. to miss the ford") (*mi jin* 迷津) is a Buddhist term referring to the condition of mortality. Soothill and Hodous, *Chinese Buddhist Terms*, 339-340, s.v. 迷.

[334] The Buddhist term *seshen* (色身) is used here. It refers to the physical body as opposed to the non-material or spiritual body known as the *fashen* (法身).

refinement [having been] completed, the transformations are inexhaustible.

Additionally, [if you] are able to apply [your] inner nature to examine into the true teaching,

[and can] fully comprehend the marvellously efficacious [way of] no [re]birth,

[you] will not have to wait for another body in a later life,

[because] in this present [life you can] obtain the supernatural powers of a Buddha.

Ever since the *Naga* maiden[335] acquired this merit

so, afterwards who [has been] able to follow in her footsteps?

Studying The Token of the Three in Accordance with the Book of Changes [336]

The marvellous function of the great elixir imitates *qian* and *kun*.

Qian and *kun* revolve; the five phases divide.

[When the] five phases go along [with things]; the constant Tao has life and has death;

[When the] five phases go against [the flow]; the form of the elixir is constantly numinous and constantly preserved.

---

[335] The Naga Maiden (*long nu* 龍女) is the daughter of Sāgara-nāgarāja, the dragon king who resides at the bottom of the ocean. The *Miaofa lianhua jing* describes the conversion mission of the Bodhisattva Mañjuśrī who descended to the palace of the Sāgara dragon king. One of the beings he converted was the eight year old Naga Maiden: "She has unembarrassed powers of argument and a compassionate mind for all the living as if they were [her] children; . . . Kind and compassionate, virtuous and modest, gentle and beautiful in her disposition, she has been able to attain Bodhi." Katō, Tamura, and Miyasaka, *The Threefold Lotus Sutra*, 212.

[336] The translation for the title of this text (*Zhouyi cantong qi* TY996, DZ623) is taken from Pregadio, "Time in the Zhouyi Cantong qi," 157.

Unity emerging from empty non-being manifests substance; the two *yi*[337] are fixed as one.

In establishing the root, the four signs[338] are not separate from these two forms,

and thus the eight trigrams together are the ancestors and decendants.[339]

The myriad forms are produced through transformative movement;

fortune and misfortune, grief and happiness[340] are thus apportioned.

---

[337] Weng Baoguang identifies the two *yi* (*er yi* 二儀) with *yang* which is heaven and *yin* which is earth. *Zhushi, xia*, 4a.

[338] The "four signs" (*sixiang* 四象) represent the next level of division from the original *taiji* and the subsequent division into *yin* and *yang*. The result of this division is the generation of "greater *yin*" (*tai yin* 太陰), "greater *yang*" (*tai yang* 太陽), "lesser *yin*" (*shao yin* 少陰) and "lesser *yang*" (*shao yang* 少陽). *Zhongguo zhengtong daojiao da cidian* (Taipei: Yiqun tushu youxian gongci chubanbu, 1983), 240, s.v. 四象.

[339] Weng Baoguang describes the cosmogonic process from the Tao's production of the unified *qi* which, through a process of transformation, gives rise to *yin* and *yang* (heaven/*qian* and earth/*kun*). The next step is the creation of the "four signs" (*sixiang* 四象), which are correlated with the four seasons. Next he refers to the creation of the eight trigrams which results from the binding together (*suo* 索) of *kun* and *qian* and then *qian* and *kun* which generates the "three male elders" (*san nan chang* 三男長) and the "three female elders" (*san nu chang* 三女長) which he names according to the remaining six trigrams. The whole process leads to the orderly cycliing of the *yin* and *yang qi* through the eight directions and through the twelve hourly divisions of the day. The eight trigrams embody this whole sequence of generation from simplicity through the complexity of successive phases of division and so are refered to in terms of ancestors and descendents. *Zhushi, xia*, 4a-b. Wang Mu explains that *qian* and *kun* are the ancestors while the sixty four hexagrams constitute the descendants. There is nothing in the text or commentaries which directly supports this suggestion. Wang Mu, *Qian Jie*, 166, n.8.

[340] The two characters translated here as "grief" and "happiness" are *hui* (悔) and *lin* (吝) which ordinarily mean grief or regret and to be stingy or tight fisted. Their occurrence as a pair in this line is almost certainly an allusion to the *Yijing* which pairs *hui* with (*you* 憂) meaning "grief" and *lin* with (*wu* 虞) which means "joyful" in the following phrase: 悔吝者憂虞之象也. *Yijing, Xici zhuan, shang*. Richard, J. Lynn translates this line as "Regret and remorse involve images of sorrow and worry." Richard, J. Lynn, *The Classic of Changes: A New Translation of the I Ching as Interpreted by Wang Bi* (New York: Columbia University Press, 1994), 49.

The one hundred families daily employ [them but] do not understand.

[However], the sage[341] [was] able to examine into [their] source

[by] concentrating on the wondrous way of the [*Book of*] *Changes* which exhausts the principle of

qian and *kun*,

and employed its signs in this text.[342]

If *pi* and *tai*[343] interact then *yin* and *yang* will sometimes ascend and sometimes descend.

[Once] *tun* and *meng*[344] are formed there will be movement and stillness at dawn and dusk.

Kan and *li* are the water and fire of men and women.

Zhen and *Dui*[345] are the *po* souls and the *hun* souls of the dragon and tiger.

[If you can] guard the centre then [you will have] the great fortune of yellow garments.[346]

---

[341] The sage being referred to here is almost certainly Wei Boyang, author of the *Zhouyi cantong qi*.

[342] The text referred to here is the *Zhouyi cantong qi*. Weng Baoguang explains that Wei Boyang, the author of the *Zhouyi cantong qi*, observed that way of the *Yijing* was very similar to that of inner alchemy and therefore chose to employ (*tuo* 托) (lit. to depute; to commission) the signs of the *Yijing* to enlighten people on the purport of the great elixir. *Zhushi, xia,* 5b.

[343] See footnote 229 for details concerning the hexagrams *pi* and *tai.*

[344] See footnote 230 for details concerning the hexagrams *tun* and *meng*. The four hexagrams, *pi* and *tai* and *tun* and *meng* are all being employed here to describe the fire phase within the body while the four hexagrams mentioned in the following two lines are being used to discuss the work of re-establishing unity within the adept: *kan* and *li* are south/fire and north/water; *zhen* and *dui* are east/wood and west/metal. The centre, mentioned in the next line, represents earth, the last of the five phases, which fuctions as the stable centre and as the site of reunification.

[345] See footnote 217 concerning these two hexagrams.

[346] The mention of "yellow garments" in this line is an allusion to the centre which, according to the five phase theory, corresponds with the colour yellow.

[If you] entertain arrogance you will lack station and honour.[347]

[Regarding] "already" and "not yet" be cautious [concerning] the end and beginning of all things.

[As for] *fu* and *gou*,[348] bright is the return and haste[349] of the two forms of *qi*.

The waning and waxing of the moon correspond to the decline and increase of the essence and spirit.

The appearance and disappearance of the sun causes the cold and warmth of flourishing and defensiveness [in the blood and *qi*].[350]

Originally [these] words were established in order to illuminate the signs;

[once] the signs are attained forget the words.

Similarly, the signs are established in order to indicate the underlying idea;

[once you have] awakened to this idea then the signs can be abandoned.

---

[347] This is an admonition not to become arrogant and, therefore, careless once the elixir has been attained. Constant vigilance is required of the adept to regulate the fire within so that the sacred foetus can be nourished. The need for "station" (*wei* 位) is associated in the commentaries with the need to provide a focus to the fire so that it does not simply flow at random through the six voids (*liu xu* 六虛). *Zhushi, xia*, 7a. The six voids are heaven, earth and the four directions, though this term can also refer to the six lines of the hexagrams. *Daojiao da cidian*, 310, s.v. 六虛. It should be kept in mind that the progression of *yin* and *yang* through the lines of the hexagrams is, as has been shown previously, often used as a means for representing the advancing and retreating of the fire phase.

[348] See footnote 184 on the hexagrams *fu* and *gou*,

[349] I have chosen to heed the observations of Wang Mu which suggests that the two words *gui* (歸) and *ben* (奔) should retain their own meanings for the purpose of preserving a twofold allusion to the cycling of the internal fire. *Gui*, he suggests, alludes to completion while *ben* connotes stirring or arousal. This approach would make the use of these two words an amplification of the symbolic function of the two hexagrams *fu* and *gou*. Wang Mu, *Qianjie*, 167, n.21.

[350] "Flourishing" (*rong* 榮) and "defensiveness" (*wei* 衛) are employed in chapter 26 of the *Huangdi neijing siwen* to describe the relative vigour or weakness of the blood and *qi*. *Huangdi neijing siwen*, 2nd ed. (Shanghai: Shanghai kexue jishu Chubanshe, 1989), 319. Also see chapter 31. Ibid, 247.

For those who understand it is simple and easy,

[but] those who go astray will be even more deluded and troubled.

Therefore the scholar of high standing who understands the cultivation of the real

studies the *Concordance of the Three* and does not dwell on obfuscating signs nor cling to texts.

Ode to the Ground of Buddha-nature

1. Buddha-nature is not the same nor is it different;

   one thousand lamps together are one brightness.

   [If one] tries to increase it, any excess is nullified;

   [try] decreasing its radiance and still it is not harmed.

   Taking or rejecting, both are erroneous concepts [in this case];

   neither burning nor floating cause any harm.

   With the various modes of apprehension: seeing, hearing and knowing,

   in not even one instance can [Buddha-nature] be fathomed.

2. The marvellous body of the Tathāgata is as pervasive as the sands of the Ganges;

   its myriad forms, dense and close are without delusion or hindrances.

   [If I am] able to attain the universally penetration of the perfect Dharma-eye

   thus [I will] realize that the three realms are my home.

3. Looking at it, it is impossible to discern its form;[351]

and yet when I call out to it there is still a response.

[But] do not say that this sound is like an echo in the valley;

for if there is not even a valley, what sound would there be?

4. [If,] in all things, one restrains hearing, seeing, apprehending, and knowing,

then [the Buddha-nature], hidden within the dusty realm, will manifest its inner power.

In [the perspective of] numinous constancy, not one thing exists;

[so, as for] the four modes of perception,[352] what [can one] rely on to make [them] trust-worthy?

5. Do not move [even] a single step to arrive at the Western Heaven;[353]

sitting upright [in meditation] all regions are before [your] eyes.

Behind the neck there is a brightness yet this is an illusion;

clouds arise beneath [your] feet, [but you have] not yet become an immortal.

---

[351] The opening five characters of this line are the same as the first five charadters found in chapter 14 of the *Daode jing*.

[352] That is, "hearing," "seeing," "apprehending," and "knowing" mentioned in the first line of this verse.

[353] "Western Heaven" (*xi tian* 西天) refers to the Western Paradise presided over by Amitābha. Through invoking the name of this buddha with complete faith the devout adherent believed that salvation was possible. Within the context of this Chan inspired text the reader is urged not to depend on notions of the Western Paradise for enlightenment.

6. As for seeking the origin of birth, it is from no-birth;

[as for] dreading annihilation, has temporary annihilation[354] ever occured?

Seeing [with the] eyes does not compare to seeing [with the] ears;

speaking [with the] mouth, how can it compare to speaking [with the] nose?

No Sinfulness or Blessedness

The whole day [you] walk around [but you have] not walked;

the whole day [you] sit [but have you actually] sat?

In cultivating goodness [you will] not attain merit;

doing evil is originally without fault.

[If] people today do not yet understand the mind,

[then they] must not cling to these words and act chaotically.

[If they do, then] after death [they will] certainly see Yawang,[355]

and it will be difficult for them to escape being boiled or ground up.

---

[354] "Annihilation" (*mie* 滅) can refer to Nirvāna though here the term appears to be contrasted with life or birth mentioned in the first line and so has been translated to reflect this implied contrast. Soothill and Hodous, *Chinese Buddhist Terms*, 405, s.v. 滅.

[355] Yanwang (閻王) is the Chinese equivalent of Yama who appears in the *Rig Veda* as the god of death. In Buddhist mythology he serves with the assistance of eighteen generals and an army of eighty thousand he serves in purgatory. He is described as ruler of the fifth court of purgatory or as the ruler of the eighteen judges of purgatory. *Chinese Buddhist Terms*, 452, s.v. 閻.

The Three Realms are Only Mind

[In the perspective of] the marvellous principle of the three realms[356] being only mind,

the myriad things [of the world are] not this, not that.

There is not one thing which is not my mind;

there is not one thing which is my self.

If You See Things You See Mind

[If you] see things, [you] see mind;

without things the mind would not be manifest.

In the ten directions it penetrates through hinderances;

the true mind cannot fail to be everywhere.

If you generate speculations based on knowledge and intelligence

still, [all it will] produce are upside down views.

[If, in] observing the world, [you are] able to be without intentions,

you will begin to see the face of perfect wisdom.

Universal Penetration

Having seen true emptiness, emptiness is not empty.

As for universal understanding, where does it not completely penetrate?

---

[356] The "Three Realms" (*san jie* 三界) are those of desire (*you* 欲), form (*se* 色), and the formless (*wu jie* 無色). Soothill and Hodous, Ibid., 70, s.v. 三界.

Objects of the senses and objects of the mind are all without substance;

[only with] marvelous methods does one understand being the same as things.

According with Others

The myriad things are present everywhere before the eyes;

accord with their movement and stillness and tolerate the hubbub and clamour.

Through complete enlightenment, *samādhi*,[357] and wisdom [there is], in the end, no stain;

[this is] just like the lotus produced in water—the lotus itself is dry.

The Precious Moon

The disk-like, bright moon [is suspended] in emptiness;

thus, the myriad kingdoms are clearly illuminated without obstruction.

[Try to] enclose it and it cannot be gathered; try to disperse it and it cannot be separated;

[move it] forward and it does not advance; [move] back and [it] does not withdraw.

[Its] "that" is not far away; [its] "this" is not near;

[its] surface is not outside; [its] interior is not inside.

Within sameness there is difference and within difference there is sameness.

I ask you, puppet,—do you understand or not?

---

[357] *Samādhi*, which is a translation of *ding* (定) refers to "composing the mind" or "intent concentration" which can occur during meditiation. Soothill and Hodous, *Chinese Buddhist Terms*, 254, s.v. 定.

Ode to the Heart Sutra[358]

The [five] aggregates,[359] [four] truths, the [six] roots of perception,[360] emptiness and form;

in all cases there is not a single *dharma*[361] that can be talked about.

---

[358] The *Xin jing* T250 is part of the *Banruo boluomijing* T223, 227 which gives a systematic exposition of the Mahāyāna doctrine of emptiness (*kong* 空). It was translated into Chinese by Kumārajīva (fl. 385-409 CE) and his assistants. Jan Yün-hua, "Buddhist Literature," in William H. Nienhauser, ed. and comp., *The Indiana Companion to Traditional Chinese Literature*, 2ⁿᵈ rev. ed. (Taipei: SMC Publishing Inc., 1986), 8-9.

[359] The five aggregates (*yun* 蘊) are the components which comprise an intelligent being. They are: 1) form (*se* 色), 2) sensation (*shou* 受), 3) perception (*xiang* 想), 4) mental formations, (*xing* 行), 5) consciousness (*shi* 識). "Form" refers to things with form and color, especially the body; "sensation" includes three groups: pleasant, unpleasant and neither pleasant nor unpleasant; "perceptions" is the forming of mental images or representations; "consciousness" is the power of mental formation and refers especially to the function of volition or the will. The notion of the five aggregates was an early Buddhist doctrine employed to demonstrate that ultimately the Self is not permanent nor whole. Akira Hirakawa, *A History of Indian Buddhism: From Śākyamuni to Early Mahāyāna*, trans.and ed. Paul Groner (Hawaii: University of Hawaii Press, 1990), 43-45. See also Soothill and Hodous, *Chinese Buddhist Terms*, 126, s.v. 五蘊.

[360] The "[six] roots of perception" is a translation of two Buddhist terms which appear as a binary term in this verse. The term is comprised of *gen* (根) meaning root, a cause or foundation and (*chen* 塵) meaning dust or dirt. In a Buddhist context *gen* refers to the sense organs: eyes, ears, nose, tongue, body and mind; *chen* refers to the objects of the sense organs: sight, sound, fragrance, taste, touch, and idea. *Ciyuan*, 846, s.v. 根 塵. See also Soothill and Hodous, *Chinese Buddhist Terms*, 327, s.v. 根; 422, s.v. 塵.

[361] *Dharma* (*fa* 法) has a very wide range of applicability. It can refer to "law, truth, religion, thing, anything Buddhist." Soothill and Hodous, *Chinese Buddhist Terms*, 267, s.v. 法. In this context it should be taken to refer to a component of existence form an enlightened perspective. This definition follows the suggestion of Daniel Overmyer. An additional set of definitions for *dharma*, including a brief account of its use in different schools of Indian thought is found in John Grimes, *A Concise Dictionary of Indian Philosophy: Sanskrit Terms Defined in English* (New York: State University of New York Press, 1989), 113-114.

[When] upside down views[362] are finally exhausted

the substance of stillness and silence is suddenly present.

Others and Myself

I am not different from others; the minds of others are themselves different.

Other people have "close" and "distant;" I am without "that" and "this."

In water, on land, flying and walking, creatures of these [various] classes [I] see as one substance.

Noble and base, honoured and lowly, [from] head to toe [they are the] same as I.

I furthermore am not I. How can there be you?

"That" and "this," neither exists; all of these bubbles return to the water.

---

[362] "Upside down views" (*dian dao* 顛倒) are erronious beliefs. Soothill and Hodous, *Chinese Buddhist Terms*, 475, s.v. 顛.

On Studying Chan Master Xue Dou's Anthology on Eminent Adepts[363]

The one stream of the Caoji[364] divides into a thousand branches

illuminating the past, clearing up the present without obstruction.

Recently, those who study do not thoroughly investigate the source,

[thus, they] mistakenly point to a puddle left by a hoof-print and take it to be the ocean.

The teacher Xue Dou understands the inclinations of the real;

the sound of a great crash of thunder extends [from] the *Dharma* drum.

When the roar of the lion king comes out of a cave,

the hundred [kinds of] beasts and [adherents of] a thousand heterodox ways are filled with fear and

dread.

[With] songs and verse, discussions and sentences

[he provides] repeated injunctions to lead deluded people [along] the road.

[His] words are numerous and their meaning is lofty and profound;

[like the] sound of striking jade and beating on gold [resonating] eternally.

---

[363] Xue Tou (980-1052) was a poet and master in the Chan lineage traced back to Yun Men (864-949). According to Heinrich Dumoulin, his primary goal was to "forge the essence of the masters' words and deeds into poetic form." In doing so he established the groundwork for the composition of the *Biyan lu* (*Hekiganroku*). Xue Tou, through his exceptional literary ability, is also credited with restoring the Yun Men school which had fallen into decline by the beginning of the Northern Song dynasty (960-1127). Heinrich Dumoulin, *Zen Buddhism: A History, vol. 1: India and China*, trans. James W. Heisig and Paul Knitter (New York: Macmillan Publishing Company, 1988), 233.

[364] The Caoji is a stream located in north-central Guang Zhou in the prefecture of Qujiang. The sixth patriarch of Chan Buddhism, Hui Neng is also said to have spoken on the *dharma* at a temple called Baolin near the Caoji. Subsequently the name of this stream became associated with Hui Neng. Caoji is also another name for the Chan sect of Buddhism. *Ciyuan*, 793, s.v. 曹溪. See also Soothill and Hodous, *Chinese Buddhist Terms*, 352, s.v. 曹.

But alas, deluded people are detained in pursuit of [their] surroundings;[365]

still [they] take hold of words and appearances[366] seeking to name and enumerate.

[But the] true thusness[367] underlying reality is fundamentally without words;

without low, without high, [completely] boundless;

Without form [yet] not empty, no duality of substance;

the field of qualities [which extends] through the ten directions is a single complete mandala.

Has true concentration ever distinguished between speech and silence?

[It] cannot be attained by grasping [and it] cannot be attained by rejecting.

Simply do not devote attention to all the differentiating characteristics [of things];

accordingly this is the true guiding rule of the Tathāgata.

Do away with illusory appearances and hold to the true response;

[if the idea of] illusion is not produced [then] truth also remains obscured.

[If you] are able to realize that neither truth nor illusion exist,

then [you will] attain the true mind which is without hindrances.

[Being] without hindrances [you] are able to be self existent;[368]

---

[365] "Surroundings" is a translation of the Buddhist term *jing* (境) meaning any objective mental projection regarded as reality. Soothill and Hodous, *Chinese Buddhist Terms*, 421, s.v. 境.

[366] "Appearances" is a translation of the Buddhist term *xiang* (相) meaning external appearance. Soothill and Hodous, *Chinese Buddhist Terms*, 309, s.v. 相.

[367] "True thusness" (*zhen ru* 眞如) is what underlies all of the appearances of conventional perception, described in the preceeding line. "It resembles the ocean in contrast to the waves. It is the eternal, impersonal, unchangeable reality behind all phenomena." Soothill and Hodous, *Chinese Buddhist Terms*, 331, s.v. 眞如.

[368] "Self existent" (*zizai* 自在) denotes a king, master, or a state of independence and hence the mind in a state of freedom from delusion. Soothill and Hodous, *Chinese Buddhist Terms*,

once awakened, suddenly the crimes of a *kalpa*[369] will be entirely dispersed.

[There is] no need to expend earnest effort to realize *Bodhi*;[370]

henceforth [you will] for ever[371] part from the ocean of life and death.

My teacher approached, then discoursed on the joyful;

[he] stays in the world to serve as a model.

Last night he was invited by me to come,

with nostrils open wide, on a staff.

[I] asked him what the first principle is like

and [he] said that words are all misleading.

An Explanation Concerning Discipline, Concentration, and Wisdom

Well, as for explaining discipline, meditation, and wisdom

they are the marvellous functions within Buddhism.

Though Buddhas and patriarchs have talked [about them],

those who have not yet understood have things that [they] cling to.

218, s.v. 自在.

[369] A *kalpa* (*jiezui* 劫罪) is a period of time between the creation and recreation of a world or universe. One *kalpa* is three hundred and thirty six million years in duration. Soothill and Hodous, *Chinese Buddhist Terms*, 232, s.v. 劫罪. A variant on the length of a kalpa, which was supposed to represent a single day of Brāhma is four thousand three hundred and twenty million years. Sir Monier Williams, *A Sanskrit-English Dictionary* (1899; reprint, Oxford: Clarendon Press, 1989), s.v. *kalpa*.

[370] *Bodhi* (*puti* 菩提) is a state of perfect wisdom or understanding; it is also the enlightened mind. Soothill and Hodous, *Chinese Buddhist Terms*, 388, s.v. 菩提.

[371] Here "water" *shui* (水) is read as "eternal" *jiu* (永).

Now [they will be] briefly discussed [so that] the masses can depend on [them to] achieve

awakening;

thus, if mind and [one's] surroundings can both be forgotten,

and a single thought does not stir, [this is] called discipline.

[When] the complete understanding of realized nature penetrates inside and out with the lustre of

gems [this is] called *samādhi*.

[When you can] accord with and respond to things,

and subtly employ them without exhaustion, [this is] called wisdom.

These three certainly complete each other,

mutually comprising substance and function.

Suppose that discipline is the form,

then meditation and wisdom would comprise its function.

[Or,] if meditation is the substance, then discipline and wisdom comprise its function.

If, [on the other hand,] wisdom acted as substance then discipline and meditation would comprise

its function.

These three have never for a moment been separated from each other.

[This is] like supposing that the brightness of the sun [makes it] able to shine,

and supposing that the shining of the brightness thereby enables it to illuminate.

[If there was] no brightness, [it would be] unable to shine;

if not for the shining [it would be] unable to illuminate.

Originally discipline, concentration, and wisdom stem from a single nature;

as for brightness, shining and illumination, their origin is in a single sun.

One, furthermore, is not one.

Three, again, how [is it] three?

Three and one, forget them all.

[Thus there is] deeply clear purity.

Ode to the Mind Indeed Being Buddha

Buddha indeed is mind; mind indeed is Buddha;

mind and Buddha, from the beginning both are unreal things.

If [you] realize that there is no Buddha and further, no mind,

for the first time this is truly like the Dharma-body[372] Buddha.

The Dharma-body Buddha lacks any formal expression;

a single pearl of light, [it] contains the myriad appearances.

The substance which is without substance is indeed the true substance;

---

[372] The *Dharma*-body (*fashen* 法身) is one of the three bodies of the Buddha which also include the body of bliss (*baoshen* 報身) and the body of transformation (*huashen* 化身). Soothill and Hodous, *Chinese Buddhist Terms*, 77, s.v. 三身. "The Dharma-body of the Buddha is the embodiment of Truth and Law, the "spiritual" or true body; essential Buddhahood; the essence of being; the absolute, the norm of the universe." Ibid, 273, s.v. 法身. Paul Williams provides the following descrpition of the *Dharma*-body (*Dharmakāya*): "The *dharmakāya* is that which characterises the Buddha as Buddha, that is, the collection (*kāya*) of pure elements (*dharmas*) possessed in the fullest degree by the Buddha—various kinds of knowledges and understandings, together with the Buddha's five pure psycho-social constituents: pure physical matter, sensations conceptions, further mental contents such as volitions and so on, and consciousness. They are said to be pure because they are without any admixture of moral and cognitive taints. One takes refuge in the Buddha's *dharmakāya* in the same way that one might respect a monk, not because he is a physical being as such but because he possesses the qualities of a monk." Paul Williams, "On the bodies of the Buddha," in *Mahāyāna Buddhism: The Doctrinal Foundations* (New York: Routledge, 1989), 171.

form which lacks form is indeed true form.

Not solid, not empty, not not empty;

neither moving nor still, not arriving nor departing.

Not different, yet not the same, lacking being and non-being;

difficult to hold onto, difficult to let go of and difficult to hear or gaze upon.

Inside and out, universally penetrating, penetrating everywhere;

a whole Buddha kingdom located in a single grain of sand.

A single grain of sand contains the whole chiliocosm;

the mind of one body is the same as the myriad [minds].

To realize this you must understand the *dharma* of no mind [which],

[being] undefiled and unhindered, forms good karma.

[Then] the thousand types of good and evil will not be enacted;

this is homage attaining [that of] Kaśyapa.[373]

---

[373] Kaśyapa, or Mahākaśyapa, was a brahman who became one of the principal disciples of Śākyamuni and who lead the disciples and convened the first Buddhist council at Rājagrha after the Buddha's death. Soothill and Hodous, *Chinese Buddhist Terms*, 316, s.v. 迦葉. Hirakawa describes Kaśyapa a being a figure of legend. Hirakawa, *Indian Buddhism*, 21.

Ode to Picking Up the Pearl[374]

The pearl[375] within the poor child's clothing

[is] naturally round, bright, and marvellous.

[If you] do not understand how to search for [it] yourself

then [you will] count the treasures of others.

Counting other's treasures in the end will be of no benefit.

This will cause you to waste your energy.

[This is] not as good as recognizing and taking hold of what is precious in your own dwelling.

Its value in yellow gold would be infinite.

The brightness of the pearl is most extensive;

everywhere illuminating the vastness of the great chiliocosm,

it has never lessened [even] the slightest degree,

but has [merely] been obstructed by floating clouds.

From the time that this *Mani*[376] is recognized and attained,

who would continue to be attracted to illusory forms[377] and flowers in the sky?[378]

---

[374] "Pearl" (*qiu* 球) is a synonym for Buddha-truth. Soothill and Hodous, *Chinese Buddhist Terms*, 330, s.v. 球.

[375] The metaphor of a poor person who possesses something of great value can also be found in the *Nirvāna sūtra* which describes a poor woman living in a house which, unknown to her, contains a golden treasure. Soothill and Hodous, *Chinese Buddhist Terms*, 364, s.v. 貧.

[376] "*Mani*" (*mani* 摩尼) is a bright luminous pearl symbolizing the Buddha and his doctrine. Soothill and Hodous, *Chinese Buddhist Terms*, 435, s.v. 摩尼.

[377] Literally "bubble forms" (*baoti* 泡體).

[378] "Flowers in the sky" (*konghua* 空華) are spots before the eyes which represent illusion.

The Buddha-pearl, furthermore, is the same as my pearl;

accordingly my inner nature belongs to Buddha-nature.

Sea pearls[379] are not pearls and the sea is not the sea.

Within the peaceful mind is contained [the whole] dharma-realm.

Tolerate the dust and clamour, all of which is before your eyes.

Perfect understanding of the wisdom of meditation is constant and self existent;

[it is] neither emptiness nor form;

inside and out [its] brightness is unobstructed.

The spiritual wisdom of the six powers[380] is marvellous and limitless.

[As for] self benefit and benefiting others it is better to understand the ultimate.

Upon seeing this [you will] understand all affairs come to an end.

Cut short learning,[381] passing the whole day in spontaneity;

calm,[382] like the little child that has not yet manifest any sign.

Soothill and Hodous, *Chinese Buddhist Terms*, 278, s.v. 空華.

[379] "Sea pearls" (*hai qiu* 海球) can refer to things which are difficult to obtain. Soothill and Hodous, *Chinese Buddhist Terms*, 327, s.v. 海球.

[380] The six powers (*liu tong* 六通) refer to the six supernatural powers or universal powers acquired by a buddha or an *arhat* through *dhāyana* (meditation). Soothill and Hodous, *Chinese Buddhist Terms*, 138, s.v. 六通. These powers are: 1) divine eye (*tian mu* 天目), 2) divine ear (*tian er* 天耳), 3) knowing the mind of others (*ta xin tong* 他心通), 4) remembrance of former existences (*su ming tong* 宿命通), 5) the power to be anywhere or do anything at will (*shen tong tong* 神通通), 6) supernatural consciousness of the waning of viscious propensities (*lou jin tong* 漏盡通). Ibid., s.v. 五神通.

[381] The opening of this line echos the opening of chapter 20 of the *Daode jing*: 絕學無憂 "Exterminate learning and there will no longer be worries." Lau, *Tao Te Ching*, 28-29.

[382] In the *Wuzhen pian qianjie* this line begins with *bo* (泊) meaning "calm" or "at leisure." *Bo*

Whether moving or at rest accord with what is uncertain.

Do not cut off the false and do not cultivate the true;

the mind [concerned with] true and false comes from attachment to the dusty world.

From the beginning the myriad *dharmas* have all lacked form,

[but] within the formless there is the *dharma*-body.

The *dharma*-body is indeed the celestial true Buddha;

further, [it is] not human and [it is] not inanimate.

Expansive, [it] fills up the space between heaven and earth;

however, [it is] soundless, colourless[383] and indistinct.

Dirt[384] does not defile [it; its] brightness is self-illuminating.

[There is] nothing which is not produced from within the mind;

if the mind does not produce [them, all] *dharmas*[385] will spontaneously be extinguished,

---

is pronounced in the second tone which accords with the *fanqie* pronounciation suggested in the text (*Wuzhen pian*, 30.6b). This line appears to continue the allusion to chapter 20 of the *Daode jing* which includes the following line: 我獨泊兮其未兆如嬰兒之未孩 "I alone am inactive and reveal no signs, / Like a baby that has not yet learned to smile. . . ." Lau, *Tao Te Ching*, 28-29.

[383] "Soundless and colourless" is a translation of the binary term *xiyi* (希夷). Chapter 14 of the *Daode jing* contains the following line: 視之不見名曰夷聽之不聞名曰希. Lau translates this line as "What cannot be seen is called evanescent; / what cannot be heard is called rarefied." Lau, *Tao Te Ching*, 19. *Xiyi* (希夷) is defined as that which lacks sound and appearance. *Ciyuan*, 526, s.v. 希夷.

[384] "Dirt" (*gou* 垢) is whatever deludes the mind; illusion; defilement. Two sets of qualities are associated with this term: 1) vexation, malevolence, hatred, flattery, wild talk, pride; 2) desire, false views, doubt, presumption, arrogance, inertia and meanness. Soothill and Hodous, *Chinese Buddhist Terms*, 299, s.v. 垢.

[385] *Dharma* is being used here to refer to things in general. Soothill and Hodous, *Chinese Buddhist Terms*, 267, s.v. 法.

then [you] will realize that sin and blessing are originally without form.

There is no Buddha to cultivate and there is no dharma to discuss.

The wisdom and discernment of great people is naturally different.

[If] their words issue forth, [they] make the roar of a lion;

unlike the discourses of the wild ox[386] on birth and death.

A Song on Meditative Concentration[387] and Pointing Out Illusion

The still nature[388] of the Tathāgata is like water;

[his] body peaceful, the wind and waves are naturally stilled.

Whether moving or at rest it remains deep and always clear;

even when not sitting alone it is like this.

Today people sit quietly [to] grasp realization;

[they] do not say that completeness is in beholding [one's own Buddha]-nature.[389]

[When you] look into [Buddha]-nature it resembles brightness;

---

[386] Presumably, "Wild ox" (*ye niu* 野牛) refers to those who foster heterodox teachings though I have been unable to locate this term in a number of Buddhist dictionaries.

[387] "Meditative concentration" is comprised of two chracters: *chan* (禪) meaning meditation, thought, reflection, and especially profound and abstract religious contemplation; the second character is *ding* (定) meaning to compose the mind, intent contemplation, and perfect absorption of thought into the one object of meditation. Soothill and Hodous, *Chinese Buddhist Terms*, 459, s.v. 禪; 254, s.v. 定.

[388] "Nature" (*xing* 性) is the fundamental nature behind the manifestation or expression. It is also the Buddha-nature which is immanent in all beings. Soothill and Hodous, *Chinese Buddhist Terms*, 459, s.v. 性.

[389] "Beholding the Buddha-nature," (*jian xing* 見性) is a common Chan saying. Soothill and Hodous, *Chinese Buddhist Terms*, 459, s.v. 禪; 244, s.v. 見性.

[if you] look into [Buddha]-nature [you will] naturally [achieve] concentration.

[Once you have achieved] completeness of concentration, wisdom[390] can be employed without limit;

this is called the spiritual power of all the Buddhas.

[If you] are about to look deeply into its substance and function,

the only [thing you need do] is look at emptiness in the ten directions.

Within emptiness there is darkness without a single thing;

further, it lacks [even] the dimness and obscurity of that which cannot be seen or heard.[391]

The dimness and obscurity of that which cannot be seen or heard[392] certainly cannot be sought;

[so if you do] seek it [you will] just become wayward and lost.

Simply put, these two characters, 'wayward' and 'lost':[393]

do not cling to and rely [even] on them.

Still, the original mind is like emptiness;

how could [it] be a place [where one is] able to gain or lose?

Simply banish the myriad *dharmas*;

banish [them] causing [the mind] to be entirely clear, without any residue.

Suddenly universal enlightenment will naturally manifest [itself];

---

[390] "Concentration" (*ding* 定) and "wisdom" (*hui* 慧) are two of the "six perfections" (*boluomiduo* 波羅蜜多). The remaining four are charity, moral conduct, patience, and energy or devotion. These six ways of action are viewed as the means to transcend birth and death. Soothill and Hodous, *Chinese Buddhist Terms*, 267, s.v. 波羅蜜多.

[391] See footnote 383.

[392] The first two characters in this line (*xi huang* 希恍) are taken to be a reiterative contraction of the full four character phrase included in the previous line (*xi yi huang hu* 希夷恍惚).

[393] The two characters mentioned here are *guai* (乖) and *shi* (失).

as such it is indistinguishable from [the enlightenment of] all the Buddhas.

The material body acts as my fetters and handcuffs;

thus [the mind's] bright light is mixed together with the common.

In your conduct always be without intention;[394]

what right or wrong, honour or disgrace is there to contend over?

The body which is born is merely a [temporary] lodging place;

the name of this inn's landlord is Vairocana.[395]

Vairocana does not come nor does he depart,

and he understands the extinguishing of life with no residue.[396]

Some ask what Vairocana is like,

[which is] merely to consider whether or not he has form.

Karmic deed upon karmic deed, defilement upon defilement;

defilement and karmic deeds, [they] are not the same nor [are they] different.

---

[394] "Without intention" (*wu xin* 無心), refers to a state of non-intentionality, without thought, will or purpose; the real immaterial mind free from illusion; unconscious or effortless action. Soothill and Hodous, *Chinese Buddhist Terms*, 379, s.v. 無心. This referes to the individual who has transcended the false notion of selfhood and self-interest.

[395] Vairocana (*Pilusheye* 毗盧舍耶) is the Buddha of Pervasive Light. The world of Vairocana represents the realm of enlightenment and Vairocana is said to have "attained unlimited virtues, paid homage to all Buddhas, taught myriads of sentient beings, and realized supreme enlightenment. A cloud of manifested Buddhas issues from the hair follicles of Vairocana's body. He is a majestic Buddha who who opens the Buddhist path to sentient beings. His wisdom is compared to the ocean (mind), which reflects light (objects) everywhere without limit." Hirakawa, *Indian Buddhism*, 280. Vairocana is described in the *Dafang guangfo huayan jing* (T 278, 279, 293). This title is often abreviated to *Huayan jing* (The Flower Garland Sutra). Further details on the *Huayan jing* can be found in Ibid., 279-282.

[396] "With no residue" (*wu yu* 無餘) refers to final *nirvāna* without the possibility of reincarnation. Soothill and Hodous, *Chinese Buddhist Terms*, 383, s.v. 無餘.

Even more, these defilements

are all Śakyamuni and *kāśyapa*.[397]

If different then the myriad musical pipes all ring out;

if they are the same then a single wind gathers [them all] together.

[If you] want to recognize and attain the *mani* [pearl],[398]

do not [simply] say that [if you] attain *dharma* [you will] know.

[If you] are ill then employ another medicine to affect the cure;

[but if your] illness is cured why continue to use medicine?

[Thus, if your] mind is deluded [you] must avail [yourself of the] illuminating [power] of the

dharma;

[but if your] mind has wakened then *dharma* is not necessary.

Further, it is like polishing a dull mirror;

the marks and dust are naturally eliminated.

At root all of the mental *dharmas* are false;

therefore cause [your mind] to be completely rid of all appearances.

---

[397] *Kāśyapa (jiaye* 迦葉) has a broad range of meanings. It can, for example, refer to a class of divine beings, to Kāśyapa Buddha, who is the third of the five Buddhas of the present *kalpa*, and to the sixth of the seven ancient Buddhas. Mahākāśyapa, was one of the principal disciples of Śakyamuni, and after his death, became leader of the disciples. Kāśyapa can also be used to refer simply to disciples. This final sense would serve well here to emphasize the dissolution of distinctions on which non-intentionality is founded. The distinctions between right and wrong, and honour and disgrace must be let go. If *kāśyapa* is understood as referring to disciples in general then the point of these two lines is that there is also no distinction to be made even between the Buddha and his disciples which are identical with karmic deeds and with defilement.

[398] See footnote 376 for an explanation of the term "mani."

What is it like to have got rid of all appearances?

It is called unsurpassed perfect truth.

If [you] long for the adorned Buddha realm,

impartially practice compassion and rescue the suffering.

Although [your] original vow to attain *bodhi* is deep,

[I] urge [you] not to have attachments amid appearances.

[In] this [way] the pair "blessedness" and "wisdom" are made complete;

[just as] one's future salvation is predicted by a Buddha.[399]

[If you are] defiled by the smallest [concern about] annihilation or permanence,[400]

[then you] still lack affinity with all the Buddhas.

[Due to their] overturned thinking ordinary people cling in delusion;

[thus they] all suffer from the defiling habits[401] of the emotions and affections.

Due simply to desires, the proliferation of emotions is excessive,

[causing] the unceasing [re]birth of embryos, and eggs produced [in] dampness.[402]

[To] study the Tao [you] must cause [yourself to be] fierce;

a mind without emotions is as hard as iron.

---

[399] This line includes the Buddhist term *shouji* (授記) which refers to the prediction of one's future attainment of enlightenment and Buddhahood. Ciyuan, 691, s.v. 授記.

[400] "Annihilation or permanence" (*duan chang* 斷 常) refers to one's end or continuance, annihilation or permanence, death or immortality. Soothill and Hodous, *Chinese Buddhist Terms*, 464-465, s.v. 斷.

[401] "Defiling habits" (*ran xi* 染習). Soothill and Hodous, *Chinese Buddhist Terms*, 304, s.v. 染習.

[402] This line refers to the various human and animal forms into which one may be reborn.

[If you are] only forgiving of [your] parents, wife, and children,

[how are you] different from other people?

Constantly preserve the perfect brightness of the single pearl.

do not [even] look at things [you] may desire to compare.

Then the myriad dharmas, in an instant, have no [place of] attachment;

[of] what earth prisons[403] or heavenly mansions[404] [can one] speak?

After that, [you will realize that] our destiny rests with us;

within emptiness there is no ascending and no descending.

Appearing and disappearing in all of the Buddha-lands,

do not part from the original seat of *bodhi*.

[As in the] thirty two responses of Kuanyin,[405]

we also should [manifest] from inner realization.

[These] manifestations[406] are impossible to conceive of;

---

[403] "Earth prisons" (*diyu* 地獄) is generally interpreted as hell or the hells but may also be termed purgatory. Soothill and Hodous, *Chinese Buddhist Terms*, 207, s.v. 地獄. Soothill and Hodous provide further deatails on the various forms of Buddhist hell including descriptions of the various punishments associated with the different hells. Ibid.

[404] "Heavenly mansions" (*tiantang* 天堂) are the mansions of the *devas* (gods, or celestial beings) which are located between the earth and the *Brahmalokas* the second of the three realms (*sanjie* 三界), comprising sixteen, seventeen or eighteen "heavens of form." The inhabitants of these realms are beyond the desire for sex or food. Soothill and Hodous, *Chinese Buddhist Terms*, 144, s.v. 天堂; 220, s.v. 三界.

[405] "The thirty two responses of Kuanyin" (*sanshier ying* 三十二應) are various forms which this *bodhisattva* can assume. They range from that of a Buddha to that of a man, a maid or a demon. Soothill and Hodous, *Chinese Buddhist Terms*, 60, s.v. 三十二; 471, s.v. 羅刹.

[406] "Manifestations" (*huaxian* 化現) refers to the appearance or forms of a buddha or bodhisattva which are assumed for the purpose of rescuing creatures. This line is referring

[they] all emerge from an unhindered [Buddha-]nature.

I am a spontaneous Chan[407] traveller;

[I do] not know [how to] distinguish [even] ordinary affairs.

Formerly, [there was] a black ox,

today [its] whole body is completely white.

There are times [when I] sing and laugh to myself;

bystanders say that my intelligence is slight.

How can they know that my roughly clad body

[has] within its bosom a priceless jewel?[408]

Further, if [they] see me talking about emptiness,

it is [to them] very much like swallowing a jujube whole.

Only buddhas are able to comprehend this *dharma*;

could an ordinary fool comprehend the [significance in such] external appearances?

Additionally, there are the lofty people who practice meditation;

all [they do is] study arguments and flap their gums.

Boasting that their repartee is witty and quick,

---

back to the thirty two reponses or forms of the *bodhisattava* Kuanyin. The various forms that she assumes are reponses to the plight of those who are suffering.

[407] "Chan" (*Chan* 禪), denotes the sect of Mahāyāna Buddhism of the same name and also refers to the practice of meditation.

[408] These two lines echo the following saying: 被褐懷玉 "Wearing rough garments but carrying a precious gem in the bosom." Mathews, *Chinese English Dictionary*, 4999.b. See also *Ciyuan*, 1532, s.v. 被褐懷玉. A very similar phrase is found in the last line of chapter 70 in the *Daode jing*.

yet, from the beginning, [they] do not recognize a [true] master.

Now this is searching the branches and plucking leaves,

not a thorough investigation of the original root.

[If you] can attain the root [then] the branches and leaves will naturally flourish;

without the root the branches and leaves will be difficult to preserve.

Showing off the original pearl already in their grasp,

the return to [distinguishing between other] people and oneself is difficult to get rid of.

From the marvelous enlightenment of my numinous source,

[such behaviour] is separated by a vast difference.

These [people] are indeed to be pitied and laughed at;

vainly [they] explain how many years [they have] studied the Tao.

With lofty minds [they are] unwilling to enquire of others;

uselessly [they] cause [their] whole lifetime to be squandered into old age.

[This] is stupidity, confusion and dull capacity;

the cause of this is the karmic weight of heterodox views.

If, in this life, [they] fail to wake up,

how can [they] escape ruin in the next life?

The Song of Non-intentionality

[I] can laugh at my mind, like the dull, like the rustic.

Lame, lame then moving, moving; employing things with peaceful abandon.

Not understanding how to cultivate conduct and not committing any sins.

Not profiting others, and not selfish.

Not grasping the precepts[409] and laws,[410] nor avoiding taboos.

Not understanding ritual or music, nor practising humanity and moral principles.

[As for] what [I] can do in the human realm, out of one hundred [affairs] not [even] one can [I]

manage.

When hungry [I] eat, when thirsty [I] drink.

If [I] am tired [I] sleep; if [I] am awake [I] am active.

[If it is] hot [I] wear unlined garments; [if it is] cold then [I] cover [myself] with a quilt.

Without thought, without deliberation; what sadness, what happiness [do I have]?

Not regretting nor scheming; no remembering, no intending.

The glories and disgraces of ordinary life are just inns [along the road].

[Consider]the birds roosting in the forest as a comparison.

In coming [they] are not restrained; in departing [they] do not hesitate.

Not avoiding nor welcoming; not praising nor slandering.

Not detesting the deformed and ugly; not admiring the perfect and the beautiful.

Not hastening to a peaceful retreat; not staying away from the city bustle.

---

[409] "Precepts" (*jie* 戒) refer to ethical guidelines which must be followed as a precondition for religious progress. The precepts are applicable to monks, nuns, and lay devotees. The precepts (of which there are ten) include refraining from killing, not taking what is not given, refraining from prohibited sexual activity, and refraining from unjust speech. *The Ecyclopedia of Eastern Philosophy and Religion*, ed. Stephen Schumacher and Gert Woerner (Boston: Shambhala, 1989), s.v. *shila*.

[410] "Laws" (*lu* 律) are rules and regulations which, unlike the precepts, are intended specifically as a means for regulating the communal life of monks and nuns. Thus, these rules are concerned with conduct during mealtimes, manners, and extolling one's own sanctity. *The Ecyclopedia of Eastern Philosophy and Religion*, s.v. *vinaya-pitaka*.

Not saying that others are wrong; nor boasting that I am right.

Not generous with the honoured and esteemed; nor mean with the lowly or young.

[I] love [my] enemies and those great and small, inside and outside.

Grief and joy, gain and loss; respect and insult, danger and ease.

[My] mind does not see in a dual way; peaceful, it is unified in its considerations.

Not considering the start of fortune nor the beginning of calamity.

[When] influenced, [I] respond; [when] compelled [I] begin [to act].

[Since I] do not fear sharp knives; why dread the tiger and rhinoceros?

In according with the designation of things, need one cling to names?

[My] eyes do not follow colour; sound does not approach [my] ears.

Everything which has external appearance, is absurd and false.

The appearances and sounds of men and women are entirely without fixed substance.

[As for] substance and appearance, be non-intentional [and they] will not cause defilement or obstruction.

[Thus,] self possessed [I] freely wander afar; things can no longer bind [me].

The bright halo of marvellous enlightenment shines, penetrating inside and out.

Enwrapping the six directions, there is no far or near.

Brightness: there is none; [it is] like the moon in the water.

[Being] difficult to grasp or get rid of; furthermore, to what can [it] be compared?

Understand this marvellously efficacious teaching and you will far transcend it.

Some ask about [my] teachings; [it] is this and nothing more.

West River Moon

1. Do not continue forcibly destroying erroneous thoughts;

   why hopefully seek out true suchness?

   One's fundamental nature and buddhahood are cultivated in the same way;

   delusion and awakening: can there be a before and after?

   Once awakened one attains buddhahood in an instant;

   but when deluded [you will be caught up in] the current and flow[411] for ten thousand eons.

   If [you] are able to dedicate a single thought to true cultivation,

   [you] will be able to eradicate the filth of sins numberless as the sands of the Ganges.

2. Fundamentally, there is no birth and no extinction;

   the distinction between birth and death is forced.

   Just as sinfulness and blessedness, also have no root,

   how could the subtle body be increased or diminished?

   I have a round clear mirror;[412]

   it is just that [it] has always been covered up and obscured.

   [But,] today [I] polish [it and it] illuminates heaven and earth;

   the myriad forms are brightly [reflected and] cannot be concealed.

---

[411] Here, "flow" (liu 流) connotes being lost in the cycle of birth, death and rebirth (*samsara*) as in the phrase, "Transmigration which has come down from the state of primal ignorance." (流來生死). Soothill and Hodous, *Chinese Buddhist Terms*, 328, s.v. 流.

[412] The mirror is the mirror of the mind (*xin jing* 心鏡) "which must be kept clean if it is to reflect the Truth. Soothill and Hodous, *Chinese Buddhist Terms*, 152, s.v. 心鏡.

3. My nature enters the nature of all buddhas;

   in all directions Buddha-nature is like this.

   Standing alone, [its] wintry reflection shines [in] winter springs;

   a single moon visible everywhere in a thousand pools.

   [When] small [it] is like the tiniest invisible hair;

   when great [it] fills every part of the great chiliocosm.

   High or low, [it] is not be bound to the square or round;

   what long or short, deep or shallow is there to speak of?

4. *Dharmas, dharmas, dharmas*: fundamentally there are no *dharmas*;

   emptiness, emptiness, emptiness: there is also no emptiness.

   Quiet and clamour, speech and silence are originally the same;

   while within a dream, why toil to explain the dream?

   [What is] useful within the useful is the useless;

   [what] lacks efficacy within the efficacious [is that which] exhibits efficaciousness.

   Furthermore, [this is] like ripening fruit which naturally reddens;

   do not [bother to] ask how to cultivate the seed.

5. Good and evil: immediately forget [all such] thoughts;

   flourishing and decaying: do not concern the mind with either [of these].

   Dark and light, hidden or manifest, allow [yourself to] float and sink;

   be content with your lot, eating when hungry and drinking when thirsty.

The spirit, being quiet and clear is constantly still;

it matters not whether [you are] standing, sitting, reclining, singing or humming.

The jade coloured autumn flood water of a single pool is as deep as before;

[when] the wind stirs do not be alarmed; let it go.

6. As for [our] external surroundings, it is not necessary to forcibly annihilate [them];

[it is merely on] the authority of false names [that the concept of] *bodhi* is established.

Matter and emptiness, light and dark are originally the same;

stop dividing true and false as two substances.

Once awakened, [you can] call [that] the Pureland;

for there is no need of India or *Caoji*.[413]

Who says that perfect happiness is in the heavenly West?

Having understood this Amitabha appears in [this] world.[414]

---

[413] See footnote 364 concerning Caoji.

[414] *Chushi* (出世) can have three meanings: when applied to a Buddha, for example, it can mean "appearing in the world." It can also mean "to leave the world" and as such is synonymous with a monk or nun who, by definition, is one who has left the family (*chujia* 出家). Finally, it can mean beyond this world or not of this world. Soothill and Hodous, *Chinese Buddhist Terms*, 166, s.v. 出世. The central message of this verse appears to be the dissolution of opposites and the realization of the immanence of enlightenment. The opening lines turn conventional expectations concerning enlightenment on their head: external appearances are not to be forcibly extinguished from the mind, and enlightenment (*bodhi*) itself is nothing but a conventional designation, literally a false name. The fourth line equates the mystical Pureland with the very experience of awakening, making it immanent rather than something remote and distinct from the subject which must be sought out and attained. By reading *chushi* as "appeared in the world" the reader is given the impression that it is not necessary to go out and seek in India, the Pureland, or from Huineng (*Caoji*). Once one is awakened Amitabha is right here in this world. The choice of translation made here draws on Cleary's rendering of this verse. Cleary, *Understanding Reality*, 184.

7. As for [the idea that there is] a permanent lord within[415] which rules completely over life,

    [this is] preferring to divide that and this, high and low.

    The *dharma* body pervades and illuminates [all] and extinguishes I and he;

    keep in mind that it is not necessary to search for it.

    Seeing the right; when has [one] seen the right?

    Hearing the wrong; [one] has not necessarily heard the wrong.

    It has always been that all functions are not mutually understood;

    [as for] life and death who can obstruct you?

8. Abiding in appearances, cultivating conduct, and giving alms,

    the fruits of such actions will not be far from [those of] celestial beings.

    But accordingly, [this] is like staring up at an arrow shot up and floating in the clouds;

    [eventually, it] falls simply because [its] strength is exhausted.

    How is [this] like the eternal, unconditioned true form?[416]

---

[415] "Permanent lord within" is a translation of *renwo* (人我) which refers to the personality "the human soul, i.e. the false view, 人我見 that every man has a permanent lord within, 常一主宰, which he calls the ātman, soul, or permanent self, a view which forms the basis of all erronious doctrine." Soothill and Hodous, *Chinese Buddhist Terms*, 32, s.v. 人我. This "false" notion of a ruler within accords well with the use of the term "rule" (*zhu* 主) which occurs in the same line. It should be noted though, that the character *zhu* (主) has been replaced with *sheng* (生) in Wang Mu, *Qianjie*, 198.

[416] *Wuwei* (無爲) refers to that which is not subject to cause, condition, or dependence and also to what is transcendent, not in time, eternal. Soothill and Hodous, *Chinese Buddhist Terms*, 380, s.v. 無爲. *Shixiang* (實相) is a synonym for the *Dharmakāya* (*fashen* 法身), the true body or essential Buddhahood. Ibid., 423, s.v. 實相. *Wuwei fashen* (無爲法身) is "Asamskrta dharmakāya, the eternal body of the Buddha not conditioned by cause and effect." Ibid., 380, s.v. 無爲. Hence the reading here of *wuwei shixiang* (無爲 實相) as "the eternal, unconditioned true form."

Return to the [true] source; revert to the simple; go back to the pure.

Surroundings forgotten, emotions ended, and accepting underlying reality,

thereby realizing eternal *dharma* patience.

9. If the fish and the hare should return into your hands,

naturally; [you would] forget the fish trap and the snare.[417]

The raft by which [one] crosses the river, the ladder by which [one] ascends to heaven;

when [one has] reached there [they are] all abandoned.

[If you are] not yet awakened [then you] must rely upon explanations;

once awakened, [relying on] explanation is completely unnecessary.

Although these four phrases are associated with the uncaused;

even these must be cast aside.

10. Having awakened do not continue searching for calmness and extinction;[418]

according with circumstances, welcome the multitudes of the lost.

---

[417] These first two lines are reminiscent of the closing comments found in the chapter entitled "External Things" in the *Zhuangzi* and are used to make the same point about moving beyond words, beyond even the words in this text. 荃者所以在魚得魚而忘荃蹄者所以在兔得兔而忘蹄言者所以在意得意而忘言吾安得夫忘言之人而與之言哉 "The fish trap exists because of the fish; once you've gotten the fish, you can forget the trap. The rabbit snare exists because of the rabbit; once you've gotten the rabbit, you can forget the snare. Words exist because of meaning; once you've gotten the meaning, you can forget the words. Where can I find a man who has forgotten the words so I can have a word with him?" Watson; *Chuang Tzu*, 302.

[418] "Calmness and extinction" (*ji mie* 寂滅) can also refer to *nirvāna*. Soothill and Hodous, *Chinese Buddhist Terms*, 348, s.v. 寂.

Having understood the annihilation of permanence, assist [them];

using the appropriate means, direct them back to the Region of Reality.[419]

[With the] five [forms of] vision,[420] three [kinds of] body[421] and four [forms of] wisdom,[422]

the six perfections[423] and myriad ways of conduct, cultivate [complete] equanimity.

A single orb of round brightness, the beautiful *Mani* jewel;

benefitting all living beings and also able to save oneself.

11. I see [that when] my contemporaries discuss the [Buddha-]nature;

[they] merely brag about [their] quick wittedness.

In dealing with opportunities and the world [they] perpetuate foolishness and delusion;

---

[419] "Region of Reality" (*shiji* 實際) is a term denoting the noumenal universe. Soothill and Hodous, *Chinese Buddhist Terms*, 423, s.v. 實際.

[420] "Five kinds of vision" (*wu yan* 五眼): human, *deva* (divine being), Hīnāyāna wisdom, *bodhisattva* truth, and Buddha vision (omniscience). Soothill and Hodous, *Chinese Buddhist Terms*, 123, s.v. 五眼.

[421] See footnote 372 for information concerning the "three kinds of body."

[422] "Four forms of wisdom" (*si zhi* 四智) are the four forms of wisdom of a Buddha which, according to the Faxiang (法相) school are: 1) (*da yuan jing zhi* 大圓鏡智) the great mirror wisdom of Aksobhya; 2) (*ping deng xing zhi* 平等性智) the universal wisdom of Ratnaketu; 3) (*miao guan cha zhi* 妙觀察智) the profound observing wisdom of Amitāba; 4) (*cheng suo zuo zhi* 成所作智) the perfecting wisdom of Amoghasiddi. Soothill and Hodous, *Chinese Buddhist Terms*, 176, s.v. 四智; see also 272, s.v. 法相. The Faxiang school was founded in China by Xuanzang (玄奘) (600-664). The doctrine of this school is founded the central assumption that the "external world" is spun into existence by our consciousness and is, therefore, illusory. A brief overview of Faxiang doctrine can be found in Kenneth Chen, *Buddhism in China: A Historical Survey* (Princeton: Princeton University Press, 1964), 320-325.

[423] See footnote 390 for a list of the "six perfections."

again, how do [such people] differ from fools?

Having spoken of attaining, [one] must then practice attainment;

[this] then is called speech and practice without deficiency.

[If you are] able to take up the sword of wisdom and cleave the *Mani* jewel,

this is called the correct understanding of the Tathāgata.

12. Desiring to understand the marvellous way of birthlessness,

do not fail to observe your own true mind.

The true body is without form and without sound;

the clear and pure *dharma* body is just so.

This way is not non-existent, nor does it exist;

also do not search [for it] in between them.

[With the] two extremes [having been] rejected, cast aside the centre;

having seen [this] is called the highest level.

Afterword

Firstly, take [the fact of] a person's birth; this brings about vain passions [associated with] having a body. Having a body [one also] has suffering; if [one] had no body where would suffering come from?[424] Now [as for] escaping from suffering, there is nothing better than to embody the perfect Tao. Desiring to embody the perfect Tao, there is nothing better than the understanding of original mind. Thus the mind is the substance of the Tao and the Tao is the function of the mind. [If people] are able to carefully examine [their] minds and scrutinize [their] inner natures, then the substance of complete understanding will spontaneously be manifest. The functioning of natural action [will be] spontaneously completed; not relying on merit they suddenly leap to the other shore.[425] This being so [if one] lacks the luminescence of the mirror mind and the expansive brightness of the spiritual pearl, then how [can one] cause all external appearances to suddenly depart, fine dust not to contaminate, the source of the mind to be self existent, and the resolve to birthlessness to be decided upon? Thus, as for the enlightened gentleman who's mind embodies the Tao, [if his] body cannot bind his inner nature, and external circumstances cannot disorder his perfection, then how could weapons [do him] harm? How could the tiger and rhinoceros [cause him] injury? [How could] raging fires or great floods be enough to cause [him] worry? The mind of an intelligent person is like a bright mirror; reflecting, it does not receive; in responding to stimulus it accords with things; harmonizing but not advocating. Therefore, [he is] able to manage things

---

[424] Chapter 13 of the *Daode jing* includes the following phrase: 吾所以有大患者爲吾有身及吾無身吾有何患 "The reason I have great trouble is that I have a body. When I no longer have a body, what trouble have I?" Lau, Tao Te Ching, 18-19.

[425] "The other shore" (*bi an* 彼岸) represents *nirvāna* while "this shore" (*ci an* 此岸) represents life trapped within the cyclic realm of life, death and rebirth. Soothill and Hodous, *Chinese Buddhist Terms*, 257, s.v. 彼.

without injury. This is what is called the marvellous Tao of unsurpassed perfect truth. [If one] traces this Tao to its source it had no name, [yet] the sages were compelled to name it. Fundamentally, the Tao is inexplicable [yet] the sages are compelled to explain it.

Therefore, if names and explanations are silenced then people now a days will be without a means to recognize its substance and return to its reality. So the sages devise teachings and establish explanations by which the Tao is [made] manifest. Therefore, Tao relies upon explanations and afterwards becomes manifest. Explanations rely on the Tao and afterwards are forgotten. What alternative is there? This Tao is most mysterious, and most subtle, while the nature and character[426] of people in the world is deluded and stupid. Clinging to their having a body they hate death and take pleasure in life. Thus, in the end it is difficult [for them] to understand thoroughly. Huang and Lao (the Yellow Emperor and Laozi), pitying their attachment to desire, then made use of techniques for cultivating life, in accord with what they desired, and gradually instructed them [by] employing the essentials of cultivating life [found] in the golden elixir, the essentials of the golden elixir in the spirit water flower pool. Therefore the teachings of the [*Scripture on the*] *Tao and Virtue* and the *Scripture of Obscure Correspondence*[427] [can be] obtained in order [that they may] prevail in the world for a time and benefit people, [so that] they enjoy their lives. [Even] so, [their] words are hidden, [their] principles obscure. Although intoning the words, no one understands their meaning. If [one] does not meet a perfected person and receive oral instruction, in the end [they will] be unable

---

[426] "Nature and character" (*gen xing* 根性), Soothill and Hodous, *Chinese Buddhist Terms*, 327, s.v. 根.

[427] Information on the *Yinfujing* (Scripture of Obscure Correspondence) can be found in footnote 276. The translation for this title is taken from Isabelle Robinet,"Original Contributions of Neidan" in *Taoist Meditation and Longevity Techniques*, ed. Livia Kohn (Ann Arbor: Center for Chinese Studies The University of Michigan, 1989), 303.

to achieve merit or complete their task. Are not those who fail to learn as numerous as the hairs on a cow and those with intelligence as rare as a unicorn's horn?

Formerly in the year 1079 C.E., Boduan met a teacher in Chengdu who gave him the method of the elixir. That year his master passed away. Henceforth [he] repeatedly preached to people and time and time again met with calamity and misfortune. In all [this went on for] not more than twenty days. [He] then came to recall the advice of his teacher: "Some day when there are those with [you] who have untied the reigns and cast off the fetters, [you] ought to transmit [your understanding] to them, leaving out nothing." Afterwards [he] wanted to give up [his] name and hometown but [he] worried [that the] people of the Tao did not know what to believe. He then composed this *Chapters on Awakening to the Real* stating all things concerning the elixir medicine from beginning to end. Having completed [the work he] searched for students [who would] come and gather together; [those who] would study with earnest intent [and whose minds] do not go to extremes. [He] then picked out [individuals to whom he could] transmit his teachings.

None [of them] had [either] the great power or strength which would allow [them] to assist [those] in danger or to save the drowning; [nor were any of them] scholars [with] the magnanimity and exceptional intelligence [which would] enable them to speak with humanity and insight. [From] the beginning [they] repeatedly incurred suffering, [their] minds still not completely understanding. Altogether, [only] three [of them], by examining their past faults, understood that the method of the great elixir is very simple and very easy [and that] although stupid and dull, [if] the small man attains [this method] and puts it into practice [he] will immediately leap up to the level of the sages. By means of this [one can see that] the intentions of Heaven are abstruse and grudging and will not permit careless transmission to those who lack heaven's [mandate]. Yet Boduan did not obey [his] teacher's words; [he] repeatedly revealed the celestial secrets because he had a body. Therefore [he] invariably received scolding and trouble. This was heaven's warning [to him] and in like fashion the spirits also urged: "Do not dare to abrogate [your] duty. Henceforth [you] ought to manacle [your] mouth and tie up [your] tongue. Although the cauldron remains right in front of [you, as if with] a sword to [your] neck, never again presume to [offer such] explanations."

What is sung about in the *Chapters on Awakening to the True* is the subtle meaning of the great elixir medicine and the fire phase; [it] does not lack any details. Those who appreciate it had the bones of an immortal in a past life. [If they] study [it] then [they] will have [sufficient] understanding for self-enlightenment and it will be possible to understand its meaning by investigating the text. Why would they need Boduan's detailed instructions to be given to them? Thus what heaven bestows is not the hasty transmission of Boduan, as if these chapters were merely songs. [They] explain the method of observing the inner nature. Accordingly, [they] present what is called the Tao of spontaneous, marvellous enlightenment; and, being so, [it is] the Tao of spontaneous action [which] equalizes things for the mind. Although [these chapters] display the secret essentials, in the end there is no transgression or fault. What remedy is there for the ordinary man? [According to his] his destined *karma* [he will] be generous or stingy. [According to the] foundation of his inner nature [he will be] sharp [witted] or dull. [Even though] hearing [only] a single sound, [he will] in confusion form heterodox views. Therefore Śākyamuni and Mañjuśri[428] defined what is expounded [as] the *Dharma* jewel of only one vehicle. And yet, [having] heard [this],

---

[428] Mañjuśri (*Wenshu* 文殊) is the guardian of wisdom and is often pictured on Śākyamuni's left. In some representations he is holding the sword of wisdom and sits on a lion which symbolizes his stern majesty in others he is pictured as a youth. During past incarnations he is described as the parent of many Buddhas and is said to have assisted the Buddha in coming into being. Soothill and Hodous, *Chinese Buddhist Terms*, 153, s.v. 文殊.

students then consider [that they] completely understand and naturally make the error of three vehicles.[429] Henceforth, if there is a scholar whose inner nature and character are courageous and intelligent [and if he] reads and listens to these chapters then [he] will understand that Boduan attained the marvellous meaning of the highest single vehicle of Bodhidharma and the six patriarchs.[430] [And so] it will be possible, following [this] single explanation, to awaken to the myriad *dharmas*. [But] if one's habit is to add more [to this] then [one] returns to the views of the middle and the small. [This] moreover is certainly not the fault of Boduan!

---

[429] These two sentences refer to a doctrine which is found in the *Miaofa lianhua jing*. There are said to be three vehicles (*san cheng* 三 乘) or ways of conveyance across the realm of birth and death. These vehicles are: 1) that of the hearer or obedient disciple, 2) that of the enlightened for self only and 3) that of the *Bodhisattva* who attains enlightenment for the benefit of others. The first two methods are small or lesser methods while the third is greater. Three levels are designated by the terms "small" (*xiao* 小), "middle" (*zhong* 中) and "great" (*da* 大). "The Lotus declares that the three are really the One Buddha vehicle, which has been revealed in three expedient forms suited to his disciples' capacity . . ." Soothill and Hodous, *Chinese Buddhist Terms*, 58, s.v. 三 乘. The term "one vehicle" (that is the greater vehicle) designates Mahāyāna Buddhism. Ibid., 1, s.v. 一 乘.

[430] Tradition holds Bodhidharma (470-543?) to be the first patriarch of Chan Buddhism, after whom came the six patriarchs of Chan, the best known among them is the sixth patriarch, Hui Neng (638-713). A discussion of the historicity of Bodhidharma can be found in Dumoulin, Zen Buddhism, 85-94. On Hui Neng see ibid., 123-154.

Chapter Three
The Inner Alchemical Theory of Zhang Boduan

Introduction: Methodological Cards on the Table

This chapter will combine two strands of comment: It will, of course, be an attempt to gain insight into the teachings of Zhang Boduan as they are expressed in the *Wuzhen pian* but it will also be a response to the representation of inner alchemy found in the work of Joseph Needham and his many colleagues in *Science and Civilisation in China*.[431] There is no doubt that the work of Needham on inner alchemy is certainly the most detailed and widely ranging study of the subject in a "Western" language and *Science and Civilisation in China* is arguably the work which has had the most influence on subsequent scholarship. It is also obvious that any scholar working on the complex and occasionally daunting texts of Taoist inner alchemy owes Needham and his associates a debt of gratitude. Despite its stature and influence in the field, attention has not been paid to the key methodological assumption which underlies *Science and Civilisation in China*: That contemporary notions of the scientific world view can be invoked as a meta-narrative in order to represent inner alchemy as a scientific or at least proto-scientific system of practice.[432] It will be argued here that inner alchemy as it is described in the *Wuzhen pian* is first and foremost a religious or spiritual practice and that the end to which the process aims is soteriological rather than unambiguously physical, as is claimed by Needham.

In dealing with these questions a very fundamental methodological assumption will be made: It will be assumed that the text itself should be permitted a strong voice in providing answers to the

---

[431] Specifically: Needham, *Science and Civilization,* vol. 5.5.

[432] Ibid., xxx.

above questions. The loudness and clarity of that voice is certainly mediated in many ways: There is, for example, a vast temporal distance between the present translator and the composer of the text in question. There are also concerns about the many incongruities between the source language and the target language which stem from basic syntactical discrepancies which in turn are symptomatic of culturally divergent modes of configuring the world. In addition to these more passive factors one must also consider that the act of translation, and indeed of reading, is an activity involving construction by means of interpretation. In light of these concerns the aim here will not and could not be to provide a definitive account of the essential meaning of the *Wuzhen pian* but rather to enter into a conversation with the text. The outcome of such a conversation will hopefully be a heightened awareness of the ways in which the "other" culture is different. Just as in the field of semiotics it has been suggested that the differences between signs provide the mechanism by which signs signify, and thus establish their own place within the flow of discourse, it is the differences between cultural domains of language which provide a basis for identity. Thus it is the responsibility of the scholar to allow those differences to be expressed in the rendering of a text. The words of Jean-François Lyotard bring into focus the goal of such an orientation: "Postmodern knowledge is not simply a tool of the authorities; it refines our sensitivity to differences and reinforces our ability to tolerate the incommensurable."[433] This set of assumptions is inspired by ideas which have grown out of an appreciation for the destabilizing method of enquiry exemplified by Zhuangzi and Socrates (or at least somewhat ironically by the Socrates of Plato's dialogues) and more recently in Europe and North America by post-*Tractatus* Wittgenstein, Derrida's description of human discourse as writing,

---

[433] Lyotard, Jean-François, *The Postmodern Condition: A Report on Knowledge*, trans. Geoff Bennington and Brian Massumi (Minneapolis: University of Minnisota Press, 1984), xxv.

and by what is now being called the neo-pragmatism of Richard Rorty. All of these individuals have contributed to the growing discontent with meta-narratives as a means of gaining insight into human behaviour.

I. A Summary of Needham's Position

A. Needham's Mission

Joseph Needham, the figure who guided the construction of *Science and Civilization in China,* undoubtably had very noble intentions. To him it appeared that a very grave injustice had been committed and his aim was to help redress that injustice. In 1954 he noted that European scholars have been disposed to trace the history of science backwards from its present achievements to Mediterranean antiquity. The foundations which provided for the successful evolution of modern science were said primarily to have been laid by the mathematicians, engineers, and observers of nature of ancient Greece and Rome. He observed that gradually work had been done to uncover contributions made by other civilizations such as the ancient Egyptians, Babylonians, Sumerians and Hittites. With *Science and Civilization in China* Needham was determined that China would finally get *its* recognition. Perhaps Needham's own turn of phrase best sums up his intentions:

> What we know is that we have met with our Chinese brothers and sisters in the fields of science, technology, and medicine during the past twenty-five centuries, and though we can never speak with them, we can often read their words, and we have sought to give them their meed of honour.[434]

How has it come to pass that Needham and his fellow scholars have assumed the privileged position of being able to offer this meed of honour to the Chinese? According to Needham the

---

[434] Joseph Needham, *Science in Traditional China* (Cambridge, Massachusetts: Harvard University Press, 1981), x.

answer rests in the obvious fact that, from about the fourteenth century onward, the peoples of

Europe were fortunate, through their discovery and subsequent mastery of the scientific method, to

make great scientific and technical leaps forward. As the Enlightenment unfolded, the distance

between the Chinese and the Europeans grew rapidly. It is the astounding success of modern science

which places Needham and his fellow scholars in this advantaged position.

Concerning the early developments of science in China Needham is genuinely perplexed. He

finds it difficult to account for the early successes of the Chinese in developing the technologies that

they did. To an individual with Needham's faith in the scientific enterprise, with its reliance on what

he calls sophisticated theorizing,[435] the achievements of the Chinese border on the miraculous. How

in the face of their theoretical backwardness[436] could such great strides have been made?

> Why should the science of China have remained...on a level continuously empirical,
> and restricted to theories of primitive or medieval type? How, if this was so, did the
> Chinese succeed in forestalling in many important matters the scientific and technical
> discoveries of the *dramatis personae* of the celebrated 'Greek miracle', in keeping
> pace with the Arabs . . . and in maintaining, between the 3rd and 13th centuries, a
> level of scientific knowledge unapproachable in the west?[437]

It is suggested that *Science and Civilization in China* is intended to discuss these and other questions.

Part of what motivated the writing of *Science and Civilization in China* was also the desire

to extend a hand of friendship to the Chinese. These feelings of friendship were to stem from the

recognition of what Chinese civilization up to the thirteenth century had contributed to the

development of modern science. For Needham the possibility of this mission of friendship rests on

---

[435] Needham, *Science in Traditional China*, 108.

[436] Needham, *Science and Civilization,* vol. I, 4.

[437] Ibid., 1.

the universal nature of the scientific endeavour. Because science transcends the boundaries between various forms of human culture it is a language common to all people. Furthermore, it is an enterprise to which people at various times throughout history and in many different places have made contributions. While the great civilizations of the past may have pursued a variety of ends they were all unwitting contributors to the advancement of science and thus, "Their achievements should be mutually recognized and freely celebrated with the joined hands of universal brotherhood."[438] Various peoples of the world have, it seems, been toiling toward a common end for centuries. What better cement could there be between peoples than the recognition that they have all contributed, sometimes accidentally and occasionally almost miraculously, to the construction of modern science?[439] Needham states that we are living in a time of great change and possible danger and at a time when the world has become one. Thus it is important that people around the world begin to enter into friendly relationships. Before such relationships can be cultivated there must be the possibility of communication and feelings of mutual respect on which to found the communication. Science can address both of these needs: Firstly its universality by virtue of its rationality provides a universe of discourse into which people from very different backgrounds can enter and secondly,

---

[438] Ibid., 9. Also see, Needham, *Science and Civilization,* vol. V.5, xxvii: "The cultures might be many, the languages diverse, but they all partook of the same quest."

[439] Needham favors the view of American historian of science Edgar Zilsel regarding the construction of science. He paraphrases ideas which Zilsel believes comprise the ideal of scientific progress: 1.That scientific knowledge is built up brick by brick through the contributions of generations of workers, 2. that the building is never completed, and 3. that the scientists aim is a disinterested contribution to this building, either for its own sake or for the public benefit, and not for fame or personal knowledge or private personal advantage. Needham, *Science in Traditional China*, 117. Alternate views are expressed in the classic work by Thomas Kuhn, *The Structure of Scientific Revolutions*, 2nd ed. (Chicago: University of Chicago Press, 1970). and in the work of Paul Feyerabend, *Against Method*, rev. ed. (New York: Verso, 1988).

its present form is evidence that over many centuries we have actually already been working towards a common end.

It is Needham's passionate devotion to the scientific world view and his belief that it offers a potential mode of communication between peoples that has lead him to view inner alchemy in a way which does not accommodate or acknowledge the possibility that what he is studying may be a very different way of viewing human beings with its own internally coherent system of ideas but a system which may be entirely incommensurable with modern scientific notions of what constitutes the human organism.

B. Needham's Understanding of Inner Alchemy

This section will briefly describe some of the key components of Needham's representation of inner alchemy. Section C will then address each of those components in order to demonstrate how a close reading of the *Wuzhen pian* makes it very difficult to accept Needham's position vis-a-vis inner alchemical training.

i. The Goal of Inner Alchemy

While discussing the symbolic significance of the reconstitution of the trigrams *qian* (乾) and *kun* (坤) through the exchange of the central lines of *kan* and *li*, Needham offers perhaps his most telling phrase summarizing what he sees as the goal of the inner alchemist: "Such was the way in which it was possible for the *nei dan* adepts to talk about the separation and restoration of pure Yang and pure Yin—transforming as it were the greybeard to the zygote."[440] There is no question that what

---

[440] *Science and Civilization,* vol. V.5, 54.

was sought through the cultivation of the adept was the creation of the "great medicine" (*da yao* 大
藥) which would confer longevity. By longevity Needham is clear that he is referring to physical

longevity and rejuvination and not to the kind of mystic and transcendent achievement described so

beautifully in the *Zhuangzi*:

> . . . there is a Holy Man living on faraway Ku-she Moutain, with skin like ice or
> snow, and gentle and shy like a young girl. He doesn't eat the five grains, but sucks
> the wind, drinks the dew, climbs up on the clouds and mist, rides a flying dragon, and
> wanders beyond the four seas. By concentrating his spirit, he can protect creatures
> from sickness and plague and make the harvest plentiful.[441]

Needham explains that "the Chinese adept of the 'inner elixir' did not seek psycho-analytic peace

and integration directly, he believed that by doing things with one's own body a physiological

medicine of longevity and even immortality (material immortality for no other was conceivable)

could be prepared within it."[442] Religious or spiritual goals are barely mentioned in the many pages

describing in remarkable detail the practices of the inner alchemical adept. Even the possibility of

psychological transformations are relegated to an ancillary position in the scheme of practice in order

that the strictly physiological dimension of the practice may remain at the forefront.

The range of practices described in *Science and Civilisation* as comprising inner alchemy

reflect this understanding of the orientation and final goal of inner alchemy. The practices associated

with inner alchemy are divided into seven major types: 1) mental and bodily hygiene, involving

cleanliness and ataraxia, 2) respiratory exercises, 3) exercises designed to circulate the vital breath

(*qi* 氣), 4) remedial gymnastics 5) conservation of various secretions from the body 6) sexual

---

[441] Watson, *Chuang Tzu*, 33.

[442] Needham, *Science and Civilization*, vol. V.5, 23.

techniques and 7) meditation and trance.[443] While mental training constitutes one category and, under

hygiene, the banishment of the passions is allowed for, the techniques remain primarily physical as

does the final goal of the process. By placing meditation in this list with sexual techniques,

gymnastics and respiratory exercises the more mystical religious elements of the training are

subsumed under the general label of physiological training, the end of which is then more readily

describable in purely physical terms. The suitability of the above list for describing what constitutes

inner alchemy and the physiological account of the end to which the practice aims will both be

considered below by considering the ideas described in the *Wuzhen pian*.

ii. Neidan as Physiological Practice

In Needham's mind there exists a potential problem in understanding inner alchemy and that

is the temptation which some scholars may feel to equate it with the "spiritual alchemy of the

West."[444] Underlying this claim is a tacit acceptance of a Cartesian-like division between the

physiological workings of the body and the psychological functioning of the mind. These two fields

of enquiry must not be confounded if an appreciation of inner alchemy is to be achieved:

> Thus there opens out before us the whole field of Taoist physiology, a proto-science
> not exactly the same as the physiology of the physicians down through the centuries,
> but not very far different from it. No greater mistake could be made than to analogize
> *nei dan* with the 'spiritual alchemy' of the West; it was physiological through and
> through, and though certainly not without parallelisms or even connections with
> Indian Yoga, it was generally more moderate, with more emphasis on hygiene, and

---

[443] Ibid., 29-31.

[444] Ibid., 23.

always infused with characteristically Chinese sanity, sobriety, empiricism and rationality.[445]

What is being established here are mutually exclusive systems of endeavor; one in which psychological or perhaps spiritual concerns are dominant ("Western spiritual alchemy") and another in which the focus is well and truly physiological or materialistic (Taoist inner alchemy).[446] For Needham it is essential that the goal of the inner alchemist is the formation of a material entity which he designates the anablastemic enchymoma. The need for the creation of this neologism is explained by Needham as follows:

> After it was borne in upon us, therefore, that we were face to face with a physiological (indeed at bottom a biochemical) elixir, to be prepared by physiological, not chemical methods, out of physical constituents already in the body, it was desirable to introduce an entirely new word for the 'elixir within'. For this purpose we have settled upon the term 'enchymoma'.[447]

Needham's points out that this term, which is based on the Greek word *enchymōma* (ἐγχύμωμα), designates, through its prefix, that the substance in question is within the body. The second and third syllables (*chumos*) indicate the substance is juice-like and he notes the connection between this term and the English word 'chyme' which *The Concise Oxford Dictionary* defines as "food converted by gastric secretion into acid pulp."[448] The addition of the adjective, anablastemic is based on the Greek word *anablastanein* (ἀναβλαστάνειν) meaning "to burgeon again, to spring anew, to grow

---

[445] Ibid.

[446] Ibid., xxviii.

[447] Ibid.

[448] *The Concise Oxford Dictionary*, 7th ed., s.v. "Chyme."

afresh."[449] 'Anablastemic enchymoma' is intended to act as a translation for the term *neidan* (內丹) literally translated as "inner cinnabar," a term synonymous with *jindan* (金丹) which is usually translated as "golden elixir." Through his choice of anablastemic enchymoma Needham has effectively constructed a term which designates the whole tradition of inner alchemy and which now has at its root a physical significance.

The acknowledgment of the separation between the material and the psychological is of the utmost importance as one studies inner alchemy because, as was described above, this study has as its aim the recognition of a common ground between contemporary biochemical conceptions and those of the inner alchemists of Tang and Song China. Needham views religious ceremony and doctrine, and various forms of artistic and musical expression as incommensurable and therefore unsuited to his purpose of establishing a common language of dialogue. The material realms of science and technology on the other hand are tied to the material world and are therefore constant and cross-cultural. Hence the need to explain inner alchemical terminology in a manner which is as consistent as possible with the basic ideas of modern biology and chemistry.

Needham's general approach to the terminology of inner alchemy is to equate it with concepts of modern science which appear to bear some similarity. An example is his belief that it is "a truism to say that the Yang and Yin principles are present wherever there is positive and negative electricity today" which of course would include "the sub-atomic elementary charged particles, the protons and electrons."[450] He also views the five phases (*wu xing* 五行) as prefiguring

---

[449] Needham, *Science and Civilization,* vol. V.5, 28.

[450] Ibid., xxix.

modern notions of the various states of matter: solid, liquid and gaseous. It is this kind of assumption which shapes his ideas concerning the key terminology of inner alchemy.

The language of inner alchemy often parallels that of outer alchemy and thus there is much talk in the *Wuzhen pian* of the creation and refining of a medicinal substance, a substance which is produced through the careful combining of ingredients. These ingredient have to be gathered, preserved and cooked. Furthermore, it is made very clear that the ingredients are all contained within the body of the adept. One of the difficulties involved in understanding the alchemical theory described in the *Wuzhen pian* is that references to these ingredients are scattered among the more frequently used metaphors employing the hexagrams of the *Yijing* and the eight trigrams of the *Bagua*. Amid all of the synonyms and metaphors there are three primary ingredients employed by the adept and these are referred to as a group only once in the *Wuzhen pian*.[451] The term used to refer to these ingredients is *san yuan* (三元) or the "three primes." The three primes are three forms of *qi* described as "essence" (*jing* 精), *qi* (氣), and "spirit" (*shen* 神). Needham describes them as follows:

> The three 'primary vitalities' of the Taoists are not precisely translatable into terms of modern science — no characteristically medieval formulations ever are — but *shen* did some justice to the mental components of man, while *chhi* denoted the dissolved gases in his body-fluids, and *ching* those fluids themselves.[452]

There are serious problems with this account of the three primes, not only because they fail to take into account some fundamental assumptions of inner alchemical theory but also because they appear

---

[451] *Wuzhen pian*, 26.25a.

[452] Needham, *Science and Civilization,* vol. V.5, xxix.

to directly contradict other accounts of the three primes given by Needham himself. These concerns will be discussed in the following section.

A second set of terms which also play a very central role in the describing of inner alchemical theory are lead and mercury. These terms are analyzed in very similar ways to that of the three primes described above:

> For the physiological alchemists the Yin line of Li represented the 'true, or vital, mercury' (*chen hung*), and the Yang line of Khan represented the 'true, or vital, lead' (*chen chhien*). 'Our' mercury and 'our' lead were thus the vital *chhi* and essences extracted by the internal work from the juices, *chhi* or secretions of the opposite sign.[453]

Here Needham is referring to the middle lines of the trigrams *li* (離) and *kan* (坎). *Li* is composed of two *yang* lines on the outside and one *yin* line in the center while *kan* is composed of two *yin* lines on the outside and one *yang* line in the centre. A recurring theme in inner alchemical texts is the need to cause the central lines of these two trigrams to be exchanged so that they are restored to states of pure *yang* and pure *yin*. According to him the lead and mercury are juices, *qi* and secretions which have their source in the various internal organs.[454] Again this supposition requires some attention.

II. Inner Alchemy According to the Wuzhen Pian

A. The Goal

The *Wuzhen pian* often refers to lengthening one's span of life though it is far from clear that such references are to be equated in any straightforward way with the final or exclusive objective of the adept. What will be maintained here is that such references should be understood, not as the

---

[453] Ibid., 61.

[454] Ibid., 25.

central goal of the adept, but as a subordinate achievement which might be viewed as a necessary prerequisite to the primary goal of the adept. In reflecting upon the place of immortality in the *Wuzhen pian* one must consider what kind of immortality is being spoken about. Should it be understood as longevity of the body or is something else intended? Secondly, one must consider references to lengthening life without discounting the fact that the text also includes references to what appears to be a transcendent goal or at least to a goal involving a radical transformation of the adept.

Concerning the nature of the immortality being sought an important phrase near the beginning of the *Wuzhen pian* offers some clarification:

學仙須是學天仙
惟有金丹最的端

[If you are going to] study immortality then it must be celestial immortality,
Which alone is the most superior [doctrine of the] golden elixir.[455]

This is an important qualification which goes to the heart of the question concerning how one should understand the place of terms such as "long life" (*chang sheng* 長生), "perpetual longevity" (*yong shou* 永壽) and "protect life" (*bao ming* 保命). Celestial immortality[456] (*tian xian* 天仙) is but one of several[457] classes of immortality though, as the text explains it is considered the most superior of

---

[455] *Wuzhen pian*, 26.9a.

[456] The term *xian* (仙) is being translated here as "immortality" in accordance with the context in which it occurs. In other contexts it would be equally valid to render the term as "immortal" which can act as a designation for one who has achieved a high level of cultivation. In this sense its function is similar to that of the term *shengren* (聖人).

[457] Translating Ye Shibiao's comment on this question literally, he states that there are a thousand kinds of immortal or immortality. *Wuzhen pian*, 26.9a. According to the *Daojiao da cidian*, 182, s.v. 天仙, there are only five types.

the various classes. In addition to achieving celestial immortality there are also earthly immortals (*di xian* 地仙), spirit immortals (*shen xian* 神仙), human immortals (*ren xian* 人仙), and ghostly immortals (*gui shen* 鬼仙).[458] For the purposes of the present discussion the class of "human immortal" is of specific interest as it appears to correspond most closely with what Needham envisions as the final goal of the inner alchemist. Furthermore, because the text tacitly rejects the condition of becoming a human immortal as the goal it sheds light on the kind of immortality which *is* to be sought by the adept of inner alchemy. Human immortality is considered a lesser acheivement which results from the work of internal refinement (*neilian* 内煉). This class of immortality is associated with an exceptionally long lifespan the years of which number into the millions.[459] Although the text relegates such an achievement to a lesser status it does not follow that celestial immortality would necessarily exclude the possibility of a very long life span; rather, it implies an achievement which goes beyond that of merely extending one's life.

Unfortunately, the *Wuzhen pian* does not offer any definitive statements describing celestial immortality though Ye Shibiao does provide a brief and rather cryptic passage on the subject:

天仙者　形神俱妙　與道合眞　聚則成形　散則成氣
學此道者　當內外虛　明表裏瑩澈 如立一塵　則成滲漏

As for celestial immortality, the form and the spirit are both mysterious. Together
with the Tao they are joined in the real. If [you] gather, the form is completed; if
[you] disperse, then the *qi* is completed.

---

[458] Each of these five kinds of immortality is described in the *Zhonglu chuandao ji*, 14.2b-6a. This text is included in the *Xiuzhen shishu*.

[459] *Daojiao da cidian*, 45, s.v. ☐H ¥P.

In studying this Tao (method) [you] must be empty both intenally and externally and understand that inside and out the luster of gems pervades. If [you] establish [even] a single grain then there will be a complete leaking out.[460]

This passage conceives of celestial immortality as entailing practices which support the body or the form as well as the spirit. Through a process of gathering, the body is supported and through dispersing (or perhaps in this context freeing or circulating), the *qi* is brought to completion. The reason for substituting *qi* (氣) for *shen* (神) in the last phrase of the first line is unclear though the parallel structure of the phrases would seem to imply that dispersing (*san* 散) bears a positive relation to spirit (*shen* 神). A clue may be found in the forword to another text of Zhang Boduan, the *Jindan sibai zi* TY1070, DZ 741 where it is explained that the spirit relies upon the *qi* just as the *qi*, in turn, depends upon the essence (*jing* 精).[461] Perhaps what is being implied here is that the consolidation of the body by means of gathering rather than wasting the precious resources of the body provides a strong foundation for the generation and circulation of the *qi* which in turn supports the flourishing of the spirit.[462] The second line of the above passage uses Buddhist language in order to link the success of the adept to an ability to sustain a state of emptiness. Not even a single grain of dust must be permitted to compromise this state.

While the Wuzhen pian offers no other specific comment on what is implied in becoming a celestial immortal there are a number of other important passages which do help to shed some light on the nature of the adept's final goal. These passages draw upon a recurring theme of departure in a variety of ways. The opening line of the text poses a question to the reader:

---

[460] *Wuzhen pian*, 26.9a.

[461] *Jindan sibai zi*, 5.1b.

[462] See *Jindan sibai zi*, 5.1b for textual evidence which appears to be supportive of this view.

不求大道出迷途　縱負賢才豈丈夫

[If you] do not seek the great way to leave the path of delusion,
although [you] maintain virtue and ability are [you] a worthy man?[463]

The path of delusion is one which involves placing the acquisition of wealth and high social standing above caring for the body and avoiding the distress which accompanies the desire for material success. The same verse concludes by asking whether one could pile up sufficient gold to prevent death from coming. The second verse continues by pondering the fact of death's unpredictability and the inevitable negative consequences which will be brought into effect by one's negative karma (*zuiye* 罪業). This verse alludes to a connection between the path of delusion and failing to care for the body. A few verses later a second statement employing the notion of departure or escape also closely associates success in inner alchemy with a long life:

謾守藥鑪看火候　但看神息任天然
群陰剝盡丹成熟　跳出凡籠壽萬年

Slowly guard the medicine stove and observe the fire phase;
attentively observe the spirit and the breath and let them be natural.
[When] all *yin* has been entirely stripped away the elixir will have been completely prepared;
[Thus you] leap from the cage of the mundane and live a long life of ten thousand years![464]

The last line of this verse indicates that the successful adept achieves two ends: she is able to leap from the cage of the mundane and also to live on indefinitely. Even taken at face value this statement allows for the final achievement of two goals rather than the single attainment of longevity. The next

---

[463] *Wuzhen pian*, 26.8b.

[464] Ibid., 26.28b.

question concerns how the text conceives of this immortality. Should it be understood as Needham repeatedly suggests as material or bodily immortality or is something else intended?

Continuing on with the theme of departure the text also describes the alchemist's attainment in terms reminiscent of what Isabelle Robinet refers to as ecstatic flight in her descriptions of Shangqing meditative practices:[465]

只候功成朝北闕　九霞光裏駕祥鸞

Simply wait until the work is completed [then] pay court to the Northern Palace; amidst the brightness in nine rose-coloured clouds [you will] ride the auspicious Luan bird.[466]

若人了得詩中意　立見三清太上翁

If people understand the meaning within these verses, then [they] will immediately see the Three Pure Ones, the Most High Elders.[467]

寶符降後去朝天　穩駕鸞車鳳輦

After the precious talisman has descended, go and pay court to heaven; safely riding the phoenix-drawn carriage of the immortals.[468]

In each of these cases the situation being described is the culmination of the adept's efforts, the completion of the work. What is striking about each of these descriptions is the complete lack of references in their respective verses to longevity. The predominant theme in these descriptions is transcendence by means of a mystical departure from the mundane realm. The stage of cultivation being described appears to have very little to do with the body of the adept. Whatever practices the

---

[465] See for example, Isabelle Robinet, "Visualization and Ecstatic Flight in Shangqing Taoism," in Kohn, *Taoist Meditation and Longevity Techniques*, 168-178..

[466] *Wuzhen pian*, 26.11b.

[467] Ibid., 26.34b-35a.

[468] Ibid., 29.14a.

adept carried out prior to this ecstatic religious or spiritual achievement, they appear to figure as stages of preparation which are necessary if the above scenarios are to be realized.

It is, of course, entirely possible that these "journeys" should not be understood as final in a way that might parallel the Buddhist conception of *parinirvāna*. Taoist hagiographic material is full of stories relating the ability of adepts to leave their bodies in order to travel great distances. One of the hagiographies describing the exploits of Zhang Boduan tells the story of Zhang's amiable meeting with a Chan master. Zhang asks the master if he is able to go travelling to which the master replies that he can. They then retire to a meditation hut, sit down facing each other, close their eyes and "depart." The term used to describe the manner of their departure is *chushen* (出 神) literally their spirits went out.[469] An interesting feature of this story is that while on their journey the Chan master and Zhang each pick a flower. At one point Zhang asks the master where his flower has gone; it is noted that the master's "spirit hand" (*shenshou* 神手) is empty. The story also relates how the two friends stretched out and fell asleep. The assumption in this story is that the material body has been left behind while the subjects remain fully functional with their spirit bodies. This story demonstrates that the concept of a spirit-body existing distinct from the gross material body was certainly in the imaginative repertoire of the hagiographer. However, the question remains as to whether this was a possibility which Zhang envisioned for the inner alchemists who chose to follow his teachings. And, furthermore, if it was something Zhang could conceive of should it be understood as the a goal which superseded that of bodily longevity?

One way to approach answers to these questions is by considering the golden elixir and how it was understood in the *Wuzhen pian*. A chemical metaphor is often employed in the *Wuzhen pian*

---

[469] *Tongjian*, 49.7b-8a.

which speaks, for example, of placing ingredients into a kind of reaction vessel (*ding* 鼎) and also

of using lead, mercury, and cinnabar. But what is of particular interest here is Zhang's description

of the elixir as a foetus which is formed inside the adept through a gestation period of ten months.[470]

The foetus is understood to be something which represents the culmination of the adept's work and

its function within the body is described in terms which focus on it's capacity to facilitate the

departure of the adept from the mundane. On this subject the text states:

嬰兒是一含眞氣　十月胎圓入聖基

[Thus] The infant is unified and embodies the true *qi*;
in ten months the foetus is complete; it is the foundation for entering the sacred.[471]

The notion that the capacity for transcending is what the newly generated foetus confers upon its host

is also stated very succinctly in Ye Shibiao's commentary on the above passage:

五行聚於此處成丹如子在胞胎數足成形也　超凡入聲此爲基本

The five phases gather at this place completing the elixir like the child in the womb.
The foetal stages being completed so the form is complete. [This] is the foundation
for leaping beyond the mundane and entering the sacred.[472]

Another reference describes the departure of the foetus from the body, referring to the foetus as

something which escapes or perhaps is shed or cast off from the body. The term used to describe the

foetus in this context is *tuotai* (脫胎).[473] Quoting the *Zhuzhen neidan jiyao* TY1246, DZ 999 the

Daojiao da cidian describes the shedding of the foetus as the culmination of the inner alchemical

---

[470] *Wuzhen pian*, 26.30a.

[471] Ibid., 26.30a.

[472] Ibid.

[473] Ibid., 28.11b.

work which is undertaken with the greatest of care. The process is likened to the dragon nourishing

the pearl, or the chicken brooding over her eggs and it is mentioned that even the slightest of errors

will cause all previous merit to be wasted. At the end of the whole process the *Yang* Spirit finally

escapes from the body, which is referred to as the escape of the foetus from a husk or shell (*ke* 殼).[474]

A final example is found in a reference to one of the constellations known as the Purple Mystery

(*ziwei* 紫微). The text describes the adept riding a golden dragon in order to visit the Purple

Mystery.[475] Ye Shibiao comments that Zhang Boduan is here describing "the spirit of the escaping

foetus which transforms flying and ascending to pay court to the Purple Mystery."[476] In these cases

the foetus generated by the adept, the anablastemic enchymoma, looks much more like a means for

achieving transcendence or salvation than it does a biochemical elixir of immortality. The goal of

the adept is one of liberation and of realization. The aim is to awaken in order to part from the ocean

of life and death, that is to escape the endless round of death and rebirth; the rare individual who

achieves this end is considered a Realized Man (*zhenren* 眞人).

B. Neidan: Inadequacies of a Physiological Characterization

The first thing which must be considered when studying the *Wuzhen pian* is the view, related

through the text itself, concerning the function of its own language and the relationship of that

language to the process of cultivation described in the text. The place of the written text is difficult

to determine and even the usefulness of the text for the reader is called into question:

---

[474] *Daojiao da cidian*, 880, s.v. ²æ -L.

[475] *Wuzhen pian*, 28.11a.

[476] Ibid. The text is as follows: 脫胎神化飛昇而朝紫微也

契論經歌講至眞　不將火候著於文
要知口訣通玄處　須共神仙子細論

Various records, essays, scriptures and songs [profess to] explain the highest truth,
[but you] cannot grasp the fire phase if it is [merely] set down in words.
[You] must understand oral instructions [in order to] penetrate the mysterious place;
[thus you] should [enter into] careful discussions with spirit immortals.[477]

Elsewhere Zhang writes that although he wants to pass on this method of training to others he has failed to find even a single person capable of understanding what he has to teach.[478] Later on, the reader is told that the contents of the *Wuzhen pian* are "simple and easy" (其中簡易).[479] So then, this *text* tells the reader that ultimately it cannot be a means for gaining understanding of the process it describes and that while its content is simple it is nearly impossible to understand. What is one to make of this? One possibility mentioned by Robinet is that this alchemical language game may not be intended to elucidate but to frustrate if not obfuscate[480] so that in Chan-like fashion one is bemused into a state of awakening. If this is the case then it does not bode well for those who hope, by studying the textual corpus of *neidan*, to gain insight into the actual practices engaged in by the adepts. One must always consider that the language of *neidan* is intended to loosen the grip of the reader on more conventional modes of analysis. It is this message which Needham appears not to have heeded as he searched for correlates to contemporary physiological concepts in order to represent *neidan* as a phase in the development of biochemistry.

---

[477] *Wuzhen pian*, 27.21b.

[478] Ibid., 26.26a.

[479] Ibid., 27.7b.

[480] Isabelle Robinet,"Original Contributions of Neidan" in Kohn, *Taoist Meditation and Longevity Techniques*, 302.

The specific terms which Needham appears to have reinterpreted are essence (*jing* 精), *qi* (氣) and spirit (*shen* 神) and lead (*qian* 鉛) and mercury (*hong* 汞). The *Wuzhen pian* describes the ingredients employed in the formation of the immortal foetus in terms which defy any attempt to see them as familiar, or commonplace substances. Concerning the general nature of the ingredients it states:

藥逢氣類方成象　道合希夷即自然

The form is complete when the medicine encounters the [*yin* and *yang*] categories of *qi*;
Tao spontaneously brings together that which cannot be seen and that which cannot be heard.[481]

見之不可用 用之不可見

What is seen cannot be used;
what is used cannot be seen.[482]

These two descriptions can be understood as a caution to those who would interpret the chemical metaphors of *neidan* as references to actual substances whether inside or outside of the body. Weng Baoguang's commentary on the above phrase describes it as referring to "the dregs of later heaven" (*houtian* 後天) which must be differentiated from the non-substantial and pure ingredients associated with "earlier heaven" (*xiantian* 先天). During the foetal stages of development individuals are considered to be in the latter state while after they are born people enter the later heaven state of being. Weng's commentary explains as follows:

有質可見者後天查滓之類也
無形而不可見者二物初弦之氣
雖不可見而可用也

---

[481] *Wuzhen pian*, 28.16a.

[482] Ibid., 28.23a.

As for that which has substance and can be seen, it is of the class of the dregs of later heaven.
As for that which, lacking form, cannot be seen it is the *qi* of the first quarter moon of the two things.
Therefore although it cannot be seen yet it can be used.[483]

The two things are references to the trigrams *kan* and *li* which contain the central lines representing "true lead" and "true mercury" which in turn are hidden within the essence (*jing* 精) and the blood. The essence is associated with the kidneys while the blood is associated with the heart. These two "ingredients" of the alchemist are also referred to as the inner and outer medicines and are paired with the sustaining of the "life" (*ming* 命) and the "inner nature" (*xing* 性) respectively.[484] What must be born in mind is that the lead and the mercury and the three primes (essence, *qi* and spirit) are concealed within substances in the body and should not be equated with those substances. At times Needham seems aware of this fact while at others he appears to ignore it. Concerning lead and mercury he states:

> Table 121 A, B, C shows the main reagents of physiological alchemy, including the *cchi* and secretions (*i*) of the body, such as saliva and semen. It was out of all these things that the primary or vital Yang (*Chen Yang*) had to be regenerated, and these two were the entities which the physiological alchemists designated as 'true mercury' (*chen hung*) and 'true lead' (*chen chhien*). The union of these produced the enchymoma of immortality.[485]

Here he seems willing to acknowledge the need to differentiate the "true" or earlier heaven ingredients from the gross physical substances with which they were associated. Elsewhere he is content to confound the two:

---

[483] Ibid., 28.23a.

[484] A lengthy and straightforward discussion of these ideas is found in a section of commentary attributed to the *Cantong qi*. Ibid., 26.10b-11a.

[485] Needham, *Science and Civilisation*, vol. 5.5, 48-49.

But when a Chinese writer speaks of 'true mercury' or 'true lead' he is likely to be speaking about the secretion, chhi or emanation of some physiological organ or tissue.[486]

The same kind of problem applies in his descriptions of the three primes (*san yuan* 三元). Needham demonstrates that he is aware of the distinction between the "original" or earlier heaven forms of the essence, *qi* and spirit and notes that the later heaven correlates are a degenerated form of the three primes. Later on, however, he states that the three primes cannot be equated "precisely" with Western scientific ideas but that they are very similar to three ideas which are familiar to the contemporary "scientific" mind: the *original* spirit is comparable to the mental faculties, the *original* *qi* "denoted" the dissolved gases in the body fluids and the *original* essence referred to the body fluids themselves.[487] Zhang Boduan does not provide a description of the three primes in the *Wuzhen pian* though a very clear account provided in the *Jindan sibai zi* directly addresses this mistaken characterization of the three primes:

鍊精者鍊元精非淫佚所感之精
鍊氣者鍊元氣非口鼻呼吸之氣
鍊神者鍊元神非心意念一之神

As for refining the essence it is the original essence [which is refined] not the [kind of] essence which is influenced by lewd and depraved [behaviour].

As for refining the vital breath it is the original vital breath [which is refined] not the [kind of] vital breath [which is] exhaled and inhaled [through the] mouth and nose.

As for refining the spirit it is the original spirit [which is refined] not the [kind of] spirit [which is involved in] the anxious thoughts of the mind.[488]

---

[486] Ibid., 24-25.

[487] Ibid., xxix.

[488] *Jindan sibai zi*, 1a.

In this passage Zhang Bo-duan deems it necessary to make it abundantly clear to his readers that they

should not confuse the three vitalities of inner alchemy with the more mundane bodily forms. He

goes on to explain that after all of the various rarefied ingredients have been gathered together they

transform into a unified form of vital breath (*qi* 氣). This transformation is described in the following

passage:

不可見聞亦無名狀故曰虛無

[It] cannot be seen or heard; furthermore [it is] without name.
Therefore, it is called empty non-being. [489]

Empty non-being is what the *neidan* adept is moving back towards. He is engaged in an inversion

(*diandao* 顛倒) of the cosmogonic process described in chapter 42 of the *Daode jing* and echoed in

the following verse of the *Wuzhen pian*:

道自虛無生一氣　便從一氣產陰陽
陰陽再合生三體　三體重生萬物昌

From empty non-being the Tao produces unified *qi*;
from this unified *qi*, *yin* and *yang* are caused to be produced.

Yin and *yang* then come together to give birth to the third form;
these three forms further generate the splendour of the ten thousand things. [490]

The *neidan* process, which inverts the above stages, is described by Zhang as a movement involving

the transformation of each of the three primes: essence, *qi* and spirit,

以精化爲氣以氣化爲神以神化爲虛

Take the [original] essence and transform it into the [original] *qi*;

---

[489] Ibid.

[490] *Wuzhen pian*, 27.8a.

> Take the [original] *qi* and transform it into the [original] spirit;
> Take the [original] spirit and transform it into emptiness.[491]

These passages not only demonstrate unequivocally how much of a mistake it would be to equate

the three primes of neidan with organic substances but they also have some bearing on how one

should view the goal of the inner alchemist. The goal once again is couched in the language of

transcendence.

In concluding this chapter some attention must be paid to Needham's description of the

practices which he says comprise the "physiological" discipline of *neidan*. As was mentioned

previously he lists seven kinds of activity which are said to constitute inner alchemical training: 1)

mental and bodily hygiene, involving cleanliness and ataraxia, 2) respiratory exercises, 3) exercises

designed to circulate the vital breath (*qi* 氣), 4) remedial gymnastics 5) conservation of various

bodily secretions, including the swallowing of saliva 6) sexual techniques and 7) meditation and

trance.[492] It appears that the *Wuzhen pian* takes explicit exception to such a characterization.

The *Wuzhen pian* includes a number of warnings to those who might be mislead into

believing that various practices such as swallowing saliva, concentrating the thoughts, nourishing

life and breathing exercises are to be equated with the work of the golden elixir:

嚥津納氣是人行　有藥方能造化生

> Swallowing saliva and taking in *qi*; these are things people do;
> [but] there are prescriptions which are able to create and transform life.[493]

---

[491] *Jindan sibai zi* , 1a.

[492] Needham, *Science and Civilisation*, vol. 5.5, 29-31.

[493] *Wuzhen pian*, 27.4a.

更饒吐納并存想　與金丹事不同

Furthermore, [you should] overlook spitting out and drawing in and concentrating the thoughts;
all of these various techniques are not the same as golden elixir activities.[494]

玄牝之門世罕知　休將口鼻妄施為
饒君吐納經千載　爭得金烏搦兔兒

Few in the world understand the gateway of the mysterious female;
do not engage in the foolish practices of the mouth and nose.

Wealthy gentlemen practice spitting out and drawing in for a thousand years;
how can they obtain the golden raven and the hare child. [495]

房中空閉尾閭穴　誤殺閻浮多少人

In [your] room vainly shutting up the *weilu* opening;
how many people in Jambudvīpa have been inadvertently killed [in this way].[496]

These passages are concerned with practices loosely categorized under the heading "nourishing life" (*yang sheng* 養生). They warn against these methods which are bound up with the narrow concern of prolonging life. Various forms of these methods are known to have been employed at least as far back as the 4th C. BCE where references to them is found in the *Zhuangzi*. This well known reference can be found in the section entitled *Constrained in Will* (*ke yi* 刻意) where a description of one who feels it necessary to withdraw from the world is provided:

就藪處閒曠釣魚閒處無為而矣
此江海之士避世之人閒暇者之所好也

494　Ibid., 26.30b-32a.

495　Ibid., 28.7b.

496　Ibid., 28.13a.

吹呴呼吸吐故納新熊輕鳥申爲壽而已矣
此道引之士養形之人彭祖壽考者之所好也

To repair to the thickets and ponds, living idly in the wilderness, angling for fish in solitary places, inaction his only concern—such is the life favoured by the scholar of the rivers and the seas, the man who withdraws from the world, the unhurried idler. To pant, to puff, to hail, to sip, to spit out the old breath and draw in the new, practising bear-hangings and bird-stretchings, longevity his only concern—such is the life favoured by the scholar who practices Induction, the man who nourishes his body, who hopes to live as long as P'eng-tsu.[497]

It is interesting that in this inner alchemical work Zhang Boduan appears to be in full agreement with Zhuangzi's disdain for the preoccupation with what he might consider crude longevity practices. It is also worth noting the criticism directed at those who feel compelled to withdraw from ordinary society and to escape into the wilderness. This is a point which Zhang also makes.[498] Needham, on the other hand, observes that those who practice *neidan* through techniques of "redemptive bodily hygiene" would probably do so "in the service of a Taoist temple remote in the mountains, and that is the setting which most adepts preferred. That is where one has to imagine them."[499] Evidently that is not where one should expect to find Zhang Boduan.

An alternate characterization of *neidan* is provided by Robinet who provides a list of four features which would need to be found in a text if it is to be labeled a *neidan* work:

One may say that texts belonging to the current of inner alchemy are characterised by

1. a concern for training the mind as much as the body, with the mental aspect usually predominant;

---

[497] *Zhuangzi jijie* (Yangzhou, Jiangsu: Yangzhou guji shudian faxing, 1991), 112. Watson, *Chuang Tzu*, 167.

[498] *Wuzhen pian*, 26.15a.

[499] Needham, *Science and Civilisation*, vol. 5.5, 29.

 2. a tendency to synthesize various Taoist currents, certain Buddhist speculations, and specific Confucian lines of thought;
 3. reference to the *Yijing*; and
 4. references to chemical practices.[500]

This list manages to avoid including practices concerned with nourishing the life and also places the "mental aspect" of the training up front where it belongs. Certainly, if a text contained all of the above characteristics it would have to be classified as a *neidan* text. The same could not be said of Needham's list. A text may well contain references to all of the practices he mentions and yet, not only is it possible that the text may not be describing the practice of *neidan*, but according to Zhang Boduan, it almost certainly would not be a *neidan* text due to its focus on physical longevity or immortality.

Conclusion

What has been argued here is that in his attempt to locate the texts of *neidan,* and specifically here the *Wuzhen pian*, within the story of the evolution of modern science Needham has been compelled to relegate the profoundly spiritual focus of these texts to a subordinate position. In doing so he has characterized the practice as being primarily concerned with retarding the aging process rather than with the dual cultivation of the life and inner nature[501] in such a way that the individual might transcend the mundane and depart from the cycle of life and death.

If the terms of inner alchemy were intended to signify anything, and if the warnings of Zhang Boduan are to be taken seriously, then what they referred to was nothing like the "biologically active

---

[500] Robinet, "Original Contributions of *Neidan*," 301.

[501] *Xingming shuangxiu*性命雙修.

substances" and "metabolic processes" that Needham describes.[502] Perhaps the most fitting way to end is by allowing Zhang to have the last word concerning the nature of the great medicine:

勸君窮取生身處　返本還元是藥王

[I] exhort you to carefully ascertain the place where the self is born;
reverting to the root, returning to the origin, this is the superior medicine.

---

[502] Needham, *Science and Civilisation*, vol. 5.5, 298.

Bibliography

Primary References (Daozang Texts):

紫陽眞人悟眞萹註 疏 *Explanations of the Chapters on Awakening to the True.* TY 141, DZ 61-62.

紫陽眞人悟眞篇三註 *Three Commentaries on the Realized Man Purple Yang's Chapters on Awakening to the True.* TY 142, DZ 63-64.

紫陽眞人悟眞萹拾遺 *An Amended Edition of the Realized Man Purple Yang's Chapters on Awakening to the True.* TY 144, DZ 64.

悟眞萹註 釋 *Explanations of the Chapters on Awakening to the True.* TY 145, DZ 65.

修眞十書悟眞萹 *Chapters on Awakening to the True in Ten Books on Cultivating the True.* TY 263 (*juan* 26-30), DZ 122-31.

金丹四百字 *Four Hundred Words on the Golden Elixir.* TY 1070, DZ 741.

玉清金笥青華秘文金寶內煉丹訣 *The Green and Elegant Secret Papers in the Jade Purity Golden Box on the Essentials of the Internal Refining of the Golden Treasure the Enchymoma.* TY 239, DZ114.

紫陽眞人悟眞篇直指詳說三乘秘要 *A Direct and Detailed Discussion of the Abstruse and Important Points of the Three Vehicles Contained in the Realized Man Purple Yang's Chapters on Awakening to the True.* TY 144, DZ 64.

修眞十書金丹大成集 *An Anthology on the Great Completion of the Golden Elixir.* TY 263 (*juan* 9-13), DZ 122-31.

金丹大要 Great Essentials on the Golden Elixir. TY 1056, DZ 736-738.

抱朴子內篇 *Inner Chapters of the Master Who Embraces Simplicity.* TY 1175, DZ 868-870.三

洞群仙錄 *On the Concourse of Transcendents in the Three Caverns.* TY 1236, DZ 992-995.

歷世眞仙體道通鑒 *Comprehensive Survey of Successive Generations of Perfected Transcendents and Those Who Embody the Tao.* TY 295, DZ 139-148.

消搖墟經 *Scripture on [Those Who] Wandered in the Wilds.* TY 1452, DZ 1081.

Primary References

古今圖書集成(Completed Collection of Graphs and Writings of Ancient and Modern Times).

列仙全傳(Complete Biographies of the Immortals).

孟乃昌，孟慶軒，輯編。周易參同契三十四家注釋集萃 (A Compilation of Thirty Two Schools of Commentary on The Token of the Three in Accordance with the Book of Changes of the Zhou)。北京：華夏出版社出版發行, 1993.

四川通志(Sichuan Provincial Gazetteer).

四庫全書總目提要(Annotated Catalogue of the Imperial Library).

台州府志(Taizhou Prefectural Gazetteer).

王沐，淺解。悟眞篇淺解(Simple Explanations on The Chapters on Awakening to the Real)。北京：中華書局出版, 1990.

浙江通志(Zhejiang Provincial Gazetteer).

周易參同契 (The Token of the Three in Accordance with the Book of Changes of the Zhou)。林聰富，發行人。台北市：武陵出版社, 1990.

莊子集解(Collected Explanations on Zhuangzi)。揚州，江蘇：揚州古籍書店發行, 1991.

Secondary References:

Boltz, Judith M. *A Survey of Taoist Literature: Tenth to Seventeenth Centuries*. Berkeley: Institute for East Asian Studies University of California Berkeley, 1987.

Katō, Bunnō, Tamura, Yoshirō and Miyasaka, Kōjiro, trans. *The Threefold Lotus Sutra: Innumerable Meanings, The Lotus Flower of the Wonderful Law, and Meditation on the Bodhisattva Universal Virtue*. 1975. Reprint. Tokyo: Kosei Publishing Co., 1986.

Chao Yün-ts'ung and Davis, Tenny L. "Four Hundred Word Chin Tan of Chang Po-tuan." *Proceedings of the American Academy of Arts and Sciences* 73 (1940): 371-377.

Chen, Kenneth. *Buddhism in China: A Historical Survey*. Princeton: Princeton University Press, 1964.

Ch'en Kuo-fu and Tenny L. Davis, trans. "Inner Chapters of Pao-p'u-tzu." *Proceedings of the American Academy of Arts and Sciences* 74.10 (December 1941): 297f.

Cleary, Thomas, trans. *Understanding Reality: A Taoist Alchemical Classic*. Honolulu: University of Hawaii Press, 1987.

——, trans. *Immortal Sisters: Secrets of Taoist Women*. Boston and Shaftsbury: Shambhala Publications, 1989.

——, trans. *The Book of Balance and Harmony*. San Francisco: North Point Press, 1989.

Creel, Herrlee G. *What is Taoism? and Other Studies in Chinese Cultural History*. Chicago: The University of Chicago Press, 1970.

Davis, Tenney L. "Pictorial Representations of Alchemical Theory." Isis 25 (1936): 327.

Davis, Tenney L. and Chao Yün-ts'ung. "Chang Po-tuan of Thien-Thai; his Wu Chen Phien (Essay on the Understanding of the Truth); a Contribution to the Study of Chinese Alchemy." *Proceedings of the American Academy of Arts and Sciences* 73 (1939):97.

Davis, Tenney L. and Chao Yün-ts'ung. "Chang Po-Tuan, Chinese Alchemist of the +11th Century." *Journal of Chemical Education* 16 (1939):53.

Davis, Tenney L. and Chao Yün-ts'ung. "The Secret Papers in the Jade Box of Ch'ing-hua." *Proceedings of the American Academy of Arts and Sciences* 79 (1940):385-386.

Davis, Tenney L. and Chao Yün-ts'ung. "The Three Alchemical Poems by Chang Po-tuan." *Proceedings of the American Academy of Arts and Sciences* 73 (1940):377-379.

Davis, Tenney L. and Chao Yün-ts'ung. "The Four Hundred Word Chin Tan of Chang Po-tuan." *Proceedings of the American Academy of Arts and Sciences* 73 (1940):371.

Davis, Tenney L. and Chen Kuo-fu. "Shang Yang-tzu: Taoist Writer and Commentator on Alchemy." *Harvard Journal of Asiatic Studies* 7 (1942-1943):126-129.

Derrida, Jaques. *Of Grammatology.* Translated by Gayatri Chakravorty Spivak. Baltimore: The Johns Hopkins University Press, 1974.

Dumoulin, Heinrich. *Zen Buddhism: A History, vol. 1: India and China.* Translated by James W. Heisig and Paul Knitter (New York: Macmillan Publishing Company, 1988

Feyerabend, Paul. *Against Method.* 1975. Revised Edition. New York: Verso, 1988.

Graham, Angus. C., trans. *The Book of Lieh-tzu: A Classic of Tao.* 1960. Reprint. New York: Columbia University Press Morningside Edition, 1990.

Hawkes, David, trans. *Ch'u Tz'u: The Songs of the South.* Boston: Beacon Press, 1962.

Henricks, Robert G., trans. *Lao-Tzu Te-Tao Ching.* New York: Balantine Books, 1989.

Hirakawa, Akira. *A History of Indian Buddhism: From Śākyamuni to Early Mahāyāna.* Translated and edited by Paul Groner. Hawaii: University of Hawaii Press, 1990.

Homann, Rolf, trans. *Pai Wen P'ien or One Hundred Questions: A Dialogue Between Two Taoists on the Macrocosmic and Microcosmic System of Correspondences.* Religious texts Translation Series Nisaba, vol. 4. Leiden: E.J. Brill, 1976.

Huang Xinyang, ed. and comp. *Xiudao yangsheng zhenjue.* Beijing: Beijing shifan daxue chubanshe, 1993.

Hucker, Charles O. *A Dictionary of Official Titles in Imperial China.* Stanford: Stanford University Press, 1985.

Ishida, Hidemi. "Body and Mind: The Chinese Perspective." In *Taoist Meditation and Longevity Techniques,* edited by Livia Kohn. Ann Arbor: Centre for Chinese Studies The University of Michigan, 1989.

Kohn, Livia. Mirror of Auras: "Chen Tuan on Physiognomy." *Asian Folklore Studies* XLVII, 2 (1988):215-256.

——, ed. *Taoist Meditation and Longevity Techniques.* Ann Arbor:Centre for Chinese Studies The University of Michigan, 1989.

———, ed. *The Taoist Experience: An Anthology*. Albany, New York: State University of New York Press, 1993.

Kuhn, Thomas S. *The Structure of Scientific Revolutions*. 1962. Second Edition. Chicago: University of Chicago Press, 1970.

Lau, D.C. trans. *Tao Te Ching*. 1963. Reprint. Hong Kong: The Chinese University Press, 1982.

Lynn, Richard J. *The Classic of Changes: A New Translation of the I Ching as Interpreted by Wang Bi*. New York: Columbia University Press, 1994.

Lyotard, Jean-François. *The Postmodern Condition: A Report on Knowledge*. Translated by Geoff Bennington and Brian Massumi. Minneapolis: University of Minnisota Press, 1984.

Maspero, Henri. *Taoism and Chinese Religion*. Translated by Frank A. Kierman, Jr. Amherst: University of Massachusetts Press, 1981.

Marcus, George E. and Fischer, Michael M.J. *Anthropology as Cultural Critique: An Experimental Moment in the Human Sciences*. Chicago: The University of Chicago Press, 1986.

Needham, Joseph. *Science and Civilisation In China. Vol. 2, History of Scientific Thought*. Cambridge: Cambridge University Press, 1956.

———. *Science and Civilisation In China. Vol. 5.2, Spagyrical Discovery and Invention: Magisteries of Gold and Immortality*. Cambridge: Cambridge University Press, 1974.

———. *Science and Civilisation In China. Vol. 5.3, Spagyrical Discovery and Invention:Historical Survey from Cinnabar Elixir to Synthetic Insulin*. Cambridge: Cambridge University Press, 1976.

———. *Science and Civilisation In China. Vol. 5.4, Spagyrical Discovery and Invention: Apparatus, Theories and Gifts*. Cambridge: Cambridge University Press, 1980.

———. *Science in Traditional China*. Cambridge, Massachusetts: Harvard University Press, 1981.

———. *Science and Civilisation In China. Vol.5.5, Spagyrical Discovery and Invention:Physiological Alchemy*. Cambridge: Cambridge University Press, 1983.

Nienhauser, H., ed. and comp. *The Indiana Companion to Traditional Chinese Literature*, 2nd rev. ed. Taipei: SMC Publishing Inc., 1986.

Ōfuchi, Ninji, "The Formation of the Taoist Canon." In *Facets of Taoism: Essays in Chinese Religion*, edited by Holmes Welch and Anna Seidel. New Haven: Yale University Press, 1979.

Pregadio, Fabrizio. "The Representations of Time in the Zhouyi Cantong qi." *Cahiers d'Extrême-Asie* 8 (1955):155-173

Robinet, Isabelle. "Metamorphosis and Deliverance from the Corpse in Taoism." *History of Religions* 19 (1979):37-70.

———. "Original Contributions of Neidan to Taoism and Chinese Thought." In *Taoist Meditation and Longevity Techniques*, edited by Livia Kohn. Ann Arbor: Center for Chinese Studies The University of Michigan, 1989.

———. "The Place and meaning of the Notion of Taiji in Taoist Sources Prior to the Ming Dynasty." Translated by Paula A. Wissing. *History of Religions* 29 (1990):373-411.

———. *Taoist Meditation: The Mao-Shan Tradition of Great Purity*. Translated by Julian F. Pas and Norman J. Girardot. Albany: State University of New York Press, 1993.

———. *Introduction à l'alchimie intérieure taoïste De l'unité et de la multiplicité*. Paris: Les Éditions du Cerf, 1995.

———. *Taoism Growth of a Religion*. Translated by Phyllis Brooks. Stanford: Stanford University Press, 1997.

Richard Rorty, "Solidarity or Objectivity." In *Objectivity, Relativism and Truth: Philosophical Papers Volume1*. Cambridge: Cambridge University Press, 1991.

Schipper, Kristofer. *Concordance du Pao-p'u-tseu nei p'ien*. Paris, 1965.

———. *The Taoist Body*. Translated by Karen Duval. Berkeley: University of California Press, 1993.

Sivin, Nathan. *Chinese Alchemy: Preliminary Studies*. Cambridge, Massachusetts: Harvard University Press, 1968.

Strickman, Michel. "On the Alchemy of T'ao Hung-ching." In *Facets of Taoism: Essays in Chinese Religion*, edited by Holmes Welch and Anna Seidel. New Haven and London: Yale University Press, 1979.

Unschuld, Paul. *Medicine in China: A history of Ideas*. Berkeley: University of California Press, 1985.

Veith, Ilsa, trans. *Huang Ti Nei Ching Su Wen: The Yellow Emperor's Classic of Internal Medicine.* Reprint, Taipei: Southern Materials Center, Inc., 1982.

Ware, James R., ed. and trans. *Alchemy, Medicine and Religion in the China of A.D. 320: The Nei P'ien of Ko Hung.* New York: Dover Publications, Inc., 1966

Watson, Burton, trans. *Records of the Grand Historian of China: The Shih chi of Ssu-Ma Ch'ien, vol.2 The Age of Emperor Wu 140 to circa 100 B.C..* New York: Columbia University Press, 1961.

——, trans. *The Complete Works of Chuang Tzu.* New York: Columbia University Press, 1968.

Welch, Holmes. The Belagio Conference on Taoist Studies. History of Religions 9 (1969): 107-136.

Werner, Edward T.C. *Ancient Tales and Folklore of China.* 1922. Reprint. London: Bracken Books, 1986.

Whorf, Benjamin. *Language, Thought and Reality.* Cambridge, Massachusetts: The M.I.T. Press, 1956.

Wilhelm, Richard, trans. *The Secret of the Golden Flower: A Chinese Book of Life.* 1931. Reprint. San Diego, New York, London: Harcourt Brace Jovanovich, Publishers, 1962.

Williams, Paul. "On the bodies of the Buddha." In *Mahāyāna Buddhism: The Doctrinal Foundations.* New York: Routledge, 1989.

Wittgenstein, Ludwig. *Philosophical Investigations.* Translated by G.E.M. Anscombe. 1958. Reprint. Oxford: Basil Blackwell, 1984.

Wong Shiu Hon, comp., *Daozang danyao yiming suoyin.* Taipei: Xuesheng shuju, 1989.

Yao Tao-chung. *Ch'uan-chen: A New Taoist Sect in North China During the Twelfth and Thirteenth Centuries.* Ann Arbor, Michigan: University Microforms International, 1980.

Appendix I

Synonyms for Lead and Mercury from the Introduction to the *Xiuzhen shishu wuzhen pian*

Lead	鉛	Mercury	汞
husband	夫	wife	妻
lord	君	servant	臣
golden fluid	金液	watery silver	水銀
golden flower	金華	flowing pearl	流球
jade pool	玉池	jade fluid	玉液
flower pool	華池	spirit water	神水
baby bay	嬰兒	young girl	妊女
yellow man	黃人	mysterious woman	玄女
golden essence	金精	wood liquid	木液
yellow sprouts	黃芽	white snow	白雪
white-headed laozi	白頭老子	emerald eyed child	碧眼股兒
simple refined husband	素練郎君	woman in green robes	青衣女子
white tiger of western mountain	西山白虎	green dragon of the eastern sea	東海青龍
fire jujube	火棗	intertwining pear	交梨
sinking	沉	floating	浮
lead of yellow sprouts	黃芽鉛	white of the yin fire	陰火白
host	主人	guest	賓客
father and mother	父母	people	民子
earth souls	地魂	heavenly souls	天魄
elixir mother	丹母	elixir foundation	金
marrow of the red phoenix	赤鳳髓	essence of the black tortoise	黑龜精
true yang within yin	陰中眞陽	true yin within yang	陽中眞陰
golden eight ounces of the rising crescent	上弦八兩	silver half pound of the falling crescent	下弦銀半斤

Appendix II
The Inner and Outer Medicines

Outer	Inner
trigram: *kan*	trigram: *li*
lead	mercury
yang within *yin*	*yin* within *yang*
The water of primordial unity of earlier heaven is sought within *kan*.	The secretion (*yi*) of earlier heaven is sought within *li*.
referents: water, moon, / in the body: reins	referents: fire, sun, / in the body: heart
reins produce seminal essence (*jing*) [*yin*]	heart produces blood (*xue*) [*yang*]
within *jing* is *qi* of true yang [*yang*]	within blood is secretion of true unity [*yin*]
lower virtue/ golden fluid	upper virtue/ jade fluid
rises and heats	descends
tiger	dragon
metal ➜ water west	wood ➜ fire east

Taken from the *Jindan dayao, juan* 1, 33b ff.